About the Author

The author spent his career as a Chemical Engineer working in several locations around the world, and the sights and background to this book owe much to that life. His view of the World's ability to control the potential disasters highlighted in this novel is not very optimistic.

Jonathon Rafferty

SERVATUR GAIAE

AUSTIN MACAULEY
PUBLISHERS LTD.

A CIP catalogue record for this title is available from the British Library.

ISBN 978 1 78455 891 8 (Paperback)
ISBN 978 1 78455 892 5 (Hardback)

www.austinmacauley.com

First Published (2015)
Austin Macauley Publishers Ltd.
25 Canada Square
Canary Wharf
London
E14 5LB

Printed and bound in Great Britain

Acknowledgments

The many authors and publications that have tried to ensure that people are made aware, on a fairly continuous basis, of the ever increasing threats to our world, the subject matter of this book.

Contents

CHAPTER 1

The Holiday

John Fenwick looked again at the beautiful naked body of his wife Angela, stretched out on the boat's cabin roof in front of him, sunbathing and enjoying the gentle warm breeze that was playing over her body, as they sailed through the sparkling azure waters of the Aegean Sea under a cloudless, intensely blue sky. Even after two children and at twenty-nine years old, her figure was still the envy of her friends, and delighted John every time he saw her. As he looked at her, he reflected on the great happiness they shared together and marvelled at the enduring love they felt for each other, the strength of which almost scared him at times.

He was still surprised at the change that seemed to have come over her in the two days since they'd flown into the Greek island of Paros to pick up their borrowed yacht. She had somehow managed to have put all the cares and worries of her normal life behind her almost immediately after they'd arrived, and it seemed to John as though a magician had waved a magic wand and Angela was again the girl he had just married all those years ago.

For his part he, too, had felt an upsurge of *joie-de-vivre* and a renewed zest for life since they had started their holiday. Was it really only two days ago?

They were on a short holiday, a fairly belated celebration of their seventh wedding anniversary, which had suddenly and rather unexpectedly been made possible by her parents offering to look after their two young children for the week.

They had also agreed it would be an ideal occasion to try for a third child.

John was the Principal Environmental Scientist with the Ecological Worldwide Threats Institute, official acronym EWTI, but long since nick-named the "Ecowotsit" by all who worked for it. Their work was very wide ranging, and as the rather unwieldy name suggested, they were part of a worldwide organisation affiliated to, but not controlled by the UN, that tried to prevent or at least, correct ecological problems anywhere in the world, though working predominantly in their own countries.

At thirty, John had had a rapid rise in the department, having used his original University degree in Zoology as a springboard into Ecology, in which he had taken a second degree.

Due to his job demanding a great deal of mental effort but not a lot of physical activity, he kept himself fit with a lot of fairly active leisure pursuits, playing squash and tennis regularly when his job allowed and going on weekend walks or swims in the local baths with Angela. He thus had a well-toned body but without appearing to be particularly well muscled. At just over six foot tall and of a dark complexion, he certainly always appeared to be in the best of health, as indeed he was.

He had met Angela at University where she had been studying Botany. They had hit it off immediately, meeting initially on a tennis court which game they both enjoyed, and then found they shared other interests, notably swimming and sailing, when the opportunity arose. The interests had very quickly been followed by a passionate love affair that had resulted in them being remarkably happily married for the last seven years. She had taken a career break to have their children, but had definite plans to resume the research work she had been engaged in when the children were old enough. To this end she had kept up with developments in her field as much as she could while managing the demands of the small children. This holiday was thus a very welcome break for her from her very demanding double role.

Now, while also enjoying the warm morning sunshine and the gentle breeze that was blowing Angela's auburn hair about in a slightly distracting manner, John thought back to the start of their voyage two days ago. They had set off to explore some of the islands in the Dodecanese group with no particular route planned, and now on the second morning of their holiday, he re-lived the time since they'd arrived as though watching a video playback.

It had been late in the afternoon the day before yesterday when they had finally got through all the formalities and moved onto their boat, very kindly lent at short notice by one of John's old university friends from the sailing club. They had decided to stay in the marina that night and start their voyage the next morning. So that afternoon, both of them enjoying the unaccustomed sun's heat from the cloudless blue sky, they did some shopping for provisions for their trip and then decided to end the day with a visit to a good quayside restaurant. There they enjoyed an excellent fresh fish dinner with some local wine, which, while unlikely to feature in a wine merchant's list at home, nevertheless, proved a very pleasant accompaniment to the meal. John smiled as he remembered how they had walked back to the boat, with his arm round Angela's shoulders, both feeling blissfully happy.

Then yesterday morning the day had dawned in classic Aegean style with another absolutely clear blue sky, again with a gentle warm breeze that inspired one to get up and catch the day in case it turned out to be just a dream. So John and Angela had had a quick breakfast on their boat, had gone ashore to buy a few last minute items from the market and then got away to a fairly early start. About mid-day, after they'd been sailing for about an hour or two, they had passed a small beach with a large restaurant sign above a low wooden building.

"Shall we give that a try for lunch?" John had asked, "Saves us doing anything and I feel a bit lazy today."

"So do I, so port your helm skipper and heave-to by yonder taverna!" she replied with a laugh.

The taverna was surprisingly good for such a small coastal village, so they took their time enjoying a local lamb delicacy, well laced with rosemary and garlic, and an unexpectedly strong red wine, apparently (according to the menu) from the proprietor's own vineyard. They followed this with a baklava, the honey of which was beautifully scented with the local wild flowers on which the bees obviously thrived. Afterwards, they had a quick look around the little village, and bought a few items from the local shops.

On their way back to the boat John said:

"Just as well they don't breathalyse us sailors in these parts – I'm damn sure I wouldn't pass!"

"Am I going to be safe, entrusting myself to a drunken sailor?" she asked in mock alarm.

"Well at least until I get you onto the boat, then it'll depend on how fast you can climb the rigging!" he had laughingly joked, giving her a bit of a hug as they walked with his arm round her waist.

Once back on the boat, they got under way in a leisurely fashion. After sailing for about half an hour or so, they had seen a deserted sandy cove, about a hundred yards wide, nestling between high rock cliffs, which provided some shade on one side of the cove.

"Why don't we stop here for an after-lunch siesta and a swim?" John had suggested.

"Great idea, though I hope the amount of sailing we've done today hasn't tired you too much, otherwise we're never going to get very far on this trip!"

"I may not be Columbus, but I think I can manage a bit more than a couple of hours, cheeky!"

He had manoeuvred the boat into the cove and anchored in about six feet of crystal clear water, a short distance from the shore. Angela had gone below to change and get some towels, and as she was coming back up to the deck, had heard the splash as John dived into the water. As she came up to where John had been she saw his shirt and shorts lying on the deck where he had just dropped them before diving in.

John having swum a short distance away had turned to face the boat and was standing on the bottom.

"Come on," he'd called, "the water feels absolutely glorious!"

She'd dived in and swam towards him. As she came up to him she saw that he hadn't got his swimming trunks on.

"John, why haven't you got your trunks on? Supposing someone sees you?"

He laughed, having always chided her on her somewhat prudish attitude to nudity.

"And just who do you think is suddenly going to appear here? Those cliffs could only be climbed by mountaineers, and I don't see many of them around. No, the only visitors are likely to come by boat like us, and if they see our boat's already here, they'll go on and find their own beach – hell we've passed dozens of coves with nice beaches already. Go on: be a devil for once, get *your* kit off and discover what a terrifically sensuous experience you've been missing all your life!"

She hesitated for a moment, then, looking around as if to reassure herself that there really wasn't anyone else there, also feeling a bit less inhibited than usual due to the wine they'd had for lunch and the beautiful peace of the place, decided to do it.

"Okay, here goes," she said, "but if I'm ravaged by the pirates that are about to descend on us, it'll be all your fault!"

A few seconds later, and feeling a bit of a daredevil, she, too, was standing naked in the sea, noticing and immediately beginning to enjoy the unusual sensations of the water playing around her body without the constraints of her bikini.

John delighted and somewhat surprised that she'd stripped off at all, had said: "Here, give me those, I'll put them on the deck for you."

After he'd done so, they swam around for a bit near the boat.

"I'm glad you persuaded me to take my bikini off – this really does feel terrific – such a marvellous sensation of freedom, perhaps helped a little by the feeling of being a bit of a devil for defying the lifelong and well drilled in conditioning of modesty. Well, the hell with modesty now, I say, this nakedness is just great!"

They then headed for the shore; John getting there first, had turned to wait for Angela to join him. As she'd walked out of the water he'd said:

"Now I see where the ancients got the idea of Venus arising from the waves – you look absolutely gorgeous like that."

Thinking that that was the most genuine compliment he'd paid her in quite a while she was slightly taken aback, but just managed a quick, "Well, thank you, kind sir!" by way of reply, accompanied by a little mock curtsey, before he had caught her in his arms and kissed her passionately.

When they broke apart, she'd said, a bit breathlessly: "If that's what I get for spending a few minutes swimming naked, I think I'll stop wearing clothes altogether…"

He'd laughed and said, "Let's walk along to the shady bit over there – we don't want to get sunburnt on our first day." So taking her hand, they'd walked leisurely along the water's edge, and then sat down in the shade.

After a few minutes she'd said: "You know, I think this nudity business could be habit-forming. Feeling the occasional bit of breeze blow round your body, and not having a tight soggy costume clinging to you really is a marvellous sensation; very sensuous in its way, though not necessarily sexually sensuous."

"We could soon change that," he said, with a suggestive laugh, reaching for her.

"I hate to be practical at a time like this, lover, but sand in tender places can be a distinct turn off."

He'd laughed, "You're right, of course. I guess I can wait till we get back to the boat…"

Then after a slight pause and completely changing the subject he'd continued:

"I wonder how your parents are coping with the kids. It was really kind of them to offer to take them for the whole week to let us get away and have this holiday – our first alone in, what, five years or so."

"Yes – maybe we could take them out to a theatre and dinner or maybe pay for an away weekend for them, by way of a thank you," she said.

The rest of the afternoon had passed peacefully, with occasional chatter between swims, general messing around, collecting a few unusual shells, and lazing on the beach, during the course of which they decided to spend the night at anchor in the cove, feeling it should be perfectly safe as they were quite a bit off the beaten track and hadn't seen another boat or any sign of anyone since they'd been there. Eventually, Angela had realised it was time to get back to the boat as there was a meal to prepare, so they had swum back to the boat.

When they were back on board, she had said: "You go and shower while I make a start on dinner, always providing I can manage to operate all the strange equipment in the kitchen – er, sorry, I mean of course the 'galley'," and had pretended to slap her wrist for the mistake.

"Well thanks," he'd replied, "but before I go, I presume a nice, cold, large G & T would ease the slog of cooking? I'm going to have one, anyway."

"Mmm – yes please, that would make the cook very happy, thank you."

Having got the drinks and sampled his fairly generously, he'd gone off to have his shower.

When he'd come back from showering still towelling himself down, he saw she'd donned an apron that covered her front, but nothing else. Seeing him looking at her she'd said:

"I didn't want any painful accidents while cooking." Then giggling a little and wriggling her bottom at him she'd added: "Do you think my bum looks big in this…" and just had time to jump clear of his lunging arms.

"Your bum looks – grrrrrr – gorgeous, eminently molestable and an absolutely perfect size in that, anything else or preferably nothing at all, come to that! However, as I am still able (just!) to demonstrate remarkable self-control, I'll let you go and have your shower and carry on with this. What needs doing next, apart from you, that is?"

"I am definitely for afters – long afters in this case," she'd said with a laugh, "so you could do the salad and get the steak ready. I've done the starter. It's that readymade *hors d'oeuvres* we bought that just required frying with a bit of garlic, if I understood what the shopkeeper was indicating. Either way, it smells very nice."

She'd thrown him the apron and headed for the shower.

When she'd come back, still drying her hair with the towel, he'd laid the small table in the cockpit, stood aside to let her slip onto the built-in bench seat and gone back into the galley.

"A little surprise, I hope," he'd said as he came back out and put a bottle of champagne and two glasses on the table.

"Oh, lovely!" she'd said, "and yes, it is a surprise. I didn't know you'd got that."

He'd poured the two glasses, and then looking at her had said:

"Here's to you, my darling. Just in case I hadn't told you lately, I love you very much, and thank you for our seven-and-a-bit wonderful years together. I still sometimes wonder at my luck at you agreeing to marry me."

Seeing he was being serious for a moment, she'd replied:

"I think the luck was on both sides, because I have always been more than happy that we got married," and turned to kiss him.

They'd enjoyed their dinner, watching a spectacular sunset, and chatting casually. Eventually he'd said:

"I'll get that gooey-looking cream pastry thing you bought for sweet in the village – it's in the fridge, isn't it?"

"Yes, just behind the bottles of wine."

"Okay," he'd said, and a few moments later, came back with the champagne and poured out the last two glasses, saying: "I think this should be finished first before it goes flat."

He'd then gone back for the sweet, which he'd put on small flat plates, but which seemed determined to slide off as soon as possible.

As he came back to the table, carefully balancing the plates, and then leaning forward to place one in front of her, he'd said:

"They're very slippery little… damn!" The confection had slid off the plate, landed against her chest, and slid slowly down into her lap.

"Oooh!" she cried, as she felt the cold whipped cream land on her, and a second or so later, as she recovered from the slight shock said:

"I've heard of people who get their kicks from covering each other with cream or some such, and then licking it off, but…" Before she could finish, he'd said:

"What a lovely idea – here, I'll lick you clean," and before she could reply, he'd started to lick the cream off her chest, spending a suspiciously long time ensuring that none remained on her right breast before moving further down.

She'd suddenly found the sensation delightfully erotic and moaned a little with pleasure before saying:

"Are you sure that was an accident?" Then, after another slight moan, "Do make sure you do a good job of cleaning it all up…oooh …your tongue…"

"I can't get it all from here," had come his muffled reply. "We'd better get onto the bed in the cabin," he'd continued as he extricated himself from between her and the edge of the table, and stood to help her out.

"My, there must be something erotic in that licking business – it seems to have got you going pretty well," she'd said, with a slight laugh, looking pointedly at his sturdy jutting erection. "Lead me to it, lover."

Once in the cabin, she'd lain on the bed, arms and legs spread-eagled.

"I think you'd better finish that cleaning job, which you seemed to be enjoying," she'd said, with a slight smirk.

"You didn't seem too averse to it yourself," he'd countered, kneeling on the bed beside her, "now, where had I got to?"

"I think you'd better start again, just to make sure of it," she'd said, her voice going a bit husky as the desire mounted in her body.

He'd leant forward and kissed her passionately on her open mouth, to which she'd responded with her tongue, before he'd moved down to start caressing her breasts with his tongue, and licking off imaginary traces of cream.

He then slowly moved down her body, every touch of his lips and tongue being rewarded with more gentle moans of pleasure, and the occasional "Oh Yes!"

For his part, feeling the silken smoothness and softness of her skin as he kissed and fondled her with his hands added further intensity to his excitement and desire.

When he'd reached her soft brown triangle, he'd pulled her knees up off the bed and opened her thighs wide, before gently kissing the insides of her thighs, and then moving slowly down towards her mound and sliding his tongue in to tease her clitoris, the while reaching up to fondle her breasts.

His caresses were fairly quickly rewarded with more of her little moans of pleasure and thrustings of her hips towards him then:

"Come into me now or I'll come without you!" she'd urged breathlessly.

Being in the same state himself, he'd quickly moved himself on top of her, and slid his throbbing penis gently into her, slowly and gently burying most of its length into her, as she'd arched her back and thrust her mound against him, adding to the exquisite sensations he felt.

She'd felt the familiar, though this time more intense hot sensation start somewhere deep inside her, and spread throughout her body like lapping waves, lapping and overlapping until the waves concentrated around the rigid pillar thrusting ever deeper into her, until she could contain them no longer, and had her crashing, all-consuming orgasm, clutching him to her and writhing and thrusting with the uncontrollable power of it. He, for his part, could not remember her ever coming with such intensity before, and the excitement of this triggered his own climax, so that both experienced a long-lasting ecstasy together.

Several moments later, when both had recovered slightly, he said: "Darling, that was one of the best ever!"

"Mmm, wasn't it, though; you really hit my jackpot that time. I've still got a deliciously floaty-on-air feeling, and everything is tingling – even my toes are still curled!"

He'd kissed her lightly and then after a pause had said: "You know, you really are marvellous, but I need a little time to get my breath back, and then perhaps we should have the other half."

"Mmm, that would be nice – I can feel a new little stirring down there just at the thought, even though Sir Percy has slipped out. Yes, hurry up and get him standing again, I want to do that all over again."

Rolling on to his back he'd said:

"Well, maybe if you'd like to minister to him a little in the lovely ways you have, he'll oblige."

"Alright, but wait a minute," she'd said, getting up from the bed and smiling at his slightly puzzled look. "Back in a mo."

She'd come back a minute later and said:

"What's good for the goose should work equally well for the gander," and so saying had sploshed the other cream pastry that she'd hidden behind her back right into his groin and spread it around a bit. "Besides," she'd added, "I didn't get to try any of this pudding first time round!"

It was then his turn to writhe around as she'd knelt over him and set about licking the cream off his body, eventually concentrating on his penis. As she knew full well, it wasn't going to take much of this sort of attention to really get him going, and she was slightly surprised at how arousing she found it herself. It wasn't long before her efforts were rewarded by seeing he was keenly ready for more action.

"If you don't stop that now, I'll come all over the place and you'll be left lamenting..." he'd said, breathing hard, then rolling over and climbing round behind her. "This time we'll give the 'missionary' a miss and have a bit of the 'canine' position. That usually reaches the parts that other ways don't, and generally to very good effect!"

"Oh, yes please, I love it when you enter me from beh..." the rest had been lost by the prolonged moan of pure pleasure she let out as he'd entered her purposefully but gently again. This time he'd leant over her, and with one hand fondled her breasts and with the other gently rubbed her mound, causing her to arch her back even more in an attempt to take as much of him and as deeply as possible, into her.

The sensations caused by the fondling of his hands, had seemed to send little lines of tingles right through her body, gradually focussing somewhere deep inside her from which those delicious waves of feeling again had started to lap all round her, holding her, and diffusing right through every part of her until they had all concentrated on his thrusting into her and again she'd come with a climax that had blotted everything from her consciousness except for wave after marvellous wave of intoxicating pleasure.

The almost animal moans of pleasure that came from her had caused him to thrust into her ever harder and had overwhelmed such little control as he still had in holding back until she came. He could feel his climax building and suffusing through his body until he could hold it back no longer and he'd then let himself drown in the spasms of pure pleasure that fired through his body, causing him to thrust into her even faster, thus adding to her orgasm. Again she'd come with a climax that had blotted everything from her consciousness except for wave after marvellous wave of intoxicating pleasure.

After the final surge of his climax, he'd gently helped her to lie out flat on the bed and had lain on top of her, panting for breath.

"Darling...that was...wow!" she'd murmured, coming gently back to earth.

"That really was...was...oh...you darling..." he'd replied somewhat incoherently, burying his face in the hair at the back of her neck, and kissing her there.

After a few moments, he'd rolled over to lie beside her on the bed. They'd lain resting, entirely satisfied, their desires thoroughly sated.

"I hope baby number three appreciates all the hard work going into its making," said John, recovering from his exertions a little later.

"It's not an 'it' it's a 'he' this time," she'd chided him, "and, anyway, I haven't heard too many complaints about the 'hard work' so far!"

"Ah well, he or she is not a *fait acompli* yet, so we'll need a few more attempts to make quite sure about the results, won't we? Can I book you for tomorrow morni…" he'd just had time to dodge as the pillow she'd swung at him thumped onto the bed beside him.

"Oh! You're the most…most…" she'd begun.

"Lovable man?" he'd interjected, laughing, putting his arms around her and hugging her close. "Don't worry, I didn't mean this instant."

"Mmm, all right then," she'd said, "but first I must cool down and then I think some sleep is definitely called for."

"Okay," he'd said, kissing her gently on her cheek, "how about a quick swim to cool down?"

"No, I don't want to risk the precious cargo you've just given me so delightfully, so I think I'll have a quick shower instead."

"Yes, maybe that's a more comfortable suggestion just before bed, so after you, ma'am!"

As the shower cubicle was not big enough for the two of them at the same time he'd stood in the entrance and caressed the water down her body by way of helping her shower.

"I suspect your motives for assisting me with the shower, but as I said, sleep is next on the agenda," she'd said with a slight laugh, "so you can have yours now. I'm going to bed."

He'd finished his shower, was soon beside her in the bed and turning over, was asleep in moments.

The next morning she'd awoken first, and seeing John still asleep, lain quietly for a little while. She'd gradually realised that she felt a bit different and was very pleased to put this feeling down to being successful the previous night. She felt fairly sure this was the case, that they had been successful and that they had indeed started their hoped-for baby.

After a little while she'd shaken John gently and said:

"Show a leg, Cap'n! We need to make sail and get under way!"

A rather bleary-eyed John had said: "Er, wossat you said?" and then coming fully awake and seeing her naked half sitting up, had promptly switched into what Angela had sometimes called his 'lust-mode'.

"Come here, you beautiful sea nymph, I want…"

But before he could reach her, she had got out of bed.

"I'm going to have a swim and then breakfast – I'm starving!" she'd said over her shoulder as she went up on deck, closely followed by John.

They'd jumped into the sea and splashed around a bit, then come back on board to get some breakfast together. After breakfast and tidying things up a bit, John had got the boat under way again, and Angela had climbed onto the cabin roof to indulge in a little sunbathing. She had laid out a couple of deck cushions, placed a towel on them and, stretching herself luxuriously onto the towel, had said:

"I'm never going to be happy sunbathing, or indeed swimming with any clothes on at all ever again. This feels so good – such a wonderful sense of freedom!"

"That suits me just fine," John had said, with a little laugh, "and I feel the same way, too."

His pleasant reverie about the first two days of their holiday was brought to an abrupt end after about a quarter of an hour, just as he was about to go back and relive some of the best moments, when Angela suddenly sat up and said:

"Why don't we go back to our bay and stay there for the day – have a repeat of yesterday if you like – as I enjoyed it so much. Besides, there is no need to go on to the next village for supplies yet."

"What a good idea – I'd love to do that, too," he said, turning the boat back the way they'd come.

"I'll see what's in the fridge and get a few things together for a picnic lunch," she said, climbing down off the cabin roof and going below, "then I'll resume my tanning session on the cabin roof."

When they'd arrived back and the boat had come to rest, he said:

"Be an angel and weigh the anchor – oh, alright you land-lubber you – chuck the damn thing over the side while I fix up the cockpit awning."

She went for'ard and dropped the anchor over the side, and followed it into the water with a neat shallow dive.

"Oooh, the water's just as nice as it was yesterday, maybe even better," she called out, "hurry up and join me!"

"Right!" he said, and leaving the awning half done, leapt over the side and swam to her.

"You haven't finished putting the awning up," she said, treading water as he swam towards her.

"With an invitation like that I wasn't going to delay for a second," he said, coming up to her, taking her in his arms and kissing her in a way that kept the fires simmering but didn't cause an instant blaze.

"Steady, lover, I can hardly touch the bottom here."

"I can," he said lasciviously, sliding his hands down her back and fondling her buttocks.

"Oh you," she said laughingly as she pushed away from him. "You seem to have developed a one-track mind lately, and I can't imagine why! Beat you to the beach!" and so saying, swam strongly towards it, he keeping just behind her.

She ran the last bit through the shallow water splashing up rainbows of drops, turned to face him, and then bent over to catch her breath. He soon joined her, and also spent a few moments getting his breath back.

"We're not as fit as we might be," he muttered between breaths, "still, a bit more energetic horizontal PT like we had last night will improve the situation, I'm sure."

"Here, turn round!" she replied; "As I thought; you've got the beginnings of a mane and long hairy tail sprouting – trying to be a stallion is obviously getting to your body…OUCH!"

He had spun her round and given her a gentle slap on her behind. "Less of the rude remarks," he said, "and equally if I'm showing stallion features, you know what that makes you."

"I didn't say I *minded*, did I? Let's lie in the sun for a while and get over all our exertions."

After a little while, he leant over her and gently kissed her left breast.

"I'll go and get the sun-tan gunge: we don't want these pretty bits of you (or some of my not so pretty bits, come to that!) which seldom see the light of day, let alone strong sunshine, getting burnt while they enjoy their newfound freedom."

So he swam back to the boat to get their books, a couple of travelling board games and some Amber Solaire, which he zipped up in a waterproof bag and took back to the beach, where they spent the rest of the morning lazing.

About mid-day they were both beginning to feel a bit uncomfortable in the heat, as there was virtually no shade at either end of the beach at this time of day in which to shelter. So they decided to return to the boat for some lunch, sitting in the shade of the awning, which John finished putting up as soon as they got back on board.

"A nice cold drink to beat the heat of the day?" asked John.

"That'd be very welcome, thanks. A nice cold white wine from the fridge will be just the job before lunch."

They sat for a while in the shade of the awning, with a little breeze coming across the sparkling sea making the heat just right.

"I suppose I ought to rush and get lunch," said Angela, not moving.

"No, I'll rush and get it," said John, likewise staying still.

After another long pause while they finished their drinks, Angela said: "Okay, *I'll* rush and get it."

A little later she called up from the galley: "How does cold meat and salad grab you? We could wash it down with that bottle of red you bought from the Taverna yesterday, and then finish off with that smelly Greek cheese. That funny shaped loaf thing we bought doesn't seem to have gone stale so that can go with it all."

"Sounds great to me," came the reply, "what cold meat have we got?"

"Well, there's some of that well smoked ham we bought in the market and some of those sausage things whose name escapes me – I'll have it done in a few minutes if you don't mind a do-it-yourself salad."

"Bring it all on, I'm starving!"

A few minutes later when she'd finished bringing up the plates of meat, bread and a tray of tomatoes and other salad ingredients, he looked at the table and said:

"Where are the cream desserts..." and ducked quickly as she pretended to throw a tomato at him.

"Some men are..." but the rest of her comment was lost as he took her in his arms and kissed her firmly on the mouth.

A little later in the afternoon, they swam back to the beach, John taking the waterproof bag with their books and other things with them.

They tried a bit unsuccessfully to play 'Scrabble' with their travelling set, then agreed the heat and beach weren't exactly conducive to that sort of brainwork, so settled for the occasional swim interspersed with reading or just dozing.

Eventually, they swam back to the boat, had showers, made a meal and enjoyed a quiet evening. After they'd finished eating they sat finishing their wine, listening to the occasional gentle lap of the sea against the boat and watching another beautiful sunset before going to bed. After their sexual activities of the night before, they agreed, without the need to say anything, to forego any more similar pleasures that night, and so went to sleep.

CHAPTER 2

Further Aegean Pleasures

The next day, they went on to another village, bought supplies, had lunch in a small taverna on the beach, and then walked up a hill to visit an old ruined temple. On the way up Angela said:

"At the risk of stating the bleedin' obvious, it seems to be getting hotter by the minute, and there's not a breath of wind. Even the cicadas, or whatever they call them here seem to have been stifled into silence. How about we rest for a bit under that magnificent great olive tree there, and have some of that lovely cool wine you brought with us?"

"Good idea, I was just beginning to understand how a sausage must feel after a while on the barbecue. Also, after our little spell as naturists, these clothes feel increasingly uncomfortable. How about a quick return to the boat after we've seen the ruin up there and then a swim as soon as possible? In fact, let's find the next bay where we can spend another blissful day like our first."

"Oh yes, that sounds just perfect at the minute as I'm cooking too. Unfortunately, as there may be other tourists about (or even islanders we haven't seen yet) I'm resisting the temptation to strip off and cool down."

"That's a pity," he said, eyeing her lasciviously, "but as I don't see anyone at the minute, I'll just shift your blouse a bit to indulge myself with a kiss of that perky little breast I can just make out through the material."

"No, that's not a good idea," she countered, without making any attempt to stop him, "as we might get carried aw... oooh! Stop that, there's someone coming!"

He looked up. "Who? Where? I see no-one."

"It would have been me if I hadn't stopped you right then!" she said, laughing and pulling away from him. "Come on – let's get up to the temple and then back to the boat so that we can have that swim, and you can have the rest of that kiss (was it?) without interruption."

They went on up the hill getting hotter by the minute, and were pleased when the path led through an olive grove that provided at least some shade, though it was still stiflingly hot without any discernible breeze. The ground was bone dry and baked hard and reflected more heat at them when out of the shade of the trees. Having eventually found the ruins of the temple, of which not a lot remained, they found a shady pine tree nearby and sat down for a rest and to enjoy the wine.

"I'm glad seeing what's left of the temple (always assuming it *was* a temple) wasn't the only reason we climbed this hill – it's rather lost its 'wow' factor, I'd say," said Angela.

"Yes, even the moss seems to have deserted the stones," replied John, leaning back against the tree. "However, at least the view is superb and a bit of a breeze seems to be trying to blow."

Being on top of the hill, there was indeed a bit of a breeze wafting past, which helped them cool down a bit and provided a very restful sound as it passed through the tree's needle covered branches. The view compensated a bit for the effort to get there, making the climb worthwhile, despite Angela's remarks about the ruins, though a slight heat haze blurred the nearby islands on the horizon. Suitably refreshed, they returned to the boat, the walk being much easier as they were going downhill.

They decided to sail further until they reached another deserted cove, similar to the first one, and then happily went in swimming, luxuriating in the refreshing coolness of the sea. After their night of abstinence the previous night, both of them felt an increasing sexual excitement as the evening progressed that resulted in the meal eventually being left unfinished as they went to bed. Afterwards, both agreed with almost a feeling of awe that the intensity of their lovemaking was still at an amazingly high level.

The next four days of their holiday followed the same pattern and passed in a blur of beautiful sensations, and as such, went all too quickly. They had congratulated themselves on being careful not to get sunburnt while enjoying their new found freedom from clothes. In fact, they had both got so used to being unclothed, that on passing fairly close to a similar yacht, Angela forgot her nudity and waved a greeting to them.

"Oh dear, do you suppose they saw me?" she asked, stopping halfway through another wave when she remembered her lack of any clothing.

"Don't worry," he replied, "they're probably doing the same themselves, though I didn't see."

Thus, apart from their newfound enjoyment of swimming naked in deserted coves, there were visits to a couple of small villages, enjoying meals in little restaurants they found, buying bits and pieces as well as food from local shops and generally soaking up the relaxing *milieu* that came with such a complete change in their usual hectic life's activities. They also enjoyed looking at the little Shrines and Churches that they came across as well as a few ancient ruins, from the remains of old fishermens' or shepherds' shacks to larger structures, all speaking mutely of the much harder livelihoods of the long past peoples who lived there.

And, of course, after the day's adventures there was always the boat to return to and the pleasures, usually of the very personal variety, to look forward to.

Though they could not know it at the time, this holiday came at a very propitious time, as John's business life was shortly going to be very much more demanding, leaving very little time for Angela and him to have together.

On their last day, Angela awoke some time well before dawn and was suddenly convinced that she would not be having the hoped-for baby. She didn't know why, but started crying, which woke up John. Still half asleep, he tried to comfort Angela, pooh-poohing her feelings, saying half jokingly, "we'll just have to try harder, won't we! Now, try to get back to sleep because we're going to have to get up early."

Angela was still in low spirits when they did get up, but gradually perked up a bit after their swim and breakfast as they had quite a bit to do. They had a two-hour journey back to Paros to be back by twelve to hand the boat back to the yard.

A little while before they got there, John said: "I suppose we'd better put clothes back on now. It's going to feel a bit uncomfortable for a while after all our freedom from them."

"Yes, it will," said Angela, "but I suppose we'll just have to get used to it again." After a pause, she added with a slight smile: "Much as I've enjoyed being without them for so much of this last week."

After handing back the boat, there was just time for a quick browse around the shops behind the quay and a coffee on a café terrace overlooking the bobbing colourful boats in the harbour, before they took a taxi to the airport for a local flight back to Athens. The size of the Paros airport amused them, being essentially a single room building, with a corrugated iron roofed open lean-to outside, with a sign "Baggage collection."

"Heathrow it ain't," remarked John.

Arriving back in England about ten that evening, they were very pleased to be met by Angela's father, who took them back to his house. As the two children were fast asleep, Angela's mother said to leave them where they were and come back and pick them up next morning.

"Dad'll run you home, won't you, dear?" she said, which offer they were only too pleased to accept, both feeling very tired by now.

So the next morning, Monday, John went back to his office, and Angela went to collect the children.

They both had the feeling of "Holiday? What holiday?" after a couple of days as life resumed its usual pattern. However, at the back of Angela's mind was the by now absolute certainty that she was not pregnant, and a week after their return she went to see her doctor. She tried to reassure Angela and said that it was probably because her system had not completely cleared itself of her contraceptive pills, and to come back in a month's time if she still had not conceived.

A week or so later, John noticed that Angela was looking a bit down and jokingly said she must be having a dose of the post-holiday blues. She surprised him by starting to cry and said she was now absolutely certain that she was not pregnant.

John tried to comfort her, telling her not to worry, and again said jokingly, "We'll just have to try even harder, won't we?"

However, despite all their best intentions, still, she did not get pregnant.

Finally, after several more visits to the doctor, they had to accept the situation. After lengthy discussions they decided against artificial insemination, having read of the difficulties and expense associated with this course of action, and more or less resigned themselves to having no more children, though John still had a slight idea that they might succeed one day.

CHAPTER 3

Brazilian Slash and Burn

Some three weeks after Angela and John returned from their holiday, halfway round the world in Brazil, Pablo Fuentes awoke and groaned as his tired, stiff muscles complained at having to work again so soon, even if it was eight hours since he'd fallen into what passed for a bed in the shack at the edge of the shanty town, Santa Isadora, that he called home. A wiry, spare frame bore testament to the hard life he'd led. Born into a large impoverished Brazilian family, he was considered lucky to have survived childhood and spent some time in school. Since leaving there some five years ago, he had done any work he was lucky enough to find, as there was always plenty of competition for the sort of unskilled work which was all he could aspire to.

He got out of bed, splashed some water on his face from a cracked plastic bowl, pulled on his well worn tee shirt, jeans and battered trainers, and set about getting himself something to eat. All he could find was a bit of two day old bread, a few pieces of cheese in a torn plastic wrapper and coffee left in the pot that he reheated on a small paraffin stove. Thus set up for the day, he went out to the pick-up point and waited for the truck that collected him and the rest of the labour gang. This took them to the forest clearing site, where he was currently employed (and glad to have the work) on the 'slash and burn' activities used to turn the virgin Amazon jungle into so-called farm land.

An hour later he was walking across the bare earth, round the large tree roots that had been dug up and were now waiting for collection, and avoiding the smouldering fires still smoking from yesterday's incineration of brush, branches and the tops of the trees. His job was to collect the small branches and other debris the tree cutters produced after felling the trees and take it to the fires. Today there seemed to be a problem with the chain saws, none of which could be persuaded to work. The site foreman was raging that those 'bloody greens' must have raided the site overnight and sabotaged the saws. Happening on the unfortunate Pablo standing around waiting to be told what to do while waiting for the cutters to get back to work, he yelled at him and the little knot of other labourers standing round him to get sickles and go and start clearing the underbrush.

Pablo, from fear of losing his job, always tried to please the foreman and so was at the head of the little band setting off to attack the underbrush. It had been cleared to a little way beyond the last line of trees left standing by the gang the previous day, so Pablo made his way to the nearest clump. As he passed the trees he suddenly felt distinctly unwell. By the time he reached the underbrush, his head felt very tight, he had difficulty getting his breath and felt he was about to faint. More by panic and an instinct to survive than rational thought, he turned round and ran back, making it to beyond the trees before collapsing on the ground, gasping for breath. One of the others stopped by him to ask if he was okay, and getting a nod, decided not to stop. Very shortly, all those who had entered past the trees were staggering out in exactly the same way as Pablo had done.

After a few minutes, they all began to recover, and were just getting to their feet when the foreman and the tree cutters, bringing new chain saws, walked up to them. The foreman, not noted for his sympathetic understanding of those in trouble, started demanding what the hell they thought they were paid for, and why they weren't friggin' well clearing effin' brush as instructed. When no one seemed able or willing to answer him, he saw Pablo.

"Well, what the hell are you lot doing hanging about here – why aren't you working?" he shouted at him.

"I…I… I got ill," replied Pablo a bit shakily, "just after I walked past the trees."

"Bloody likely – if you want to be ill, do it in your own time, not work time! Now, all of you, get back there and start working, or I'll fire the lot of you."

With which remarks he started walking towards the trees, followed by the cutters, and the reluctant labourers.

As he walked beyond the trees, he began to suffer exactly the same symptoms experienced by Pablo earlier, and staggered back out to collapse on the ground. All the rest stopped and looked at him, but no one rushed to assist him, mainly because they were all still feeling the effects themselves, and the cutters because they weren't too sure what was going on, anyway.

They all stood like statues around him as he slowly recovered, not saying anything. As he gradually recovered, and was aware of their presence, he tried to get up, managing it at the third attempt. He was still so shaken that he didn't shout at them at first, as he would normally have done. Then realising that he must regain control of the situation as soon as possible, he said:

"Okay, so there is something there making us sick. However, if we cut down that first line of trees, then you can get the brush without feeling, er, ill. So, Francesco," he said, turning to the chargehand of the cutters, "you and your men start cutting those trees!"

Stopping a few feet in front of the tree, Francesco pulled the cord on his saw to start the small petrol engine running. The machine didn't start, so he tried again and again, each time without getting the machine to run. The other cutters were similarly being unsuccessful.

"What the sodding hell's going on here," shouted the foreman, gradually regaining his normal composure, "are we being sabotaged?"

Looking at the knot of men standing around him, he realised it was extremely unlikely that any of them would either want, or indeed even be capable of organising a disruption of this sort. Then he had a thought: "Those bloody green conservationists, or whatever they called themselves, they could well be responsible for this. He'd heard of the disruption they had caused elsewhere to contracts like his. Yes, that must be it, so he'd better phone the office right away and tell the manager what was going on, otherwise – hell they might even hold him responsible and…"

He didn't even like to imagine the likely consequences of that. Instead, he looked at the men and said:

"You lot, stay here while I phone the office and get them to come and sort out what's going on."

He came back a few minutes later and said: "Well, you might as well go and wait in the rest area, the contract manager himself is coming right away."

The men drifted off to the rest area rather disconsolately, as they realised they wouldn't be paid for this non-working time. The 'rest area' consisted of a tarpaulin strung between four trees that had been left standing for the purpose. It provided some shade from the sun at midday (or from thunderstorms), there were some rough tables and chairs under it for meal times and a plastic pipe and tap tied to one of the trees for water.

About an hour later a swarthy, fat, moustachioed man in a very crumpled dirty off-white suit arrived, sweating profusely, dabbing ineffectively at his forehead with a saturated handkerchief and extremely irate at having his otherwise peaceful air-conditioned morning interrupted. He berated the foreman for the whole episode before asking him what had happened. He cut the explanation short, making plain his disbelief in the whole story, and strode off to the edge of the forest, the foreman following a few paces behind.

The labourers, having heard the dressing down the foreman had received, watched the new arrival striding towards the trees with mounting interest, which changed to ill-concealed glee when he was seen to stagger back from the trees exactly as they had done. Because of his obvious lack of any sort of physical fitness, it seemed to take him a lot longer to recover than it had taken them. The foreman, who had carefully avoided following him into the trees, came over to the labourers, and without a word, took a mug off the table, filled it with water, and took it back to the still recumbent figure.

When he had recovered enough to realise that his dignity had suffered at least as much as his body with that sudden 'funny turn' that had hit him in the forest (and dispelled the growing fear that maybe there had been some truth in what that stupid doctor had told him about 'improving' his lifestyle), he struggled to his feet, roughly knocking away the foreman's proffered hand and started walking a little unsteadily towards the site office, the foreman accompanying him.

A little later, the labourers saw the manager get into his car and roar off in a cloud of dust, which blew gently towards them. A few moments later, the foreman appeared and told them the transport was coming back to take them home, as there would be no more work that day, but they should be at their collection points the following morning, when he hoped the problem would have been sorted out. He also added, in case there were any still naive enough to think that they'd get paid for the day that they wouldn't. As they were climbing onto the truck, a thought struck him and he shouted up at them all:

"If any of you are involved with the people who have done this to our site, you won't just be fired; you'll find yourselves in jail for a very long time. For all our sakes I hope whatever it is in there has cleared by tomorrow morning."

When Pablo got off at his collection point, he was feeling pretty low, partially as a result of the attack, but also at the prospect of possibly no work in the immediate future. He checked how much money he'd got left. As he'd been careful with it for a while, he decided to cheer himself up a bit with a beer in the little bar he passed every day. He took his beer and went and sat at a table near the only ceiling fan that was lethargically making an attempt to move the stale air around a bit. Sitting down, he tried to chase a couple of flies off the table, but they were enjoying the spilt beer far too much to take much notice of him. He hadn't been there long when he was joined by a man he knew slightly, who, like him, was always looking for work, and was prepared to take anything on offer as he had a family to support. After a while, Pablo noticed that the newcomer was crying quietly to himself, so asked him what was the matter.

"That job I was working on, well they just chucked us all off the site today, and I don't know when or indeed if we'll ever get the work back. What will happen to my family if I'm out of work, how will I pay for their food?"

Pablo had often thought it would be nice to have a wife and family, but knew he was unlikely to achieve that for a while, and in view of his companion's worry at the consequences of losing his job, was glad he hadn't.

As there were quite a few building sites in the town that required labourers, Pablo assumed the man had been on one of these.

"Don't worry too much," he said sympathetically, "there are quite a few buildings being constructed just now – I'm sure you'll find another soon," he added, without much conviction.

"No, I don't think so," came the reply, "I only know farming work. I've been out near the new farmland project by El Campo, and suddenly everyone got sick and they've shut down the site until they find out what it is…"

He tailed off when he saw the look on Pablo's face. "You…" he began, and Pablo cut in to tell him what had occurred on his site that morning. When he realised that the circumstances were identical in both cases, he realised the authorities would shut his site down too if they found out, and wondered if the contract manager had said anything to anyone. Chances were that even if he hadn't, they'd find out soon enough, so he'd better use the rest of the day to find another job. He knew one of his cousins, Alfredo, who lived in Calaxias, a town some fifty miles to the south had said he could always get him a job if he got fed up with the forest clearance, so decided he would take him up on his offer.

He went back to his shack, phoning his cousin on the way, collected his few belongings, and as he'd already paid the rent for the week, without further ado, went to the bus station.

His cousin met him off the bus and took him to his small house in the poorer area of the town, not far from the main street. They had always got on well together, having spent a lot of their childhood together as Alfredo's parents had been close neighbours of theirs in those days.

"Good to see you, Pablo," said Alfredo, giving his cousin a strong bear hug in welcome. "I've made a few enquiries, and have managed to find you a job – not much, I'm afraid, but at least it's something to keep you going until you can find something better."

After thanking him profusely, and enquiring about Alfredo's family, they took a local bus to near Alfredo's home, catching up on family news as they went.

CHAPTER 4

Pablo's Close Call

Pablo was not alone in finding the forest clearance work was suddenly put on hold. Every site north and south of Santa Isadora where he'd been working had experienced the same problems of not being able to get into the forest without feeling very ill and panicking to get away from the trees. News of this didn't take long to reach the Brazilian Land Clearance Office, and all work was stopped pending an investigation.

The 'usual suspects' in the shape of associates of the "Green Planet" movement were duly rounded up, but strenuously denied any knowledge of, or involvement in the occurrence, though admitting that they were very pleased it had happened, no matter who was behind it. After some further checking and reviewing what had happened, the Office had to admit that they had absolutely no idea what was causing it. Also, as no one from their scientific arm could identify any possible causative factors, they decided that it most probably wasn't caused by the activists.

As there was nothing the office could do to resolve the matter, it slipped comfortably into the "avrio" category to await developments. ('Avrio' is similar to 'mañana' but without its sense of urgency.)

As there was no more clearance work, Pablo was very pleased to take the job that Alfredo had managed to get for him, working land that had been cleared of forest some time earlier, and was now going to be ploughed and sown. The first couple of days had the gang of which Pablo was a member clearing away rocks and other debris left over from the forest clearance. They started at the side of the site adjacent to the dirt track that provided access to all the sites along this edge of the forest, and then moved in towards the trees. This was because it was easier to move the rubbish over the site once it had been cleared. As a result of this Pablo didn't go near the trees until his third day on site.

As he was now fairly near, he wondered if these trees would make him feel ill like the ones had the previous week. An opportunity arose when the chargehand was called over to the truck that doubled as a sort of site office, so he went over to the line of trees at the far edge of the site. He hadn't quite reached them when he started to feel exactly the same symptoms as he had before, so ran back to where he had been working before he got really affected and before anyone noticed what he was up to. He didn't say anything to anyone about this, as apparently no one else was aware of it and he wanted to keep working as long as possible.

Over the next three days, he checked it in the same way, and soon noticed that the distance from the trees where he started to feel the illness was increasing. On the fourth day, as the work was progressing towards the trees, one of the other workers started working that much nearer than the others, and ran back towards the road, before collapsing on the ground. It wasn't long before they all knew what was going on, but it was another two days before the line where the illness was felt had advanced to cover about three quarters of the width of the site. Hence the area they could plant also gradually decreased, and at the end of the day as they waited for the truck to take them back to town that evening, the foreman told Pablo and a few others that they wouldn't be needed the next day. This sickness on the site eventually found its way into the relative

Ministry pending tray, again with no one rushing to take responsibility for doing anything about it.

Having nothing in particular to do the next day, Pablo decided to walk into the shopping area of the town. He'd made a little money from his work, and even had a bit left over after paying his cousin for his stay with him, so decided to get himself another tee shirt and some small presents for his cousin's wife and children.

Having done his shopping, he was just thinking a beer would be nice. As he walked along the side of the road on his way home on the lookout for a suitable bar, there was a sudden series of short, sharp cracks just behind him. He knew gunfire when he heard it, and flung himself onto the ground, just as a man who had been walking a couple of yards in front of him collapsed. Though not immediately aware of it, Pablo had been saved from being shot as he was walking past a tree at the critical second.

He heard a car accelerate away rapidly, and looked at the dying man lying on the ground just in front of him. The man had dropped a smallish packet which lay just in front of him. Seeing it there, he pushed it over to Pablo and then lay still.

As soon as Pablo was sure the car had gone, he quickly picked up the bits of his shopping that had spilled out of the paper carrier bag he'd been carrying, stuffing in the man's packet as well. He then ran as fast as he could to the first turning off the road he had been on, ran down it a bit and then ducked into a doorway to get his breath back and to see if anyone had spotted him or if he was being followed. As there was no one in sight at that moment, he thought he had less chance of being spotted if he put on the new bright red tee-shirt he had just bought instead of the dirty white one he had been wearing. He waited a few moments then, checking again that there was no one chasing him or had seen his quick change act, started walking fairly quickly back to his cousin's house, looking behind him frequently to see if he was being followed.

As far as he could tell, he got back to his cousin's house without anyone seeing him, where he collapsed into a chair, and gladly accepted the beer his cousin gave him. He was still very shaken by the whole incident, and so described to his cousin, in a rather disjointed fashion, what had happened to him. It was only after he'd calmed down a bit that he remembered the package that he'd picked up from the victim of the shooting, and got it out of the bag of shopping. It was wrapped in brown paper tied round with string. He undid the string and carefully unwrapped the paper. The first thing he saw was the transparent plastic bag that contained what at first sight looked like it might have been talcum powder, though Pablo had been around enough to be fairly sure what it was. Had he had any doubts they were removed by the two bundles of notes, one a number of hundred dollar bills the other a large collection of smaller denominations, underneath the plastic bag.

Both men stared at the contents of the package in awed silence: neither of them had seen so much money like that before, but after a few moments the implications of the rest of the package came through with an increasing sense of almost panic.

No gangsters were going to let that amount of cash and drugs just disappear – they were probably looking for it now – and may already have found a few people who had seen what happened – and may be on their way to this house right now....

His cousin was fast becoming paralysed with fear, but Pablo, being a bit more 'devil-may-care' by nature, was wondering how he could benefit from the package, while at the same time, stay alive.

"You cannot stay here with that!" the cousin whispered, trembling with fear, "they will find us and kill us both, for sure, and my poor wife and children," he added, almost as an afterthought.

"No, of course," said Pablo, "I will leave immediately. Here," he said, giving his cousin some of the smaller denomination notes, "have this as a present for having me live with you, but be careful not to spend too much at once or too soon in case it attracts attention, and hide it now!"

It didn't take Pablo more than a few minutes to pack his few things into the tatty shoulder bag he carried, carefully hiding the money behind a part of the lining that had come adrift slightly though not obviously. He stuffed the packet of drugs into the pocket in his jeans, the easier to dump it somewhere unnoticed. He then put on a baseball cap to change his appearance a little more. After thanking his cousin again, asking him to give the other presents to his wife and children and wishing him well, he left from the back of the house.

He had no idea where he should go, and started walking back into the centre of town by a different route. Suddenly, this large black car appeared on the street, driving slowly, and even slower as it came level with him. He managed to restrain the impulse to run for his life, and his fear kept him walking steadily and not looking at the car, other than what he could see out of the corner of his eye. After what seemed like minutes, during which pictures of the man shot in front of him earlier that day kept coming into his mind, he heard the car speed up a little and continue down the road.

When he'd calmed down a bit, he began to think of the bag of drugs. What should he do with it? He just wanted to get rid of it, as he felt it was like a time bomb, waiting to blow up and kill him. So at the first available opportunity, he hid the bag in a small shrub beside the road, now well away from his cousin's house.

Gradually, his confidence growing slowly as the people in the car hadn't recognised him and no one else had challenged him, he started thinking of the money and what he should do with it. With a slight laugh he realised he didn't even know how much was there, but plenty, that was for sure, and he began to feel better. Then he thought of his parents, and wondered how he could get some money to them. Of course! Go visit them! No problem paying for a bus fare now – or was there?

If he turned up at the bus station and tried to buy a ticket with dollars, particularly peeling it off a large bundle, it might put the gangsters on his trail. No, better change a small note into reals at a bureau de change. He could always say he'd been paid by an American tourist for something. So, finding somewhere out of the way of prying eyes, he carefully extracted one twenty and two ten dollar notes and put them in his pocket, making sure the rest were still well hidden behind the lining in his battered shoulder bag, further concealed by his few belongings.

He found a Money Changing office in the main street, but walked up and down a few times, wondering if it would be safe. Eventually, seeing very few people entering and leaving, he steeled himself to go in. The man behind the counter was watching football on a small TV, and hardly looked at him as he asked brusquely, annoyed at the interruption, "reals?"

"Yes, please," said Pablo as he handed over his dollar bills. He felt a great sense of relief at not having to give a word of explanation, and as he left the office, feeling much happier, he took off the cap, just to change his appearance again. On his way to the bus station he thought a different tee shirt might help to cover his tracks a bit further, so this time got a light brown coloured model with a clear logo emblazoned across the back which could be turned inside out to completely hide the logo. Seeing himself in a mirror as he left the shop, he was pleased with how different he now looked.

At the bus station, he got his ticket and, merging into the crowd, wandered over to his bus, which was due to leave in five minutes. He congratulated himself on his lucky timing, and went to the first available seat. As he sat down, he found out why it was available. The broken springs complained bitterly with a loud 'boing' at his interfering with their easier life, and a bit of one of them took its revenge by jabbing him uncomfortably in the backside. He got up rather more quickly than he'd sat down, much to the ill-concealed amusement of others who'd had the same experience.

He moved further back and was settling down into the new seat, when glancing out of the window, he saw what he was sure was the same black car pulling up on the road outside the bus station. Two men got out and crossed into the station. Pablo picked up an old newspaper from the seat beside him and pretended to read it while trying to keep an eye on the two men who were moving swiftly among the crowds milling around. They stopped to speak to an inspector, and to his horror, Pablo saw the man point to the bus he was in. He watched, fascinated, as the pair quickly made their way towards his bus.

At that moment, the driver started the engine, closed the door, and started to drive off. The men ran forward and tried to signal to the driver to stop, but he either didn't see them or wanted to be on his way. Either way, to Pablo's intense relief, he didn't stop and they were on their way.

He was about to discard the newspaper when an advertisement caught his eye: "Labourers wanted in Portugal to work in sherry vineyards." He carefully tore it out of the paper and decided that this must definitely be his lucky day – a chance to get well away from the gangsters and a job that would probably pay much more than he'd been getting so far. The address to apply to was only another bus ride on from his parents' village, so he could be there tomorrow morning.

After an uneventful trip to his destination, as he was leaving the bus, he saw another two men carefully looking at all the passengers leaving his bus. Again, a moment of panic: should he make a run for it? He managed to keep control of himself and walked out with a small group of other passengers, taking care not to look at the two men. He felt shaken at the thought that those two men may not have been anything to do with the drug gangsters, on the other hand, they might have been. He'd been lucky so far, but how long would they go on looking for him? He had no way of knowing, but began to realise the plight of the hunted – never sure when or if the hunters will catch up with you, and forever looking over your shoulder for reassurance that is never forthcoming.

He stopped off in the little bar he'd been in the day he left Santa Isadora – "*Sacre Madre!* Was it just a week ago?" – and had a beer while he thought about what to do. The first thing was to try and get that job in Portugal tomorrow morning, which would at least get him away from the drug gangsters. He went back to the bus station and got a local service to visit his parents.

His welcome was not very warm, as his father was not well and so was not working, and his mother thought at first that he had come home simply because he was out of work and would want to be housed and fed. Her attitude was understandable, given that she was worn out with her years of raising ten children, two of whom had died very young, and the youngest was still at home, not yet in his teens. Things looked up considerably when Pablo said he only wanted to stay the night, and that he'd got some money for them.

He gave his mother a couple of hundred dollars' worth of the small bills, advising her to be very careful how she changed them, and even suggesting that she take the bus to Calaxias and visit the same bureau de change that he'd used. He didn't tell her how he'd come by the money, just that he'd been lucky to get a very well paid job for a while. He also didn't tell her about the possible job in Portugal, he could do that later, if he got it. His mother, who had never had any money to speak of, was overwhelmed at having so much at once, and assured Pablo that she would be very careful with it.

Pablo bid his family a tearful farewell the next morning, knowing that it would be a long time before he saw them again, and made his way to the office to apply for the new job. After some fairly offhand enquiries and checking his battered national ID card, he was delighted to be given the job. Almost as an afterthought he was told that the cost of the airfare would be deducted from his wages at the vineyard, and should he be so foolish as to try and leave before he had paid off the debt.... He promised that he would work hard and not leave the job early. The official nodded briefly – he was fairly sure the unspoken threat had done its work.

There was a charter flight leaving the next day Pablo was told. Then he was given a ticket voucher, some papers of introduction and told to be at the nearby San Juan Baptisto airport by nine o'clock the next morning, when they would exchange the voucher for a ticket.

It was about lunch time when he left the office, so he thought to have a look around the town. He found a cheap café for something to eat, checked on how to get to the airport and found a run-down hotel for the night, promising himself that this would be the last time he'd ever have to stay in a filthy place like this.

CHAPTER 5

Pablo's Escape

The next morning Pablo was up early after an uncomfortable night, the 'hotel' he'd chosen being almost in a class of its own when it came to ways of ensuring no one ever stayed for any longer than they absolutely had to. In the early part of the night, a water cistern in the roof overflowed and fell noisily onto a corrugated iron roof just below Pablo's window. Then water pipes banged and rattled in the thin walls, through which the televisions from three rooms away could be heard. When that quietened down a bit after midnight, the late visitors could be heard slamming doors as they left, or arguing loudly about not being paid the agreed amount. At about three o'clock there was a police raid, resulting in more shouting, heavy boots stamping along the corridors and the yells of those protesting at the rough handling they were receiving. When all that had settled down, the indigenous night life came out hunting for food. The next morning, Pablo realised that he had obviously been the 'plat-du-jour' or maybe that should have been 'plat-de-la-nuit'. Either way, he started the day with several bites that itched annoyingly and felt very jaded from lack of sleep.

He made his way to the airport, getting there in good time, and having checked in, went to buy a coffee.

He hadn't been there long when another man of similar appearance to Pablo asked if could join him at the small table. The newcomer then said:

"Hi, I think we are going to the same place and work – I was behind you at the ticket desk. My name is Miguel, Miguel Carajas." He held out his hand, which Pablo shook a little mechanically.

"Hi, I'm Pablo Fuentes," he replied, picking up his coffee, not particularly wanting to talk just yet.

Miguel, however, was keen to glean anything he could about the new job, as he had been harbouring doubts about the whole thing. He'd read a few lurid articles about people signing up for jobs that seemed to be a great opportunity, only to discover too late that they had been sold into virtual slavery. He mentioned these worries to Pablo, who had to admit that such possibilities had never crossed his mind. As they talked, Pablo gradually shook off the effects of his night in the hotel, and when they boarded the plane they both were on the way to becoming good friends.

As is often the cases with such work offers, the cost of the fare and incidental expenses in getting the workers to their new job site is recovered from their initial wages. Pablo was secretly not worried about this, as he knew he could buy himself out of the deal in Portugal if he didn't like it.

The journey to the vineyard some way above Oporto near the River Douro was uneventful, and they were all pleasantly surprised at the accommodation provided, far from luxurious but well above what Pablo, at least, had had in Brazil.

The morning of their second day on Site, due to a driver's mate being ill, Pablo was told to take his place to help the driver of a large articulated lorry taking a consignment of Port to England. His first duty was to help load the vehicle, ready for a start early the next morning. Miguel was very envious when he heard about Pablo being given this work, even if it was only a 'one off'. During their lunch break he regaled Pablo with a great deal of second hand information about England that he'd heard from a brother-in-law who'd managed to be accepted as an immigrant, he thought, though wasn't sure.

"Yes, Manuel told me it is marvellous," continued Miguel. "Actually, he got in illegally but it's all okay now, I believe. He'd heard it was so good he jumped ship and said he came from Bolivia and was running away from a drug cartel's hit men, so could he please have asylum. Okay, they said and gave him somewhere to stay, lots of money and said to stay there while they checked his story. After about a year, as he had not heard anything from the immigration department, he got fed up with doing odd jobs and managed to get a really good job in the north of the country. So he decided to leave the house where they had put him without telling anyone. When I last heard from him a few months ago, he still had the good job, he was still getting money from the immigration people and no one had come to ask him why he'd moved. Great place! If I get a chance, I'm going to try to get there."

Not surprisingly, given this glowing account of how easy it was to enter this land of 'milk and honey', Pablo started to think seriously about how to use this amazing opportunity that had been presented to him. This truck was going to take him right into England. Surely, it would be easy to just jump off and stay as an immigrant as Manuel had apparently done? However, not to let Miguel suspect that he might try to follow the brother-in-law's example, he kept up a pretence of not being particularly interested in his forthcoming journey, and would be glad to be back working the vines, which work he liked and knew well.

Notwithstanding his replies to Miguel, Pablo kept going over various plans in his mind for the rest of the afternoon and evening. It should be easy: once he had landed in England, he would use the first opportunity to run away from the truck. No, better wait until they were in a large city. Yes, that would be much better. The driver wouldn't follow him (why should he bother?) and it would be a long time before anyone thought to look for him. The more he thought about it, the easier the whole scheme seemed. So in a state of suppressed excitement, he went to bed.

Everything seemed to be absolutely routine the next morning as they started out on their journey, which they broke for two overnight stays at the usual truckers' hostels in France. They then caught a cross channel ferry early the next morning. If anything, the boredom of the journey had begun to impinge on Pablo's thoughts of his escape, and for a while he thought tending the vines would have been better than this. However, when they arrived at Dover around mid-day the following day, he had decided he would try and stay. After all, if it failed they would only send him back to Portugal.

The worry that rapidly grew into near panic started, when he asked the driver why they were waiting in this queue of trucks.

"Passport check," came the reply.

For a few moments Pablo sat almost paralysed. He hadn't got a bloody passport, only his National ID card! They'd probably chuck him in a cell to be collected by his driver on the way back, if he was lucky. He couldn't run now, far too many police and officials around: he'd most likely get shot before he'd got ten metres from the truck. Clutching at straws, he thought they might, just possibly might accept his Brazilian ID Card instead of a passport. He fumbled in his pockets to make sure it was still there. Relief! He hadn't forgotten to bring it with him. His fear grew as their truck gradually neared the front of the queue, and eventually it was their turn. The driver wound down his window as the official approached.

"Good morning," he said, looking into the cab at the two of them, "your passports, please."

The driver handed his over, and after the customary perusal had it handed back. Then looking at Pablo said:

"And yours ple…what the hell…" He'd stepped back from the truck and was looking behind them, where a very noisy commotion had occurred and had officials from all over the concourse, including the one who had been about to inspect Pablo's non-existent passport, run over to try to restore order.

After a few minutes, the official returned, looking somewhat dishevelled and out of breath. Seeing and remembering the driver and evidently forgetting he hadn't seen Pablo's passport, he waved them on.

Pablo had difficulty breathing for quite a while, and had gone rather pale.

"You okay?" asked the driver.

Pablo was on the point of telling him about his predicament, but decided against it, saying he'd felt a bit sea-sick, but it was easing off.

A little later, Pablo's luck decided it had supported him for quite long enough and it was time to move on. They came across a spot-check road block, and had no option but to stop. This time there was no avoiding the inevitable, and Pablo was taken off to an immigration holding station. The driver, whose papers (which fortunately listed Pablo as Driver's Assistant by name) were in order, convinced the authorities that he didn't know the silly idiot hadn't brought his passport with him, was allowed to go on his way.

As Pablo was put into a cell, he was almost relieved. He'd got into the country, and from what Miguel had told him it should be easy to stay, though he had to admit that wasn't the impression the various officials he'd come up against gave him.

His interrogation started later the next morning, with an immigration official and a Portuguese interpreter. It seemed to Pablo that it lasted for a very long time, and the official became very interested when he heard about Pablo's account of his sickness by the rain forest. As Pablo obviously could not say what it was, the official thought it sounded like some sort of fever, which, for all he knew may be infectious. However, as Pablo was obviously in reasonably good health at the minute, he continued his interview while waiting for a doctor to come and examine him.

After the doctor had completed his examination and could find nothing wrong, the official wondered if Pablo was lying about the sickness to help him get into the country. Eventually, he decided that he probably wasn't, and in that case, the Ecowotsit outfit might be interested to check out the story. He'd had a few contacts with them before about immigrants, and spoke to George Powers, someone he'd dealt with before, who also happened to be a colleague of John Fenwick. George, who at that moment had a quiet spell in the project he was handling, was sufficiently interested to go down to talk to Pablo the next day and find out more of his experiences.

He listened to (and recorded) Pablo's story from the first time he'd encountered the 'tree sickness', as he called it, until his arrival in the UK. George had heard a few rumours that there was something odd going on in the tropical rain forests, but had never heard anything specific. Hence Pablo's experiences were very enlightening, and something George could hardly wait to get back to the office to discuss with John, which he made a point of doing as soon as he'd arrived in the office the next morning. After John had listened to George's recorded account of Pablo's story, they decided they ought to bring Mark Bedford, their boss, up to date with this information, as there had been some rumours about this doing the rounds in the office for some time now.

"That certainly seems to back up what the rumour mongers have been spreading for a little while now," said Mark. "How reliable do you think this Brazilian character's story is, George?"

"Bearing in mind that he's trying for asylum and claimed to be fleeing a drug cartel there's good reason for him to fabricate it. However, my opinion after listening to him, an opinion shared by the immigration official I spoke to, is that the man didn't seem to be the sort who could make up a story like that, and be entirely consistent in the telling of it two days apart. So yes, I think he's telling the truth as he remembers it. What to make of the story, assuming it's true, I don't know. Doesn't sound like anything I've ever come across. Have either of you ever heard of anything like it?" he concluded, looking at the others.

"No," Mark replied, "but I wouldn't be surprised if we hear more about it before long! Let me know if either of you hear anything else about it."

After some deliberation, it was decided that the easiest option was to send Pablo back to Portugal on the same truck in which he'd arrived. So they arranged to have the truck held at the company where its cargo had been delivered until secure transport could take Pablo back to rejoin the driver. An electronic tag was placed round his ankle, and he was advised of the dire consequences if he left the truck, as he would be found very quickly due to the tag, and then thrown in jail.

However, on the way back to Dover he decided to chance it, and escaped again.

Due to a glitch in the monitoring and recording system, by the time it was suspected that he was no longer on the truck, an urgent message to the ferry established that Pablo was definitely not on the truck. When asked, the driver claimed he'd stopped for a pee at the last service station before the port, and when he came back out Pablo had disappeared. He said he looked around for him but couldn't wait longer otherwise he'd have missed the ferry and in any case, there were no police about to report his absence. He said he had intended to report it once his lorry was on the ferry, but they'd found him before he could do so. He also didn't want the delay that telling the police would have caused him, though naturally he didn't tell them this.

As a result an extremely sparse file was opened about Pablo's case – just another illegal immigrant – and placed with a few hundred thousand others to await investigation.

CHAPTER 6

Back in the Office

On the Monday morning, some six weeks after their holiday cruising the Greek Islands, John took the train into his office as usual. He'd been getting gradually less than enthusiastic about his job since the holiday, but for the first time in as long as he could remember, he felt really down at the prospect of another week on his current assignment. He realised that this was probably in part because Angela and he were very depressed at her not becoming pregnant, either whilst on holiday or in the following month and secondly, because of the way his current project was developing. He'd been working on it since some three months before going on holiday; it had virtually stalled and didn't seem to be going anywhere fast. He had started out with high hopes that it would be very interesting and would advance his career if he completed it successfully. However, as the whole thing seemed to be getting progressively buried by an increasing tide of new EU Directives and 'red-tape' regulations, he had to spend most of his time dealing with this rather than the investigations and research that was his normal, and fulfilling area of work. So with his interest in the project waning, his work was becoming a boring chore that had to be endured rather than something he could look forward to, as he had usually been able to do in the past.

Having stopped to get his first cup of coffee on the way to his desk, he was looking at it rather morosely in a worse than usual fit of the Monday morning blues when his phone rang and he was called in to see his boss, Mark Bedford.

"I was sorry to hear of the personal problem you and your wife have been going through lately, but in a way it may help us with the next assignment I'd like you to undertake. You'll have to leave your current one, but I think Simon can handle that on his own for a while."

At the prospect of a new job to get his teeth into, John perked up.

"Great," he said, "what is it and when do I start? And yes, I'm sure Simon can handle it," he added.

Smiling slightly at John's sudden enthusiasm for Simon taking over his job, Mark went on:

"Well firstly, you've got to realise it is a job of an extremely confidential nature, that you mustn't discuss with anyone outside this office. Any leaks attributable to you will result in your instant dismissal. That's the first thing you've got to understand and accept. Also, it's going to involve a fair amount of travel, and you may have to be away from home for a few days at a time. Do you want to go ahead on that basis?"

John, somewhat taken aback both by what Mark had said and the unusually formal way in which he had said it replied:

"Well, yes, I'm obviously keen to progress my career with the Ecowotsit and have always done what was required of me, but can you tell me some more about it before I commit myself? Also, if it involves being away from home often and for several days at a time, I obviously need to discuss it with Angela, my wife. As you know, we have two very young children, and she may not want me to take it."

"Well, obviously I understand that, but I can't tell you the nature of the work until you agree to take it on and sign the special secrecy agreement. One consolation for her though is that it may help to resolve the difficulties I understand you've been having lately trying to add to your family."

John was somewhat surprised by this. Firstly, he didn't know that the fact Angela wasn't pregnant had travelled round the office so far (he was fairly sure he'd only mentioned it to one or two of his colleagues), secondly, what the hell could be the reason for all this secrecy and travelling?

Nothing, as far as he knew that his office had ever undertaken before had involved anything like that. What on earth could it be? But as the thought of operating like some latter day James Bond started to intrigue him, he couldn't imagine Angela agreeing to it very happily.

Seeing that John was worried by the prospective job and secretly hoping that he would take it as he was the best staff man he had for this assignment, Mark continued:

"What I can tell you is that you will be involved in making very confidential enquiries both in this country and possibly in Europe, and the information you collect may, as I mentioned, ultimately and indirectly help you with your wish to have another child. I can't tell you how or anything else about it unless you accept the post. Oh, and of course, there would be a considerable uplift in salary to cover the greater responsibility and a generous disturbance allowance to help you with the disruption to your home life. Think it over very carefully because I'm sure you're the right man to carry out this difficult assignment. Let me know your decision tomorrow."

John went back to his office, his whole mood lifted by this news. He thought carefully about the whole prospect, which the more he thought about the more he liked, and decided he would take, always provided he could get Angela to agree. So,

he set to thinking how best to explain it to her to achieve that end. With this occupying his mind almost to the exclusion of everything else, he found it difficult to concentrate on starting to hand over his work to Simon.

When he finally got home that evening, he tried not particularly successfully to conceal his enthusiasm for the new project from Angela, while hoping that she would want him to take it. For her part,

she'd seen how lacklustre John had been in relation to his job. She'd noticed the increasing despondency with which he left for the office each morning, and had heard his disinterested replies when she enquired about how his day had been, so when he came home that evening, obviously in much brighter spirits, she realised something must have improved with his job. In reply to her questions as to why he was so much more cheerful, he said he could only tell her that it involved collecting a lot of statistics in person from the people involved, and was sorry he couldn't tell her anything more about it just yet, under pain of being fired. However, she was pleased for him that he had this new opportunity which had so evidently cheered him up, and so agreed readily to his taking it.

"Great," he said, catching her in his arms and doing a pirouette holding her off the ground. "Let's see if your mother will baby sit for us tomorrow, and we'll go out and have a celebratory dinner somewhere nice. Might even bring back a cream dessert for afters," he finished with a suggestive smirk.

"Humph," she replied, thinking of the night of passion they'd had on the boat with the last cream desert, but which abandoned behaviour had been a bit off the agenda since their return for all the usual domestic reasons associated with a family of two small children.

"Hey – what's happened to that gloriously sexy goddess I had the great pleasure of being with for a few days in the Aegean? We are in danger of just becoming another staid 'curried mapple' – oh, all right, a staid 'married couple', if you must!"

She smiled: he was so obviously in better spirits that she was swept up a bit with his mood. He hadn't indulged in his enjoyment of his own variety of Spoonerisms for quite a while.

"Yes, that'd be lovely – going out to dinner, I mean," she added hastily, "though I suppose I might be persuaded to indulge in some of..." she finished with a theatrical 'come-hither' look.

"Oh, you darling!" he said, "I'll phone your mother right away."

Back in the office next morning with a definite spring in his step, he went to see Mark to tell him he'd got the required matrimonial blessing on taking the new assignment.

"So can I now know what I'm letting myself in for?" he asked.

"Right. Sit down and I'll give you an outline of what you'll be doing. The details you'll find in this folder," Mark said, handing him a slim buff file. He went on:

"Firstly, you must sign this undertaking about not revealing anything of this assignment, as I mentioned yesterday, so if you'll do the dotted now, I'll continue."

John duly signed and handed the form back.

"There have been reports gathered from various medical practices around the country that indicate that there has been a very significant drop in the number of new pregnancies that are, as they so quaintly put it, 'presenting' at the surgeries. There have also been rumours that the same thing may have been happening in continental Europe. We need to get a far more definitive handle on these reports, such as how big a drop, where they are − you know, regional distribution anomalies, or is it fairly general all over the country. In order to get some solid information, we, or rather, you are going to visit a dozen large practices spread across the country and get the necessary statistical information so that we can see just how big a drop there's been and how it's distributed. The addresses and contacts are all in the file, so work out how you're going to get round them all, ideally in two weeks. Thereafter, dependant on whether the similar reports from Europe are substantiated, you may need to go over there to compare statistics."

"As you can well understand, the Environmental Minister is taking a personal interest in this, so do a good job with this – a lot hangs on it, not only for our department, but also possibly for the country as a whole. So get started right away. You'll need to arrange to see the various people listed in the file there, so hit that first, and I expect you to start your travels tomorrow morning.

As I think you will appreciate from the nature of the enquiries the reason for the secrecy. If the rumour-mongers got hold of this it could cause quite an amount of public panic, so hence why we're keeping it secret for the time being.

"Any questions?"

John was somewhat taken aback at the scope and apparent urgency of this new project, his mind racing through the likely problems and how he would handle them.

"Can't think of any right now, so I'd better get on with it – and thanks, it looks like the sort of challenge I could use to get my teeth into rather than ploughing through miles more red tape and EU regulations on the old one."

John spent the rest of the day organising his various visits and planning his itinerary. It was going to be tight, but he reckoned he could do the first four and get back home for Wednesday night, then the next four and be home for Friday night. Just as he was getting on top of the travel arrangements, he remembered he'd asked Angela's mother to baby sit for them on Tuesday night, which she could no longer manage. A quick call to her and, a big sigh of relief, she could do tonight for them, no trouble. Now, to check with Angela. She, while surprised at the speed with which his new assignment had taken off and a bit put out at the short notice, nevertheless, said it would be alright. He also remembered to phone and book a table at their favourite restaurant, one that by mutual unspoken consent was reserved for special occasions.

John got home in good time, and for once, the fates conspired to ensure their evening got off to a happy start, everything working out as planned.

After a thoroughly enjoyable meal, they arrived home in a very happy frame of mind, to find all had been quiet and peaceful at home. They phoned Angela's father, who had been visiting his brother only a few miles away, and, as previously arranged, he came to pick up Angela's mother.

They all had a 'thank you' drink and then her parents left. Angela and John were just finishing their top-ups of the drinks they'd started while her parents were still with them, when John said, in mock seriousness:

"Damn! I forgot to get a gooey cream desert!"

"Oh, that's a pity, I was quite looking forward to it," she replied, and after a slight pause added nonchalantly:

"However, being a good ex-girl guide and thus prepared for all eventualities, I took the precaution of making something similar this afternoon. Care to try it out?"

He was so delighted, surprised and excited by this that he could do no more than whisper, "You are the most delicious, desirable…" and pulling her to him kissed her passionately. He then followed her into the kitchen to pick up her cream 'desert' and then up the stairs, partially undressing her as they went.

Afterwards, they agreed that, while it may have lacked something of the ambience of the last occasion on the boat, it came pretty close.

The next morning, he woke early at the alarm's unsympathetic insistence. He thumped it into silence. He then paused to look at Angela in the dimmed light he'd turned on, and was pleased to see it had only slightly disturbed her. God, but she looked so desirable, her hair in splendid disarray, her bare arm out of the bed that the temptation to creep back in and cuddle up behind her was nigh irresistible. However, he controlled the urge, got washed, dressed and packed an overnight bag. As he finished, Angela turned over and suddenly awake said:

"Gosh, is that the time? Why didn't you wake me? I'll get you some breakfast."

The sight of her getting naked out of bed nearly wrecked his resolve to catch the planned train. Instead, he took her in his arms and said:

"What a lovely sight to greet the hunter off to 'hunt and gather' to feed his family! But don't bother with breakfast for me. I'll just have a plate of flakes and a coffee now, and maybe treat myself at the department's expense to a slap-up breakfast on the train." Having said that, he suddenly remembered that these were no longer available, but didn't mention that to Angela in case she felt obliged to get breakfast for him.

She put on a wrap and checked the children before going downstairs to sit with John and join him in a coffee.

"Hope it all goes well for you, darling," she said at the front door as she kissed him goodbye. "Give me a call this evening to tell me how it went, and see you tomorrow night."

"You bet!" he said and left to catch an early train to a practice in Birmingham, which he'd arranged as his first visit.

On the Friday at end of the second week, John felt fairly exhausted by the travelling and the series of nights in different hotels. Also, having to gather information from quite a number of different people had proved a bit of a strain as not all of them had been very co-operative, and some had complied with barely concealed hostility – another bloody man from the ministry wasting their time with damn fool questions, being a not uncommon attitude.

Having a few spare minutes at lunch time on that Friday, he called Angela's mother again and asked if she could baby sit for them on Saturday evening. Hearing him sound rather tired and despondent, she offered to take the children on Saturday morning and bring them back on Sunday afternoon, so that John could surprise Angela with a night away somewhere, or even have some time to themselves at home.

This offer was accepted with delight by John, who phoned Angela with the news.

"Well, I'd love to go away for the weekend, but aren't you fed up with staying in hotels every night?" asked Angela

"Not if I'm going to be the Mr. of the 'Mr. & Mrs. Smith' having an illicit tryst somewhere!" he said, trying a bit unsuccessfully to sound lascivious. He went on: "Anyway, it won't even seem like a hotel if you're with me – with any luck it might seem like the boat again, though I doubt if we could manage the swimming part of it!"

They had a thoroughly enjoyable weekend at a small country hotel that had been recommended to him by a colleague, and John returned to the office on the Monday feeling much more able to tackle the preparation of the statistical data and report of his visits.

On the Wednesday he went to see Mark with his finished work.

"The most surprising factor to emerge from this survey is the consistency of the data reported," John began. "With very little variation across all the practices I visited, the end result of all of them is that firstly there hasn't been a single woman presenting who has already got two children, and the numbers overall are down quite a bit. One other curious fact: there were extremely few under eighteen, virtually unknown previously, particularly in the inner cities. Most of those who did see their doctors were 'primo parti', (i.e. those having their first baby, as one doctor witheringly enlightened my ignorance of the medical term!). The other, not so surprising thing to come out of my questions, was that none of them could give me a good reason of even theory as to what might be causing this. On that aspect we're still none the wiser, though there is no doubt whatever that the number of births in those twelve practices compared with the same month last year is down by some five to ten percent."

Mark had been listening carefully as John recounted his findings, and after a few questions to clarify some details, said:

"One thing you'll probably be glad of: you won't need to repeat this exercise anywhere in Europe. The what-used-to-be Benelux countries have all done a similar exercise, and from what we've heard so far, have come up with results very similar to yours. I'm seeing the minister this afternoon to go through your report and decide what we do next, so be ready to come and answer questions."

"How long is the secrecy of all this to be maintained?" asked John. "Because it seems to me that with these enquiries going on all over Europe, it's not going to be long before it becomes general knowledge. I really just wanted to know if it'd be alright to tell Angela what I've been up to, and it may help her to feel less upset about not having another baby."

"You're probably right about it soon being public knowledge, so I guess you could tell Angela, but keep it to yourselves until it is in the papers, okay?"

"Yes, sure, and I'll be on hand to answer any questions the minister may have," John replied, thinking that with a bit of luck he wouldn't be needed. He was disappointed in that as barely a quarter of an hour later, he was called in to the meeting with the minister and spent the rest of the afternoon going through details of his findings. He was a bit surprised to find how seriously the minister took the whole matter, considering what he'd heard of his interest or rather, lack of it, in earlier work done by others in John's department.

An hour later John left the meeting with the certain feeling that, in this case, the minister was more concerned for his own job than the wider implications of his survey's findings. As he had not been the minister for long, his was naturally keen to show how well he had everything in his department under control, and to have something like this come up, the reason for which no one could explain and, therefore, did not know what to do about it, did not reflect well on his ability to take decisive action to handle the problem. John also felt, with some justification, that it was going to be 'spun' into a minor blip in statistics, or worse, the statistics would be described as flawed. Having done what he thought was a conscientious and carefully carried out piece of work, he felt depressed at the prospect of it being buried somewhere in a government file and lost.

CHAPTER 7

A logging problem in Africa

About the same time as Pablo was landing in Portugal, some four thousand miles away at the edge of a West African jungle being progressively decimated by logging, one of the crews engaged in the almost certainly illegal activity was setting out for another day's work.

"God, I swear it's even bloody hotter than it was yesterday! I'm going to go back and crew ice-breakers when this effing contract is finished – I've had it with jungles, their stifling heat, humidity and their voracious inhabitants, treating me as walking fast food!"

Thus spoke Sven Pedersen the boss of this particular crew, to no one in particular, while flapping his sweat soaked shirt in a futile endeavour to provide a little cooling, as they bumped their laborious way in a well-worn truck along a rough logging track leading into the jungle. He was a second generation Canadian in his early thirties, and a classic Scandinavian blonde giant of a man: six foot five tall and turning the scales at a very muscular two hundred fifty pounds, his body honed by many years of hard outdoor manual work from farming, through lumber-jacking to oil roustabout with time out playing serious American Football and some amateur wrestling. He looked, and was, as tough as the hardwood trees he was currently employed in felling, and his face, while reflecting the hard life he'd led and bearing a few small scars from his sporting activities, still retained most of the youthful good looks he'd had in abundance at the end of his teens, but now matured with a slightly battered charm about them. He had taken this contract mainly to start a new life after a very painful though not especially acrimonious divorce from his wife. This had been caused by the accumulation of many problems, most of which are typical of not particularly happy marriages, but in this case, their inability to have children had been one of the final factors. By throwing himself into this totally different, bachelor status environment, he hoped he could get over all the hurt of the divorce and get himself back onto an even personal keel.

Turning to the Nigerian sitting behind him he said, "Pedro, how many of these damn trees are we due to chop down today?"

Before the man had a chance to reply the truck's engine suddenly cut out.

"Goddamit, Joe," he said to the driver, "I thought you said that mechanic you knew would do a good job. What the hell's up with this bloody truck now?"

"Geez, boss, I dunno. He told me he'd fixed it real good and it would be fine."

"Well, it bloody isn't and now we're going to be stuck in this stinking heat until the others get here. I'll show that mechanic of yours a few unusual ways of using a spanner when we get back. Meantime, have a look and see if you can see what's up with the damn thing."

The driver, having tried the starter unsuccessfully a couple of times, got out, opened the bonnet and peered inside. Sven, never the most patient of men, was soon at his side.

"Well," he said, "what is it?"

"Can't rightly say, boss, it all looks okay to me."

Sven, restraining a scathing reply, got back into the truck to await the arrival of the rest of his logging crew with the tree transporters. After a few moments of the suffocating heat in the stationary truck, he got out and decided to walk back along the track a bit to meet them, as they couldn't be that far behind. He stopped in the shade of a tree, thus getting a little relief from the blazing heat of the sun.

"I might also stop them ramming the back of my bloody truck and adding to today's problems," he reflected morosely while waiting for them to arrive.

In due course the first tree-transporter arrived and stopped at the top of the slight incline where Sven was standing.

"The bloody truck's broken down again. To avoid you getting stuck on the muddy slope as well, pay out your winch cable and we'll pull the bugger back up here and try and start it by running it down the hill." They started doing as Sven had instructed, without an overdue show of enthusiasm, and soon had the truck back up the slope in front of the transporter.

"Okay, Joe, you know how to give it a running start?"

"Sho' thing, boss," Joe replied grinning, jumping into the truck. He turned the ignition key, and out of sheer habit turned it fully to the 'start' position. The engine sprang into life.

"What the f…" Sven started, staring at the hapless Joe, then said to the transporter driver: "Wait here a minute to make sure we keep going up the other side of this dip, then follow on."

Curtly telling Joe to move over, Sven got into the driving seat of the truck and set off along the track again.

When they got to the bottom of the slope, the engine cut out exactly as it had done before.

Sven got out, still cursing and walked back up the slope.

"I'm going to give this one more try," he said to the transporter crew as they winched his truck back up. "Only this time I'll go very slowly to see where it stops and then try to figure this damn thing out. I'll leave the winch wire attached, so let it freewheel. I'll shout if the engine cuts again, and you can pull us back up. I'll also try starting the engine again on the way up, so stop winching if I signal that I've got it going."

After a few trials, he established that the engine cut out at exactly the same spot every time, and marked the spot with a small heap of rocks at the side of the track. He also realised it could be restarted anywhere back up the slope. He signalled the men to winch the truck back up to the top of the slope and was still thinking about the problem, when the second transporter arrived.

"Okay, tell you what we're going to do," Sven told the men. "We're going to send the first transporter down the slope to see if we get the same result. If we do, we'll use your winch to pull it back," he added, nodding to the driver of the newly arrived transporter. "Hastings here will fill you in with what's been going on. If it happens again, we're all going home for the day and I'll try and find out just what the hell's been going on here."

The transporter stopped in exactly the same place, twice, just beyond Sven's rock marker.

"Right, that's it! Let's go home," Sven said, unable to keep the annoyance out of his voice, and getting into his truck added: "All of you be at the yard, usual time, tomorrow."

When he got back to the small town of Arbreville where they were based, he went to see Harimoto, the Contract Manager, who was apparently responsible for his and several other logging operations in the area, the legality of which probably would not have withstood any serious scrutiny, but was well buried under fistfuls of US dollar bills. He was a small Japanese man in his mid-forties, of unpleasant manner and appearance, who spoke English with difficulty. He and Sven had taken an instant dislike to one another, but Sven treated him as just another disadvantage to this job that had seemed a worthwhile opportunity when he started it, not least because of the high pay that was US dollars in hand, no questions asked. Harimoto, for his part disliked Sven mainly because of his size and strength and the latent fear this induced that he certainly wouldn't admit to, not even to himself, that any sort of physical confrontation would certainly result in his suffering a very painful and humiliating conclusion. Also, Sven's easygoing can-do manner, the aura of authority that seemed to surround him and the ease with which he did things that Harimoto couldn't even begin to attempt, reinforced the fairly well hidden inferiority complex that he'd had most of his life.

Sven entered his office, which was a large part of a rather ramshackle wooden building, with a window air-conditioner that had long since died of neglect and the rank stale air inside would have seriously challenged an industrial chemist's expertise to analyse. He described the morning's events to Harimoto. The latter, perhaps with some justification as he had not fully understood the import of Sven's story, could not see why, just because there was apparently some difficulty with getting a transporter up a hill, he had to lose a day's logging.

"We go see ploblem. Come! Now!" Harimoto said, abruptly, starting towards the office door without looking at Sven and calling to his chauffeur.

"Drop me off at the yard and I'll bring the truck," said Sven, "you won't want to be stuck in the jungle when your car stops."

Harimoto shrugged his shoulders and went to his car. When they got to the yard Sven said:

"I'll lead the way and show you where it all happened."

When they came to the slope, Sven stopped and walked back to Harimoto, who had remained sitting in his car, still in a truculent frame of mind.

"Just down there," said Sven, "go slowly so that you're not too far beyond the point I marked with that little pile of rocks beside the track, otherwise I won't be able to tow you back."

Harimoto grunted by way of reply and said something to his driver in Japanese. It was obvious from the way his car drove forward that he didn't believe Sven's story. He was intent on demonstrating his annoyance at this needless interruption to his day and hoping to humiliate Sven at the same time. He would have to see if he could dock his pay for the lost production. Yes, that would be good. At this thought, he brightened up a bit and told his driver to get on with it.

Sven, who by now was almost beginning to wonder if he hadn't imagined the whole episode – it was so damned unlikely, after all – watched the car gain speed down the hill. To his slight relief, it stopped some distance beyond the point where his engine had cut out. He got back into the truck and drove cautiously down the slope, stopping well short of his rock marker: he had no desire to be stuck out here with Harimoto.

He walked up to the car. Trying reasonably hard not to appear too sarcastic, he opened the door and said: "Having trouble?"

Harimoto, by now livid at the humiliation of being in the wrong and thus unable, in turn, to humiliate Sven, replied with ill-concealed anger: "Get lope! Pull car back!"

Sven, now beginning to enjoy the other's discomfort replied: "Sorry, but as I warned you, you are now too far away for my towrope to reach you because you went too fast.

We'll have to go back in the truck and send one of the transporters out here to recover your car."

For a moment, Sven thought Harimoto was going to explode, but sanity, in the shape of realising the likely outcome (extreme pain and further humiliation) of any physical assault on Sven prevailed and he eventually managed to control himself enough to get out of his car. His driver, terrified by his boss's rage, ran ahead to open the truck door for him. The uncomfortable journey back in the truck did nothing to improve Harimoto's mood. He sat with a face like thunder and didn't speak until Sven dropped him at his office. He then said something briefly to his driver, who stayed in the truck, then to Sven, "Get car velly quick and make work – must have by night time."

Having organised the recovery of the car, Sven decided he'd earned a drink so went to the only half decent bar in the town, somewhat incongruously named 'The Ritz', and sat down to enjoy a cold beer, wondering idly why the canned music being played seemed to mangle the English language so much, the language he'd spent many an hour struggling to learn:

"Ay-e-e-e jer-r-r-ss won-n-n-na ler-r-r-r-ve yee-o-o-o, Buy-bee…" the pop singer informed her captive audience.

He'd no sooner sat down than a fellow logger by the name of Mike Harrington he'd got to know in the bar sat down alongside him.

"God, I hate this dump," Mike started, "the stinking heat, things that bite you, nothing bloody works, you can't get anyone to do anything, and this morning one of my blasted trucks broke down – stuck out in the wild." Picking up his beer he went on: "Cheers, or should that be depressions?"

Having taken a drink he continued, "Anyway, how come you're skiving in here at this time of day and not sweating your nuts off for that charming oriental you have to answer to?"

"Cheers," responded Sven, in a far from cheerful tone, before downing a good draught of his beer and continuing: "I'm here because of a most extraordinary thing this morning. My trucks didn't break down, like yours, they just cut out, and the really astonishing thing was that they all did it at exactly the same spot, and worked perfectly when we pulled them back. It happened again just now when old Quasimodo, who didn't believe me, insisted on going out there to see for himself. I was delighted when his Merc cut out in exactly the same way at the same spot, and he had to enjoy the discomfort of my truck to get him back to his office. Almost made the whole charade worth it just to see his face in the truck!" he added, smiling as he recalled seeing the anger and humiliation fighting for control of Harimoto's face. "Anyway," he went on, "I've just had to send some of my crew out to retrieve his car. I'm damned if I know what's caused it all, it just doesn't make any sense to me one way or another."

"Bugger me – that might well have been what happened to my truck! One of our transporters was leading the convoy and it just stopped on a bend over a stream, completely blocking the track. Up until then it had been perfectly okay, but just cut dead, according to the driver. Our crew truck was following it, so we all just came back and I sent some mechanics out there to fix it. Maybe I'd better get out there quickly and see if pulling it back works like it did for you."

A slight pause, then he continued: "Well, fairly quickly, anyway – I've got a beer to finish first!"

Just as he was getting up to leave, another logger of their acquaintance, Pierre LeFevre, came in. He too was an expat Canadian with a fairly similar background to Sven, and was working under similar conditions.

"You two must be being paid very well to be able to take an afternoon off like this," he said, by way of greeting as he sat down and signalled the barman to bring him a beer.

"Funny you should say that," said Sven, "we were just about to say the same to you! Anyway, we've got a very good excuse for being here – our vehicles have run into trouble. What's your excuse?"

"Vehicle trouble?" repeated Pierre eyeing them suspiciously, "what sort of trouble?"

So they told him, and it very soon became apparent that Pierre had encountered exactly the same problem.

"So, have you two bright sparks arrived at a theory as to what could have caused this to happen to our three sets of vehicles this morning, each several kilometres from the others, when they were all working perfectly yesterday, and apparently work as soon as you pull them back from this 'no-go' zone?"

"No-go zone! Hey! That's very good, Pierre, you're English jokes are improving!" laughed Sven, "but you're right – it does appear to have a very clearly defined boundary, this 'no-go' zone, and no, we haven't the slightest idea what's caused it or perhaps more importantly, whether it will continue to do so."

"I tell you one thing," chipped in Mike, "if it *is* still there tomorrow, it isn't going to be long before the word gets around the natives that there's a powerful evil spirit loose in the jungle and they won't go near the place. Even if we get the trucks to work, we won't be able to hire any labour!"

"Christ, I hadn't thought of that," said Sven, "but you're absolutely right. We'll have to get this resolved bloody quickly, but how?"

"Wish I knew," commented Mike, while Pierre nodded and stared thoughtfully into his beer.

"Wait a cotton-pickin' minute," said Sven, "what if some bugger's put an electronic gizmo beside the track that kills the ignition as you go past it? That could have caused it!"

"Great thinking, Batman," laughed Mike, "but it was also diesel trucks that packed up, remember? They don't have an ignition system so it can't be that simple."

"Yeah, you're right, and just as I was thinking I was on to something."

"Another thing," continued Mike, "who'd want to play a trick like that in this Godforsaken hole?"

"A sacked labourer with a grudge, perhaps," ventured Pierre, before correcting himself, "but no, couldn't be that – none of them would have the know-how."

"What about those eco-something people, whatever they call themselves, they're always protesting about cutting down trees," said Sven.

"Now, that is a distinct possibility," said Mike. "I might go out and have a look round where our transporter stopped, see if I can see any suspicious-looking gadgets."

They sat for a moment in silence, considering these possibilities.

"Tell, you what," said Sven, "let's make this a serious investigation – I mean carry it out methodically. For instance, let's see if we can plot any sort of boundary to Pierre's 'no-go' zone – you know, see how far it stretches.

"Now you're talking a lot of sense there, Sven. Let's have another brain stimulator in the shape of another round of what passes for the 'amber nectar' in these parts," replied Mike, signalling the barman for another three beers, "and then put together a proper plan of action. But first, I think we need a good map of the area."

"I've got one in my truck – back *toute de suite*, er, in a second." So saying, Pierre hurried out to his truck.

A quarter of an hour later they had agreed what to do. There were several tracks shown on the map as entering the jungle. As they would obviously have to travel in pairs, one some distance behind the other, Pierre said he had a friend in Mayanda, a small town some ten miles to the south of Arbreville, who would probably be able to join him. Pierre and his friend would take an agreed area going south along the edge of the jungle, marking up each track with the position where the no-go zone started. Sven and Mike would do the same going north. Both would cover as much ground as they could by nightfall, and then meet in the Ritz again that evening at seven to compare the results of their surveys.

CHAPTER 8

How far does the problem stretch?

Sven and Mike, having stopped to buy an identical map to the one Pierre had and one or two other necessities for the trip, set off. They went via Mike's yard so that he could arrange for his stranded transporter to be recovered. He gave the necessary instructions to ensure that a second vehicle was not also stranded, and then they set off for the first track they were going to check.

It wasn't long before Sven, who'd said he'd go first down this track, came to an abrupt stop. Mike, who'd been following a short distance behind, stopped, and picking up his tow rope, walked up to Sven's truck.

"Exactly how my truck stopped this morning," said Sven "no warning, just cut dead. And," he added as an afterthought, "I reckon it's about as far from the edge of the jungle proper, say that line of trees, as it was this morning. Before you pull me back, let's just make a note of roughly how far it is by walking over and both counting our paces to those trees. Then we'll mark up on the map where my truck stopped."

They walked to the first of the trees, which were fairly small and scattered, and then on to where the jungle could really be said to start, with near impenetrable underbrush and no discernible way through, other than the track itself. They stopped level with this line of trees to compare and note the distances they had each measured. Mike had just got out a small notebook to record these when he suddenly felt distinctly unwell.

"Are you okay?" asked Sven, seeing his friend's sudden change of demeanour.

"Well, since you ask, no. I suddenly feel as though something nasty and microbial has just decided to attack me. I need to get back to the truck as soon as possible. Do you feel okay?" he asked over his shoulder as he set off back along the track.

"Yeah, I think so," replied Sven, "though I was just beginning to feel a bit queasy. However, it's eased off now that we're clear of the trees," he added, a few seconds later.

"Bloody odd, that," said Mike. "But yes, I'm beginning to feel okay now myself. Oh, it was probably the goddamned heat and maybe a rotting carcass or gases from a swamp beside the track. Even stranger, though, I could feel a sense of almost panic developing, a compulsion to run away from the trees as fast as possible. Anyway, that's eased off as well, so let's get out of here and try our next track."

At the next track they had swapped places, and it was Mike who came to a sudden halt. Again they measured how far it was from the trees (but didn't venture into them, as it was so nearly the same distance), and marked up the map as before.

After they'd explored some half dozen tracks, including one where an abandoned truck had stopped just past the point where Mike's truck cut out, they decided to call it a day and headed back.

"I'm going back to my place for a shower and change," said Sven. "We might as well all go to Ricky's together to get a meal after we've had that drink at the Ritz."

"Good idea," said Mike. "After I've showered, changed and cooled down a bit, I'll be about ready for some food by then, too."

The others were already into their first beers when Sven and Mike arrived. As they approached the table, Pierre stood up and introduced his companion.

"Sven and Mike," he said, turning to each in turn. "I'd like you to meet my friend, compatriot and fellow sufferer Jean. After we'd found out he had the same problem, he decided he'd come up and stay with me for a day or two to learn what he could. It won't take him long to get back if the whole thing blows over."

Jean stood up and shook hands with the other two, adding with a laugh as he did so: "I'm glad to know that Pierre and I aren't the only two idiots who were conned into thinking this was a good place to come for a job! What got you two – the lousy greenback, I suppose, there can't ever be any other reason!"

"Got it in one!" replied Mike with a laugh, "trouble is, you don't find that out until too late. Anyway, glad to meet you."

They settled down to discuss the findings of their respective trips, and it very soon became apparent that they were almost identical, after they had copied their stopping points onto a single map.

"What is it, Pierre, what have you noticed that has dodged our close scrutiny?"

"But, do you not see it *mes amis,* allowing for a bit of error in our markings and measures, all these points we have marked are practically in a straight line."

"God, you're right!" said Sven. "I was looking mainly at the points in relation to how far they were from the trees, but yes, it is a straight line, even though the line of the edge of the forest isn't particularly straight. Why the hell do you suppose that is?"

They all fell silent for a moment, pondering this finding.

"One thing that might be worth mentioning," said Jean, breaking the silence, "did either of you actually go into the jungle? Well, we did at the first track we tried, after we'd

81

measured how far the trees were from the 'no-go' zone point, and we both felt very ill and scared suddenly. It passed off almost immediately when we left the trees. Any ideas on that?"

Sven looked at Mike, who replied in a slightly agitated manner: "But that's exactly what happened to us, too. Not so much to Sven, but it hit me pretty hard. I guess that's probably because he's such a big hard bugger that no bug would dare to have a go at him, but yes, it definitely hit me, and as you said, cleared as we left the trees. Either way, we seem to have identified one problem just to find another!"

Sven smiled slightly at that particular reference to himself but added: "As a matter of fact, I didn't notice it this morning when the gang and I were going to start work first thing, and I don't think it was the case when old Quasimodo (or Harimoto, to give him his correct name) was out there later on, or at least I didn't notice him being other than his usual objectionable self!"

Mike rejoined with a slight laugh: "Quasimodo is so unpleasant that you'd be hard-pressed to tell even if he was ill, but maybe that illness thing didn't start till midday or a bit later. What the hell do you suppose is going on out there?"

"More to the point," cut in Pierre, "what the devil are we going to do about it? If it doesn't disappear as quickly as it came, we're all going to be out of a job."

"Dammit, you're right," said Mike, "I hadn't thought that far ahead."

They all sat in silence for a few moments, which Sven was the first to break.

"What I suggest is this. Let's all set out as normal tomorrow morning and see if this 'thing' is still out there. Also, let's check this illness and fear thing to see if that's still apparent. If, as I suspect, it is all exactly the same as it was today, we'll have to pack up for the day, anyway, so let's meet here again tomorrow at, say midday. Everyone okay with that?"

They all nodded their agreement, finished their beers, and in a far from cheerful frame of mind, went on to Ricky's for a meal and then back to their respective houses.

The next morning Sven found his truck stopped at *exactly* the same spot as it had the previous day. However, this time he took his driver with him and they both walked a little distance in toward the trees. This time Sven did experience both the fear and ill feeling, but not half so much as his driver, who took quite a while to recover.

After returning his crew to the yard, trying to give them some words of reassurance and telling them to be there again the next morning, he went to see Harimoto. The latter seemed to have undergone a complete change of mood, and Sven nearly convinced himself that the man was actually trying to be pleasant. More likely, he thought, that he'd got wind of the problem being more widespread than just his contract, that it wouldn't simply go away, and he'd be severely out of pocket. Sven confirmed his fears as quickly as he could with a brief account of the morning's expedition. Sven said they'd try again the next day, to which Harimoto agreed limply.

By midday they had all returned to the Ritz, each one having found no change in his particular part of the 'no-go' zone.

Sven started the serious discussion after they'd all settled down with drinks. "Well, unless any of you have had any startling revelations this morning, I don't think we're any further ahead in solving the problem, right?" They nodded their assent. "So, we'll need to get some expert advice. However, we don't want to start a panic so we need to keep it quiet and confidential as much as possible. Obviously, it won't be long before word gets around – we saw an abandoned truck out there yesterday morning which had stopped at the no-go boundary – but we can try to keep a lid on it. One thing I thought might be worth a try. I have a friend in London, one Pat O'Hanlon who is a terrific news hound. He can get information out of the proverbial clam as they say, and in fact once got information out from behind the 'Iron Curtain' as it was then, and we've been in some pretty good scrapes together. I'll give him a call and see if he can ferret anything out. For instance, is it just our little patch, or have others experienced the same thing? If that's okay with you guys I'll follow it up and let you know."

They all agreed and spent a while rather morosely drinking and discussing possible future plans, as suddenly they were at an unexpected loose end and had nothing immediate to do.

Sven, having got clear in his mind how he was going to ask O'Hanlon about the problem, went back to his house to call him.

CHAPTER 9

Help from Outside

Pat O'Hanlon was a freelance journalist, very much a larger-than-life character, who would always be found at the noisy end of a bar, swopping ever more outrageous stories, which in his case were quite likely to be true, as his life had packed in more events than most people could ever have imagined, never mind experienced. He had about him an air of the Irish 'Blarney', always enjoyed life to the full and had an unending fund of funny episodes and jokes, usually of the non-repeatable variety in polite company. He laughed loudly and often and with something of a mischievous twinkle in his eyes, which he used to good effect when trying to get a story from female interviewees.

Today, having had a somewhat late lunch, he was propping up the usual section in his favourite bar just off Fleet Street in London, where a few of the older press men still congregated, despite nearly all the newspaper offices having left the area. He was passing the time of day with an acquaintance, when Sven's phone call came through on his mobile.

"Sven, you old bugger, how the devil are you?" he greeted his caller. "Are you in serious trouble this time or have you just decided on a social call?"

After a few moments listening to Sven, O'Hanlon's whole demeanour changed – an obvious sign to his acquaintance that he was onto something interesting of a professional nature. The conversation was distinctly one sided, as Sven related what had happened, and he finished up with: "Any ideas, Pat, or do you know anyone who might be able to advise?"

"Leave it with me, Sven; I'll get back to you as soon as I can."

And with that, he forestalled the question from his acquaintance by tapping the side of his nose, saying, "Gotta see a man about a dog, as we used to say – can't stop now but looks like something big is brewing, so see you anon chum. Cheers!" He downed the last of his drink, and left the bar hurriedly.

O'Hanlon had heard a few whispers on his own grape vine from a friend in Africa of odd goings-on in their logging operations, nothing definite, but enough to make it worthwhile calling him again to find out any developments.

Half an hour later and he was on the train to Heathrow. He'd heard enough from Africa and a couple of other leads to convince his editor that he was onto something very unusual and possibly very serious, and that he ought to get out to Arbreville as soon as possible. On the way he called Sven.

"I don't know what you've stumbled onto," he began, "but I'm on my way out there to join you. It's going to be a great journey – here to Lagos, Lagos to Libreville and then on via your newly created Bariari national airline, the only one that flies to Arbreville, apparently. God knows what time (I'm beginning to think 'If') I'll arrive. Perhaps you could try and meet me at the airport (I suppose they *do* have an airport and it isn't just a field?). I'll call you later to let you know when I'll get there."

"I don't envy you that trip at all," replied Sven. "I've done it a couple of times now, and yes, it is an airport, of a sort. Still, you will have one advantage. The Bariari airline recently announced that they'd just upgraded to a Mark 3 Dakota…"

He laughed through the splutterings from the other end and then went on:

"Don't worry, I'm assured the plane has been thoroughly overhauled, er, in Lagos, I believe, so it should be fine. See you later."

"Thanks, and with that far from reassuring comment I sincerely hope you do...bye."

It was later, much later, early the next morning in fact, before a tired, dishevelled and distinctly unhappy Pat O'Hanlon arrived at Arbreville, where, true to his word, Sven was waiting for him.

"Pat, me boy," he said, hamming up the Irish accent, "how the divil are yis?"

"Feeling as rough as an elephant's arse, and it was only the scent of a possible scoop that's got me here at all. Can we go and get a decent cup of coffee and something to eat, then I'd like a shower and after that I may start to feel a bit human again."

"I see you've had the deluxe VIP treatment on our local airlines," said Sven with a laugh, "and yes, we can get you some breakfast, quite a good one, in fact. My truck's outside."

On their way to Ricky's, where the proprietor provided breakfast for a few 'special' clients, they went over the recent happenings in a bit more detail than had been possible on the phone, and Sven told Pat that he'd arranged to meet the others in the Ritz later that morning so that Pat could get the full picture.

After they'd eaten, they went back to Sven's apartment, a fairly newly built block that had been put up by an oil exploration company when they had thought there was a good prospect of finding oil in the area. Unfortunately, that thought was subsequently found to have been based on 'information' provided by some ministers in the junta that ran the country then. Hoping to try and attract some foreign money into the impoverished bank accounts of those same ministers, the information bore precious little resemblance to the actual surveys on which it had been based, and the oil company, on discovering this, stopped any further work and left.

"I can put you up here for a day or two, no problem," said Sven, "not high class, but as good as the best local hotel, and I'm glad to say, with less opportunity to observe the wildlife at extremely close quarters, and even less chance of being relieved of items of personal property!"

"That'd be great. I certainly prefer getting up in the morning with roughly the same amount of blood in my veins as when I went to bed! If it's okay, I'll have a shower and change, then we can go and meet your buddies, then I'd like to go visit the scene of the action."

The others were already there when Sven and Pat arrived, and after introductions, they all briefly described their different experiences, and answered Pat's questions, most of which he caught on his pocket recorder as the conversation progressed. Sven checked that Mike had already driven out that morning to establish that the no-go zone was unchanged, which he confirmed. When they'd all finished, Pat grabbed their attention by saying:

"Without wanting to alarm you more than necessary, I've heard from contacts in some areas where something like this has been going on, that the local population, led by some rabble-rousing wannabe land-grabbing dictators has been persuaded that it's the ex-pats' activities that have caused it all by angering the Forest Spirits with their logging, mining, oil exploration or whatever. The result has been some nasty small scale riots with some of the expats not getting out quickly enough to avoid the whipped up fury of the mobs. Now there doesn't seem to be much sign of anything like that here at the moment from what I've seen, but be warned, it doesn't take long for it to get started. So my advice is get packed up and have an escape plan ready. For instance, don't reckon on flying out, and ad hoc roadblocks, with drunks armed with AK47s manning them looting anything they can get, make driving out extremely dodgy."

"Wow! That's quite some happy future scenario you just painted, Pat," replied Mike. "Still, I don't doubt you're correct. However, I think I may just have an ace up my sleeve in the shape of my ex-naval patrol boat, as you know, Sven. It's quite a big beast with a good long range. I got it a while back when I was diving for a living, and now use it mainly for fishing trips. By a happy coincidence, she's fully fuelled up and ready to go. She's moored, fairly well concealed, in the mouth of a creek in a deserted part of the coast away from the main road, and it's about two miles out of town down rough tracks most of the way to get there. Being an ex-navy ship, all the access doors are solid steel plate with good locks on. Also the windows on the bridge have steel plate covers, so she's pretty well impregnable to the sort of light fingered gentry we're likely to encounter in these parts, otherwise I wouldn't leave her there. Also, I have a couple of rifles locked away on board, and keep a revolver in my apartment. So you would all be very welcome to join me on board if we have to do a runner."

"Thanks, Mike," said Sven, "that's very good of you and a great relief to know. I hope it won't be necessary, but as Pat said, it's better we be prepared."

"Yes, I second the thanks and will be very happy to join you all on the boat," Pierre chipped in, closely followed by a few similar words of thanks from Jean.

"Right," Sven cut back in, "I suggest we all get packed up now ready for a moonlight flit, and meet up back here in a couple of hours time – say at three o'clock. Pat wants to have a look at the no-go zone, so we'll go and do that after I've packed a few things."

While the others went off to pack up, Sven and Pat drove out to where he'd first encountered the no-go zone. When they got to the slope, Sven stopped the truck and they both got out.

"See that marker, the little pile of rocks beside the track?" asked Sven, "that's as near as I could tell was where the truck cut out, so I suggest we walk on from here, and see what happens. Don't want to drive too near in case it has moved."

They got out of the truck and, with the breeze caused by driving with the windows wide open stopped, the heat suddenly hit Pat, being unused to anything like it in quite a long time.

"Jeez, how do you guys put up with this heat?" asked Pat, mopping at his face with a handkerchief already soaked with sweat.

"Just have to get used to it. You can, after a while, but it's never easy or pleasant," replied Sven.

They walked on slowly down the track to the marker and then on a bit further towards the start of the forest proper.

"Whatever it is it doesn't seem to bother the inhabitants. Just listen to that racket!" said Pat.

"Yeah, they are a noisy bunch, but after a while you don't notice them very much, particularly when the chainsaws are operating."

As they walked on past the edge of the forest Pat suddenly stopped, looked at Sven and said:

"I think whatever it is is attacking me now. I suddenly feel distinctly ill. You okay?"

"Yeah, just about. Want to try a bit further?"

"Okay, if you do – let's do it, but slowly, huh?"

Five paces on, Pat suddenly turned tail and ran back along the track as though a tiger was chasing him until he was clear of the forest, and then stood there, leaning heavily against a tree, sweating profusely and gasping for air at the unusual exertion. Sven, meanwhile, was also beginning to feel ill, but before following his friend back out, put a mark in the track with his boot.

When he reached him, Pat was bent over double, still struggling to get his breath back.

"Okay now, Pat?" he asked.

"Yeah, it's settling down a bit. God, but that was weird! Firstly, I was just feeling ill – you know as though I'd got a bad dose of 'flu, bones starting to ache, shivering, that sort of thing, and then after we'd walked that bit further, I was suddenly filled with the most all-consuming panic I've ever experienced. I just had to flee from this God-knows-what that was about to devour me so I ran away as fast as I could. That feeling of dread eased off after I'd left the trees and the 'flu' has nearly gone now. Man, that was the most bloody awful thing I've ever experienced, I can tell you. He sat down on a rock beside the track, mopping his brow and gradually calming down.

Sven said: "I was feeling the same flu-like effects as you, but not the fear, though maybe I didn't go in quite far enough. I marked where I got to, so I'll go back, and then a little further to see if affects me the same way."

"For Christ's sake, don't do it man, it's bloody terrifying," came the almost shouted reply.

"I think I ought to so that no one can say it was just you getting the heebie-jeebies. However, if I lie on the ground screaming for help, be a good mate and pull me out, huh?"

"If you think I'm going back in there you're very much mistaken," said Pat, still visibly shaken by his experience, "so don't bloody fall over – I don't think I could come in to rescue you. And besides, you're far too heavy for me to shift – I'd need a bloody bulldozer or crane to move you!"

Notwithstanding these unreassuring words, Sven decided he had to do it.

"I'll be okay," he said over his shoulder as he started walking back along the track. As he got close to the mark he had made, he felt the illness symptoms enveloping him again, feeling very bad as he got to the mark. Steeling himself, he walked on another pace. Two. Three. Four.

At his fifth step, the feeling of indescribable terror that Pat had experienced engulfed him. The feeling that he was drowning in wet concrete grabbed him with the force of a whirlwind and he realised he was running for his life back out of the forest.

It was Pat's turn to ask anxiously if Sven was alright. Eventually, he calmed down, and they both got rather shakily back into the truck.

"I think we can safely say the no-go barrier is firmly in place, and judging from our experience, no one, but *no one* is ever going to get into this, or any other bloody forest past it," said Sven, as he started the truck.

"I'll go along with that, one hundred percent. In all my life I don't think, in fact I *know*, I have never experienced anything like that, and I've been in some pretty rough situations, as you know.

Also, I have never been so bloody scared, and of what, I wonder? Anyway, I sure as hell don't ever want to be that scared again!"

They sat in silence for a while as Sven drove them back. "We might as well go past my yard to see if anything's happening there, then on to my apartment to pack."

As he pulled up opposite his yard, he noticed the five bar gate was open, and he thought he saw a couple of figures disappear behind one of the sheds.

"I'll have that bugger's guts for garters – he knows he not supposed to leave the gate open," said Sven, as he went to get out of the truck.

"Hold it!" said Pat, quickly grabbing the other's arm. "You don't want to walk in there on your own unarmed, when something doesn't look right. It could mean trouble."

"You're right. I'll call my foreman and ask him what's going on down there," said Sven reaching for his phone, and punching in the keys.

"Funny, there's nothing. No ring tone, engaged signal or anything. He usually answers immediately. Let's go via the office and see if Quasimodo knows what's going on. For all I know, he may have decided to save a bit of cash and fired the whole lot of them. Meeting Quasimodo (or Harimoto, to give him his proper name – he's the bod I have to report to) is another unpleasant experience you won't forget."

Arriving at the office, another surprise awaited them. Harimoto's car was not in its usual place alongside the building, and on entering his office a scene of chaos greeted them. The place was a shambles, some remnants were still smouldering in what had been a wastepaper basket, the window had been pushed out from the inside and was lying smashed on the ground outside and the desk had been upended.

"Looks like he had quite a party here," said Pat eyeing the wreckage, "but at least there isn't a body or any blood splattered around."

"No, but it looks as though someone has run off with the loot – look at that safe! And there *is* a bit of blood on the floor beside it."

The rusty hulk was standing on its plinth, the door open and just a few papers scattered inside. The blood Sven had noticed consisted of a smeared patch about the size of a tennis ball, with a line of drips leading to the window.

"I wonder if they found his secret stash?" mused Sven. "He kept cash in the safe for day-to-day expenses, but I caught him one day when I knew he'd just picked up a goodly wad from one of his nefarious dealings and he wasn't expecting me to visit. He'd actually locked the door, but when I tried it, I just assumed it was a bit stuck, so leant on it a bit hardish. The lock gave way and as the door swung open old Quasimodo was standing by that cupboard, which was a bit out from the wall, looking guilty as hell with his hands behind his back. He screamed at me to get out, which I did, as I hadn't intended to break in. When I went back a little later with an apology and promise to repair his door he calmed down a bit, but never mentioned what he'd been up to with the cupboard. I thought he was probably hiding his loot, but I didn't give it much more thought at the time, but now, I wonder…"

"Here, grab that end and let's see if there is anything behind it," said Sven, going over to the cupboard.

"Hold it a second," said Pat, moving to what was left of the window and looking out. "You always were a bit impetuous. Let's just make sure there isn't some chancer out there hoping that someone like us comes along to show them where or if there is anything else in here worth looting."

"You're absolutely right, Pat," Sven replied with a slight laugh, and after a slight pause while Pat looked out through the window. "Reckon it's clear out there now?"

"Yep – let's get on with it and get out of here. If there is any law round here and they find us like this, well, I wouldn't fancy our chances!"

They moved the cupboard a couple of feet away from the wall, only to reveal nothing but some lethal looking spiders' webs, a few bits of paper and plenty of dirt. There were, however, signs on the floor that one end had been pulled out several times.

"Ah, I thought so!" Sven bent down, and fishing a penknife out of his pocket, prised up a short length of floor board that was clearly not nailed down and showed signs of having been lifted recently. There was an open empty biscuit tin in the space beneath.

"Damn, the buggers have beaten us to it!" he muttered.

"Try lifting that out," said Pat.

Sven did so, to reveal another closed tin underneath. "I thought that might be the case," said Pat. "They've been using that trick since they built the pyramids! But careful how you lift it out – it might be booby-trapped."

Sven did a careful but thorough check all round the box and couldn't find any trace of a trap. So having retrieved the second tin, they quickly replaced the first tin, the piece of floor board and the cupboard, scuffed over the dirt to remove traces of the cupboard having been moved and, after checking that there was still nobody hanging around outside, left.

Once they were safely in the truck and under way, Pat said:

"It might be a good idea to report the break-in we've just found to the police now, otherwise some clever bugger might start accusing us of doing it, as someone may have seen us enter the building."

"Good idea, Pat, I'll do it now," Sven replied, pulling in to the side of the road and reaching for his mobile phone. "As a result of a bit of trouble I helped him sort out a little while ago, I get on pretty well with the local police commissioner, and have his own number stored on the phone."

It didn't take more than a couple of minutes to get through and report all they knew about the incident, except for the removal of the second tin box, which (they reasoned) obviously had nothing to do with the event as it was still in its hiding place, and, anyway, they hadn't opened it yet to find out what was in it.

They arrived at the Ritz bar to find the others already there.

"I hope you're all packed up and ready to go," said Pat, quietly as they sat down, "as it looks as though things may have already started to go downhill – not sure, but…"

Sven then took over to recount their discovery at Harimoto's office, and was about to carefully open the tin, when he saw a uniformed policeman come into the bar, and without hesitation, walk over to their table. Sven slipped the box to Pat under the table, making sure that the policeman didn't see the manoeuvre. They stopped talking and turned round enquiringly to the new arrival, who without any preamble, and addressing Sven in heavily accented French said:

"You were seen leaving the premises of Mr Harimoto, which was subsequently found to have been ransacked. You have to come with me to the police station."

Picking up his phone from the table, Sven replied: "There seems to have been some misunderstanding as I have already reported the break-in to Edouard, er, that is your Commissioner Ricard, personally, so if I may have your name, I think we can clear this up right now."

The man, clearly somewhat flustered at the mention of the commissioner's name and that this man seemed to know him personally, said: "Just a moment, please, I need to phone my office," and so saying, left the bar rather more quickly than he had entered.

"Mike, quick," said Sven urgently and quietly, "follow him out and check if there's a police car out there and what he does, but don't let him see you."

Picking up an empty glass and making as though he was going up to the bar, Mike was able to do as requested without the policeman noticing, and watched him through the slightly open door to the bar. He came back a few moments later.

"Very funny behaviour for a policeman," he said, as he sat down again. "He went over to a car with a couple of other men in it (not a police car, need I add), then got in, and they all buggered off down the street at a fair old rate. What do you suppose that was all about?"

Pat replied: "I'm afraid it bears out my worst suspicions of a little earlier. That was no cop, but probably part of the mob that raided your boss's office, and they must have seen us arrive. I wouldn't like to be in his shoes if they've kidnapped him – most likely for ransom. Maybe they thought they could add you to the list of bargain offers. Either way, we'd better stick together – you know – safety in numbers." He went on after a slight pause: "I'd feel a lot happier if we'd got a gun."

"We have. I thought to bring mine with me, just in case!" replied Mike quietly.

"Good, that makes me feel a bit better. Now, while we've got a few moments, let's have a look in that box. Sven, you found it so you open it, but carefully. No, on second thoughts, don't. You'd be better doing it by remote control somehow and not in this bar, in case it explodes on opening."

"Gee, thanks, Pat – you're all heart! Still, you're probably right. It'd be just like that little shit to leave a bomb like that in case someone got to his loot. We'll try it later. Right now we've got to decide what to do."

Following a general murmur of assent, Pierre asked: "Does anyone of us have a reason to stay here until tomorrow, because if not, we might as well hightail it to Mike's boat before it gets dark and get the hell out of this dump. From what Sven and Pat said, this additional no-go zone for people seems to be a fixture that's been there for two days to our knowledge and there doesn't seem to be any reason to suppose it's just going to go away, does it?"

"Fortunately, I brought everything with me of any value that I've got out here (and I've kept that to a minimum for obvious reasons!) for my stay with Pierre, so I'm quite happy to go tonight. However, I had got quite a promising date set up for tonight," said Jean, "but I guess she'll have to console herself at her great missed opportunity with someone else – which won't be for the first time, I'm sure," he added with a laugh.

"Okay, that's agreed then, we go tonight," said Sven. "I suggest we use my truck, which can carry us all and a fair amount of baggage. It'll attract less attention than a mini-convoy of us all using our own trucks."

As unostentatiously as possible and putting on a show of lighthearted banter, they left the bar and got into the truck.

"Let's make it look as though we're going to have a party at your place Mike, being the nearest to your boat," said Pierre "and we'll go round to Sven and my place to pick up the luggage, but make it look as though we're bringing out crates of beer, some bottles of scotch or six packs – whatever, but try to conceal the luggage."

"Right," said Mike, "then when we get to my place we'll start a bit of noise as though we're settling down to a good night of it, leave the music blasting and sneak out to the truck and drive away quietly. I think I know a good back way that won't get us noticed."

CHAPTER 10

The Moonlight Flit

The plan went without a hitch until they were about halfway down the track to the boat, when they saw the track was blocked with an apparently dumped car.

"I don't like the look of that one bit," said Pat, "we're likely to be ambushed, but it's going to be difficult to get past that car. Got your gun handy, Mike?"

As they tried to get between the trees and the car, a man stepped out into the headlights, pointing a rifle at the car. A second man appeared alongside him holding up his hand for them to stop.

Sven, who was driving, said, "I guess we'd better stop – there may be more of them in the trees."

The second man came up to Sven, pointing a pistol at him and ordered him to get out. As he was doing so, the bogus 'policeman' they'd seen earlier joined the group and said:

"We think you stole a box from the office of Mr. Harimoto this afternoon. You will hand it over now!"

Sven started to say something when the man covering him hit his arm hard with the revolver and said:

"You, shut up! Just stand by car. You!" he said to Pat who was on the back seat on the driver's side. "Get box and give it to 'policeman'. Hurry!"

Pat got out carefully and said, "OK. It's in the back. I'll get it."

He moved slowly to lift the tin out of the back of the truck and handed it to the 'policeman', who put it on the ground while fishing in his pocket for a torch.

The events that followed were almost a blur they occurred so quickly. Firstly, the 'policeman' opened the tin. There was a loud popping sound and the 'policeman' reeled back, choking and holding his hands over his face, while the stench of ammonia reached the truck.

The man covering Sven with his revolver made to move towards the 'policeman'. In the split second it took for Sven to react, he was on him, at the same time shouting to Mike: "Get the guy with the rifle!"

Sven grabbed the man's wrist, holding it with such force that he couldn't move it, and at the same time smashing a straight left punch, that a world heavyweight champion would have been proud of, into the man's temple. He collapsed without a sound, dangling like a damp cloth from the wrist that Sven still held. Sven then removed the gun from the limp hand, gave it to Pat, and let the body drop to the ground.

Mike didn't have to 'get' the man with the rifle as, though he couldn't see past the car's headlights, he'd heard enough to trigger urgent thoughts of immediate self-preservation, had dropped the rifle and run off into the trees without waiting to see what happened to his erstwhile 'friends'.

Mike went over and picked up the rifle. Surveying the prostrate ex-gunman and the 'policeman', still sitting on the ground with his hands over his face, alternatively coughing, choking and moaning said:

"Well, that seems to have sorted them out. Want to take the bodies with us or leave them here?"

"Good question," said Sven, gently rubbing his knuckles. "God, but that bugger's got a hard head! Anyway," he went on, "I think we should just leave them here. Old buggerlugs here will come round eventually and can help his cop friend along to a doctor's, though with the packet of ammonia he took in the face I don't fancy his chances of a recovery very much. However, let's move them off the track a bit, so they don't get run over to add to their ills, and commandeer their weapons. Oh, and let's not forget old Quasimodo's tin – think there are any more nasty surprises in it, Mike?"

"Doubt it, but I'll put it in the back of the truck again, very carefully, and we can examine it on the boat," said Mike, gingerly picking up the still-smelling box. "And with a bit of luck the smell will have cleared by then, too!" he continued, trying to avoid breathing in the vapour.

They picked up the revolver moved the comatose gunman just into the trees and then lifted the 'policeman' and placed him alongside the gunman. He moaned while they were doing so, and between coughing fits said to them in a barely audible fashion, "You can't leave me here like this!"

"No? Watch me!" said Sven, uncharitably. "You expect us to help you after what you were going to do to us? When your friend here wakes up he can get you to a doctor. Your other friend has run off, and I wouldn't be surprised if he's taken your car and left you two here – obviously very concerned about your welfare! Still, it's not a hellova long walk back to the town. Next time, pick your friends a little more carefully. Oh, and I'd get out of that police uniform if I were you. Edouard will not take kindly to someone trying to join his force via the back door like that!"

They then got back into their truck and drove on down to the boat.

"This is as far as we can go in the truck. Let's get out and wait a few minutes in case anyone else is following us before we go to the boat. It'll take us a few minutes to get everything on board, unlock the mooring chains, get the engine started and be on our way, and I'd rather not do that while we're being shot at if we can avoid it! Also, I'll do a quick recce to make sure we don't have any undesirable visitors awaiting our arrival," said Mike.

After getting out of the truck and turning off its engine and the lights, Mike made his way very quietly up to his boat, while the others hid by the truck in the bushes at the side of the track armed with their newly commandeered weapons. After a few moments of near absolute silence, the insect population resumed its interrupted night time cacophony.

Having ascertained that there was no one on board or near the boat, Mike came back to the group. They then all waited in silence for a couple of minutes. Nothing. No noises of approaching people or vehicles, only the insects. Eventually, Mike said quietly:

"I think we're okay now, but let's get moving as quickly but as quietly as we can. Starting the boat's engine will make quite a racket, so that has to be when we're absolutely ready to go."

Fortunately, there was enough moonlight for them to make out where they were going, and so with a minimum of trouble and very little noise they put all their bags and other bits and pieces into the boat, managing not to lose anything or anyone when walking along the very rickety plank to get on to the boat. Mike, who'd been first on board, had unlocked the various steel doors and covers on the bridge windows while the others were loading all the equipment. He then unlocked the mooring chains, lowered them quietly into the water and pushed the boat clear of the bank. There was enough of a small flow in the creek to get them drifting out towards the sea. When it looked as though they had got a clear run ahead of them, Mike started the engine. Because they'd been so quiet, the sudden noise seemed as though it must have been audible for miles, but they were quickly under way and heading out to sea, with no sign of anyone being aware of their departure.

CHAPTER 11

Farewell to Arbreville

Once they were clear of the creek, cans of beer were handed out and they all drank to their successful escape, and then discussed where they should go to. Pat needed to get back to London to give his editor the story as quickly as possible, and Sven said he'd like to go with him. Pat was keen for him to do so, to give another slant on his story.

So after checking the charts and the amount of fuel left in the tanks, Mike said there was enough to get them to Douala in the Cameroon. This was the nearest town of any size which they could reach early the next morning, and from where Pat and Sven could get a flight back, after a few changes, to London. So Pierre was nominated as helmsman to keep the boat on a steady course, nor-nor-west to clear Port Gentil, while Sven and Mike cooked up a somewhat sparse meal, having only ingredients taken from Mike's kitchen and deep freeze that they'd brought with them during the unexpected escape.

About half an hour later, during the meal, they discussed what they would be doing next. Mike would sail back down the coast to Cape Town, where his home was, and would treat it as a bit of a holiday, as he felt he owed himself one after his time in Arbreville. Pierre and Jean accepted his offer to travel with him to Cape Town, after which they would go their separate ways. Both liked the idea of a 'cruise' holiday, and happily agreed to chip in to the cost of fuel and other supplies.

In the middle of these discussions, Jean suddenly remembered Quasimodo's tin which was still sitting in the heap of bags and other belongings they'd stowed hastily on the boat when setting sail.

"How about checking that stink bomb tin?" he said, "we might as well see what was in it that those three were so anxious to get their hands on."

"Good idea," said Pierre. "I'd forgotten about that while indulging in the culinary delights you two cooked up! Yes, let's see what's in it."

"Right, I'll go get it," said Jean, going out of the cabin to retrieve it from the heap.

There were collective 'Whooshes' of amazement from the four, as the contents were put onto the cabin table: bundles of US hundred dollar bills and a small leather pouch with quite a few beautifully cut diamonds in it, some quite large.

"Bet that lot wasn't acquired by purely legal means!" exclaimed Mike.

"Jeez, those stones must be worth a packet in their own right!" said Pat. "The only time I seen better was through a stocking mask!" he joked. "So, what are we going to do with this lot?" he finished up, to no one in particular.

After a lot of discussion they decided that they would use some of the cash for Sven's back pay, and some of it as an 'advance' for the others to tide them over. The rest, together with the box and diamonds would be put into a safe deposit box in Cape Town by Mike, who promised to advise the others of the details of the bank and the safe deposit number later in case of accidents. They also agreed that in the unlikely event of Harimoto reappearing and it transpiring that the cash was all legitimate, they would repay it. Finally, they set a date for three months later to meet up again at Mike's home in Cape Town to decide what to do about the money and diamonds.

That decided, they drew up a watch schedule, each of them acting as helmsman and lookout for three hours each.

When they arrived at the Douala harbour early the next morning, they all went to the immigration office on the docks to clear their entry into the country. After they'd cleared all the formalities, Pat and Sven spent some time finding a trustworthy looking taxi to take them to the airport. Mike set about sourcing suitable fuel while Pierre and Jean went in search of a shop to stock up on food, beer and other essential supplies for their trip to Cape Town, which Mike reckoned would take at least five days, unless, of course, they decided to break the journey with visits to towns on the way.

The road was fairly new to the airport, so Pat and Sven got there without incident. They then had to do a fair amount of 'negotiating' to get a flight out – Pat using his journalist ID plus a small bribe to get them both on the first available plane, which took a somewhat circuitous route back to London but got them there just before midnight.

Meanwhile, Mike and the other two, having successfully reprovisioned the boat, had a quite enjoyable and uneventful trip to Cape Town, where the three stayed at Mike's house for a few days while they made their own arrangements as to what to do and where to go next.

On arriving back in London, Pat called his editor from the airport and arranged to meet him early the next morning. He invited Sven to stay the night with him so that he could be at the meeting with Pat's editor the following morning.

After Pat and Sven had told the editor, Matthew Lloyd, all about their experiences, he was delighted to be in a position seemingly to have got a virtual exclusive on what looked to have all the makings of a world scoop. However, it would be even better if he could suggest a likely cause, attributable to an authoritative source, of course.

Consulting his file of 'Useful Contacts' he came up with the name of John Fenwick, and prompted by the file, remembered the occasion they had met and the reason for the meeting. By one of those lucky coincidences that happen from time to time, Matthew was on the spot when a construction team digging out some foundations came across the remains of a body. Because of several factors relating to the proposed new use of the site and its previous use, the Ecowotsit were called in to assess if there was an environmental risk due to the presence of the remains. Yes, he remembered him well then – John had struck him as a thoroughly competent and professional man who knew his subject extremely well, and they had got on well together.

So it came about that John received a surprise phone call from Matthew the next morning, and agreed to meet him over lunch to learn what it was that Matthew needed to know.

After a few preliminaries and reminiscences of their previous work together, Matthew handed over the story to Pat and Sven, who between them, summarised most of what had been going on at Arbreville in relation to the 'no-go area' and fever since the first day when Sven's truck had stopped. After a lot of questioning, John had got a pretty clear idea of what had happened, but had to admit that he didn't know what the cause could be. However, he promised to try and find out and said he'd get back to Matthew as soon as he had anything positive to report. Matthew asked that this be done very quickly, as he wanted to publish the story as soon as possible. He already knew that rumours and anecdotal stories were being published about this phenomenon, but, as far as he knew, no one had established the cause of it. He wanted to be the first with that information.

When he got back to his office, as it was Saturday, John phoned his boss Mark, at home to bring him up to date on what he'd just been told, and to get his agreement to make some discreet enquiries.

This John did, but was unable to get any hard information for Pat. However, he did get a tacit agreement from the Environment minister, George Bentley, that there didn't seem to be any reason at this time not to publish a straightforward press report of the loggers' story, as it didn't add very much to what was already fairly general knowledge. He did, however, suggest that the actual location be suppressed, referring only to a 'West African' country.

CHAPTER 12

Organise a Scientific Expedition

Three days after George Powers had had his interview with Pablo at the immigration detention centre; Mark called him and John Fenwick into his office.

"Well, rather as we thought, it's started to hit the fan with a vengeance!" he began. "Those rumours we've heard recently and that Brazilian's story now seem to have some more substance to them. The Foreign Office has been asked by the president of Nimeroon if the UK could help them to find out what is causing this so-called 'forest fever' as it has hit his country very hard. This is because most of their foreign earnings come from their lumber exports, and for quite a while it appears they have been unable to get into their forests at all."

Seeing the slightly blank looks on both faces of his audience, Mark added, with a trace of sarcasm: "I see your schooling in geography was sadly deficient. Nimeroon is a small ex-colonial coastal country on the west coast of Africa, someway south of Nigeria." Then, relenting a little, added: "Okay, I didn't know that either, but we're all going to have to bone up a bit on the place, as it's going to involve us quite a lot in the very near future – you particularly, John."

Mark continued: "Firstly, the reason for their request is that their president was given one of the bursaries that were given to quite a number of students of ex-colonial countries in the sixties. He studied at Imperial College in London, has very happy memories of his time as a student there and fortunately has held this country in the highest regard ever since, so naturally we want to help if we can."

"So it has been decided on high that we are to put together a team of expert scientists to go out there and investigate what's going on with their forests as soon as possible. It goes without saying that, of course, we will have identified the cause and put forward remedial action within a couple of days of arrival, so don't forget to put new batteries in your magic wand, John!"

Noting John's startled expression, he went on: "Yes, I'm afraid you've drawn the short straw again, and will be part of the team that goes out there. So start scouring your address books for names of suitable people that are available who would like to go on this expedition and who we can propose to the Foreign Office. Tell 'em it will carry huge kudos and help their careers no end. The F.O. is going to make all necessary logistics arrangements with the Nimeroon government, and we are assured by their president of their utmost co-operation. So having identified the team, they'll have to tell us what equipment they need to take with them to carry out as many of their investigations as possible on the spot – mobile field laboratories, if you like. Arrangements are in hand with RAF Transport Command to fly the team and their equipment out to a suitable air field (Nimeroon doesn't have one yet)."

"Douala is the preferred one (though the F.O. hasn't got their agreement yet but our Consul out there is working on it) and then transfer them all onto a Royal Navy frigate that fortunately happens to be on a goodwill visit to several states in that region at the moment. They will be disembarked at the small harbour of Djambaville, the capital of Nimeroon, where there will be a boat provided for them that can act as a floating base and accommodation for the team. All clear so far?"

Before they had a chance to ask anything, Mark went on: "There is a pretty large river that flows out to sea through Djambaville that rises in the mountains many hundreds of miles inland. The idea is to get to the forest via this route for two good reasons. The first is security. The president doesn't want any more people than necessary to know the purpose of our expedition until a positive result can be proclaimed. Also, of course, apart from protecting the team and the equipment from the unwelcome attentions of the local population, it'll be a lot easier to transport everything on a boat upstream to the forest. One reason of ours is that there are known to be some primitive tribes living near the river, and it would obviously be advantageous to see how the fever is affecting them. Finally, there is a coastal plain some twenty-five miles wide that has to be traversed before you reach the forest, again a lot easier by boat. Hell, man you could almost say it was a holiday cruise!" he finished with a smile.

"One other point not to be overlooked is security in the sense that the purpose of the expedition must remain as secret as possible. This is because, even though it's been officially requested by the country's president, there is a lot of public feeling out there that the fever has been caused by the Spirits becoming angry at the destruction of their forest, entirely attributable to the logging carried out by foreigners. They, of course, turn a blind eye to the fair numbers of the indigenous people who have gained employment of one sort or another from the logging, not to mention the shady deals with some of those in positions of authority and the fortunes safely tucked up in Swiss banks that they have made. However, this has turned into a fair amount of suspicion of all foreigners, and outright hostilities to anyone involved in logging – in some cases lethal attacks. So the less anyone knows about the expedition the better."

"Well, that gives you a general overview, and here are two files, one for each of you, with a lot more detail in them that you will need when speaking to your potential travellers. There are also some suggestions as to possible participants though you should also check with any people you know who might either be interested, or more importantly, could make a useful and definitive contribution to the expedition. Any questions?"

Having had a lot of their questions answered, John and George set about their task without too much enthusiasm: John could already hear the most likely response: "You gotta be joking!" However, after an exhausting and battering day of calls, they had managed to put together a proposal to submit to the F.O. that fitted most of their requirements and constraints.

The team eventually selected comprised:

Professor Andrew Kowalski, who held the Chair of Tropical Diseases and Medicines at Bonneville University, and who was currently on a three-year Sabbatical with the Norton University in England. Having led many field trips during his career, particularly in the tropics, he was also invited to be the expedition's leader. John was delighted when he not only accepted, but even sounded keen to join the expedition.

The Professor was a man of distinguished appearance in his early fifties with a naturally authoritative manner, who still had a good head of grey hair. He wore rimless glasses, which gave a distinct American flavour to his appearance, though in fact he was born in England. His parents were both Polish who had managed to flee the Nazi invasion of their homeland, his father having subsequently distinguished himself in the Royal Air Force during World War II as did many of his countrymen. His manner was a little intimidating, as being a man with a formidable intellect, he tended to be rather curt with those who could not follow his line of argument immediately, as some of his students had found out to their cost. He was married to **Myra,** whom he had met when they were both PhD students, she extending her studies as a Pharmacist.

Martin Airedale, a postgraduate research student, who had worked very successfully with Professor Kowalski for more than a year and who the Professor insisted had to accompany him. He was not yet twenty-five, he had excelled academically all his life, was rather quiet and self-effacing and had tended to use his work as an excuse to himself for not socialising more. Physically he was of medium height and very thin, a legacy of little exercise, cursory eating habits and sedentary studying.

Geoff Smith, a medical laboratory technician, who would be responsible for all the equipment the Professor required and for operating it on site. A very conscientious worker in his mid-thirties, he had worked with the Professor during his sojourn at Norton, as a result of which the Professor had implicit trust in all the practical work entrusted to him. A large man, whose size owed as much to a fondness for beer as to physical prowess in a sport, he had a very cheerful disposition and got on well with anyone he worked with.

Dr. Denise Carter, a Tropical Botanist with the Gladstone Arboreal Research College, who had carried out a lot of research into the diseases of tropical trees and plants in West Africa previously. A disastrous love affair that went horribly wrong for her during her undergraduate days had nearly terminated a promising career in her chosen field. Her recovery from that had taken the form of throwing herself totally into her studies to the exclusion of practically all other activities. It had also resulted in her throwing up an impregnable emotional shield, which gave her a cold and aloof manner that in turn increased her isolation outside her immediate work field. Despite this, she still looked physically attractive, which several men had found to their pain, was completely without warmth or encouragement.

Carol Spencer, who was currently working for her PhD in Dr. Carter's department at Gladstone's, and who Dr. Carter had wanted as her assistant. In her early twenties, she was a beautiful girl who seemed to take a perverse delight in detracting from her natural looks by following unsuitable fashion trends. Thus she favoured dressing in shapeless army fatigue style overalls and had her hair done into a frizzy mop that conveyed a totally unkempt appearance. Despite all appearances to the contrary, she had an engaging personality, and had initially been a bit loath to accept the assignment, having recently started a relationship that for the first time in her life was serious. However, encouragement from her boy friend and the intended short duration of the trip decided her to go.

Diane Jameson, a horticultural laboratory technician who had worked for a long time with Dr. Carter and would have similar responsibilities to Geoff Smith. In her early forties, she had the comfortable appearance of one who had a very happy and satisfying life, both professionally and with her husband and two children who were just starting at university, and of whom she was justifiably proud.

John Fenwick, Ecowotsit's Principal Environmental Scientist, who had already had quite a lot to do with earlier reports on the fever, and who Mark wanted to be present, as Ecowotsit would ultimately be responsible for the finished findings of the expedition.

Pat O'Hanlon, the freelance journalist, who was invited because of his firsthand knowledge of the fever and prior involvement with the problem. He would also act as reporter and photographer for the expedition, both on behalf of the team and his editor. It had also not escaped his thoughts that he would be in a great position to write a nontechnical, possibly adventure-style book about the whole enterprise that could help his bank account recover from some recent serious assaults occasioned by some indiscretions on his part.

Sven Pedersen was also invited because of his direct involvement with the fever and knowledge of the forest, local conditions and bush craft gained from his time in West Africa. Also, Pat had specifically asked that he be included.

So this was the team that met up at RAF Brise Norton three days later for the trip to Douala. They were seen off by Mark Bedford and a minister from the Foreign Office, who used the opportunity to stress the importance of their expedition and the need to complete it successfully as soon as practicable. After a final check to ensure that all their equipment had been clearly identified and none was missing, they flew out on the first leg of their journey to Gibraltar, for a refuelling stop and then on to Douala.

They were met at the airport the next morning by the British Consul and the First Officer of the frigate, and were pleasantly surprised at how well everything seemed to have been organised there, as indeed had the whole flight.

As they were leaving the aircraft, the pilot went over to Professor Kowalski and drawing him slightly to one side said:

"I was given this packet by an aide to the minister from the Foreign Office just before we boarded at Brize Norton, with instructions to give it to you personally on arrival at Douala, so here it is."

He quickly handed over a small fairly stiff brown manila envelope, having first looked around to make sure they were not observed. "He didn't say what it was or anything else about it, just to keep it confidential, so better stick it in your pocket right away. Hope you have a successful trip," he concluded, shaking the Professor's hand and then going off to join his crew.

Wondering idly what it might be, he put it in the inside pocket of his bush jacket and then forgot about it, joining the others about to go through the Passport and Immigration Control at the airport.

There was a minimum of delay with the immigration authorities, and all necessary paperwork for the transfer of themselves and their equipment to the frigate had been taken care of by the Consul. Being a bit jaded after the long journey, they were glad not to have to worry about that or the equipment, the Consul having also made the necessary arrangements to have it all offloaded onto trucks for the journey to the harbour and then stowed on board the frigate.

The team were then taken in cars provided by the Consul directly to the frigate. Once there, they were shown to their cabins for the overnight journey to Djambaville, and invited to 'freshen up' before returning to the ward room where they were given a very welcome breakfast. As all the equipment would not be loaded before mid-day and having nothing else to do, most of the team returned to their cabins to relax and recover from the tiring effects of the flight. Though jet lag was not a problem, the time difference only being one hour ahead, most still felt a bit jaded by the journey.

The Professor, perhaps feeling the effects a little more than the others, took off his jacket prior to lying down. Draping it on a chair, he saw the envelope the pilot had given him sticking out of the inside jacket pocket. Wondering what it could possibly be, given to him in an almost conspiratorial way by the pilot, he opened it. He could hardly suppress a laugh when he saw that, apart from a folded covering letter, sellotaped to a piece of card were nine military style 'dog tags' complete with neck cords.

Bloody typical of a ministry mentality to issue us with Identity Discs! he thought, chucking them on to his bunk before turning his attention to the letter.

The letter apparently originated from a military research group, was addressed to the minister who had seen them off at Brize Norton personally and referred specifically to the Professor's expedition. After wading through an amount of jargon relating to 'official secrets' and other admonitions as to security, the gist of it was that these discs were specially developed to appear as normal dog tags, but built into the plastic film on the back was a new electronic system that was primarily intended to ensure that the malaria bearing Anophele mosquitoes and some other fever bearing parasites would not come anywhere near the wearer. Apparently, it was important that the tag be 'primed' by direct contact with the wearer's skin (and, therefore, must be worn under all clothing), must be worn at all times and once 'primed' by one person could not be transferred to another, as it would not then work.

Picking up the discs again, the Professor was slightly surprised to see that they were already engraved with the names of each of his team members and the supposedly secret code name for the expedition – "UK Savers". A rebellious streak in his nature tempted him to throw them into the wastepaper basket in his cabin, but with a sigh of resignation at the workings of ministerial minds, decided instead that he'd better hand them out to the team at lunch as instructed. Besides, if they really worked against the mosquitoes, providing a successful field trial for them would not be a hardship, and indeed would a benefit to the expedition. If they work, he added to himself as a morose afterthought.

So after lunch he called the team together and gave them their individual discs, appraising them as to the contents of the letter. He finished up by saying that they must ensure they all wore them, but he didn't suppose they need to do so until they docked in Djambaville, as he hadn't noticed many mosquitoes out here in the open ocean, (thereby giving his rebellious streak some satisfaction).

CHAPTER 13

Start of the Expedition

It was mid-day the next day before they were moored alongside the quay in the little harbour of the small town of Djambaville. The party, much refreshed after their short journey on the frigate, disembarked, with Pat O'Hanlon, followed by Sven, leading them down the gangway, the Professor as leader, being the last, staying to thank the Captain for his hospitality.

"Jesus H Christ! What makes you think this is a fishing port?" asked Pat O'Hanlon of Sven, holding a handkerchief over his nose.

"Over there," came the slightly muffled response from Sven, similarly trying to prevent his olfactory nerves being decimated by the piscatorial assault, and pointing to the other side of the quay to which they were moored. All the small local fishing boats were tied up there, with baskets of their catches stacked up on the quay and trestle tables laden with fish being picked over by local buyers. There was also a mass of fishy remains, scattered all over the quay that had been accumulated over a long period of time, and were now well trodden in and being slowly cooked by the midday sun, raising the appalling stench that greeted the team. It was so strong that it even prevented them from initially realising just how hot it was, particularly in contrast to the air-conditioned ship they had just left.

The team were soon following the lead of Pat and Sven as they made their way quickly towards the exit from the quay to escape the smell. Halfway there, they saw a rather flustered looking figure in a neat white suit hurrying to meet them. It was the local government official who had been instructed to look after them and give them every assistance necessary, and was about to introduce himself to the Professor and his team. Being entrusted with this important task that may well lead to his promotion into higher echelons of government, the official was determined to make a good impression on these very important visitors and ensure everything went smoothly. To this end, he had driven his few subordinates into near dementia with constant demands, counter demands and enquiries as to their progress. To his credit, the end result was satisfactory, and so he was quite pleased with himself.

"Ah, Professor Kowalski," he began, beaming his best welcoming smile and holding out his hand to Sven.

"I'm the Professor," said the Professor rather coldly, as he stepped forward and took the other's hand.

"Oh, a thousand apologies for my stupid mistake! I was misinformed!" gushed the embarrassed official, but pressed on hurriedly to try and recover from the initial blunder. My name is Claude Kindusa, the government's special representative in this region, and I have been told to do everything necessary to help you with your expedition. Here is my card, and please feel free to call on me any time you need anything, anything at all," he finished, beaming at them all again.

"Thank you," replied the Professor, surveying the medium height figure, fat round face and tinted rimless glasses in front of him. "It's good to see that all the official lines of communication seem to have worked well. I hope our stipulation that all must be done to maintain the secrecy of purpose of our expedition has been adhered to, as the subject is still extremely sensitive, and we have your President's assurance that this will be so."

"*Mais absolument, Messieurs,*" replied M. Kindusa, unintentionally relapsing into French and trying to ensure that some of the kudos of being directly responsible for carrying out his president's instructions rubbed off on him. "Outside my department, and even within it, the purpose has only been revealed on a strictly 'need-to-know-basis'."

"Good," said the Professor. "Now, can we please see the boat that's going to take us up river?"

"Er, that is being fuelled, provisioned and final preparations for your voyage are being completed as we speak. Your equipment, which I see is being offloaded on to the quayside this minute, will be loaded on board this afternoon, and all will be ready for you to start tomorrow morning. In the meantime I would like to take you to the hotel we have arranged for you to stay the night and rest after your journey. The cars are over there," he concluded, pointing to further along the quayside.

"I would have preferred to have gone straight on to the boat so that we could get settled in, but if it's not ready, I suppose we'll have to stay at the hotel," replied the Professor in the mildly annoyed tone of voice that in earlier years would have boded trouble for his students.

"Please make absolutely sure that it *is* ready for first thing tomorrow, as we have a very tight schedule, and I also have your science minister's personal phone number and his offer to step in if things go wrong anywhere in the arrangements, which offer I shall not hesitate to accept if the need arises."

"Of course, and I fully understand. Please rest assured that everything will be absolutely ready. When I have taken you to your hotel, I am going back to check all areas of the work personally to make sure that they will all be absolutely ready in time, *absolument,*" replied the by now thoroughly rattled official. The various underlings responsible for this work, and who had not had the boat ready today would certainly see the other side of his nature. The obsequious fawning official would rapidly become the brutal, bullying tyrant.

In view of the secrecy surrounding their expedition and possible hostility of the people to foreigners, it was decided that they should stay in the hotel for the rest of the day, where they had a good dinner that evening and a fairly comfortable night in what they were assured was the best hotel in town.

They were met by Kindusa in the lobby after breakfast the next morning to return to the docks. He was both happy and very relieved to tell them that all was now ready for their journey, and that the cars were outside to take them there now.

First impressions of the boat as she lay alongside the quay were quite favourable. While not exactly luxurious, the team was pleased to see she looked in good condition, and had obviously been well cleaned up for their trip. Once on board, they found that the rooms were quite comfortable with accommodation for twenty guests and crew, so there was plenty of room for them. There were other rooms that they could use as their laboratories, and an airy lounge with a small bar at one end, a dining area at the other, and what, in the boat's earlier career, had been a small dance floor in the middle of the room.

Kindusa introduced them to the boat's captain, who he claimed had been specially assigned from the country's navy at the president's insistence for the task, and a similarly well connected captain from the army who would be responsible for the small squad of armed guards on the boat for their security during the trip.

Some of the guards would accompany the team into the jungle for their protection, though John felt they would not be necessary. This was because there would only be the indigenous tribes to worry about, or possibly crocodiles, there not being any reports of dangerous animals in this area of the jungle, or indeed any workers from what had been the lumber industry, they all having left when the fever first struck. However, they could not object to them accompanying the team as they were unlikely to interfere with their work.

Pat and Sven were delighted to see a proper barman in neat white jacket already in position behind the bar, polishing glasses and giving an impression of dedication to his job that was most gratifying to them.

Having spent about half an hour with the team showing them round the boat and making the introductions, Kindusa then left and they started on their trip up-river. It took the best part of the day to get to within sight of the start of the forest, and the captain chose a spot to anchor about a quarter of a mile short of the forest, a little distance offshore and opposite a small sandy beach that looked as though it owed its origins to an animal watering place.

During the journey up river the Professor held a meeting of the team to outline his proposals as to how the expedition would go about its work. For his part, he was going to look for any new disease causing agents that might be present in the air, water, particularly stagnant water in the forest, on leaves or on plants in general. Also, he would be able to examine any of the team should they fall victim to the fever.

It turned into an open forum thereafter so that the Professor could get input from the others as to preferences and particularly the work that Denise Carter wanted to carry out, as he recognised she would have different priorities from him. She outlined the type of work she wanted to carry out, which would mainly involve seeing if there were any plants, fungi or other vegetation she didn't recognise that might be responsible. Both she and the Professor would bring samples back to the laboratory from their forays into the forest for analysis, overseen by their two assistants, Martin Airedale and Carol Spencer.

John Fenwick, who had initially studied Zoology prior to expanding his expertise into general environmental science, would look out for any signs of animals, including birds, insects or river life that seemed to be sick.

The Professor then asked Sven and Pat to tell them of their experience of the forest fever, and how you knew you were being attacked by it so that they all knew what to look out for. Pat started by saying forcefully: "You'll know, alright, within a couple of seconds, you'll bloody well know," and, with a few enhancing additions from Sven, they then gave a very graphic description of their experiences, such that no one was particularly keen to experience them at firsthand, and the lab technicians, Geoff Smith and Diane Jamieson were in two minds as to whether to venture from the safety of the boat at all.

By lunchtime, the Professor had got a fairly good general agenda mapped out so that everyone knew what was required. They broke for lunch and were all very pleased with the standard of food prepared by the galley staff. As Geoff Smith remarked, "I could quite happily continue my trip on this boat as a holiday if they keep up this standard," to which there were general murmurs of agreement. As an afterthought, Geoff added: "And the beer's pretty good too," raising his glass to the bar tender, who smiled back, delighted to have been noticed.

After lunch they rested through the worst heat of the day, even though it felt somewhat cooler on the moving boat than it would have done had they been driving overland, and then got on with various tasks in preparation for the work to come. In particular, getting all the equipment into their new 'laboratories', setting it up and testing occupied all of them, bar Pat and Sven, pretty well full time, though they did help with the physical moving of equipment.

When the captain announced that they had arrived at what would be their base, as there was still a good hour of daylight left, the Professor organised the first trip ashore, saying they might as well use the time if for no other purpose than to see how the land lay and modify plans if necessary.

They had anchored opposite some flat featureless land that had not long ago been cleared by the removal of the forest and some work done to prepare it for crops; it was some distance away from where the jungle itself began. The Professor told the guard's captain that there was no need for his guards to accompany them on this first outing as they would be, more or less, within sight of the boat and there was no risk of attack on this open ground.

So they all went ashore at the small sandy beach, including the lab technicians Geoff and Diane (who had overcome their initial worries but determined to stay at the back of the party), in the inflatable dinghies that were part of the boat's equipment added for the expedition.

When the outboard motors were switched off, they were immediately struck by the silence of the place.

"Well, that's certainly announced our arrival," said John with a short laugh. After a few moments, however, the insect noise, which had been temporarily silenced by the noise of the arrival of the boats, started again, and an occasional bird was seen flying about.

Otherwise the land, for as far as they could see, was deserted. It had all the usual signs of having had its forest removed fairly recently, with little vegetation remaining, other than a few stunted bushes, and occasional wiry grass cover, and no sign of any animal life. One or two tiny shoots showed where the trees were trying to re-establish themselves; otherwise it was verging on a desert. They'd all climbed up the short river bank and stood at the top looking around when the Professor said:

"Let's make a start by seeing if we can establish contact with the 'enemy'. Sven, you and Pat already know what the fever symptom are, so you two lead us up to the forest, and we'll stop when and if we meet it. We'll be right behind you."

"A bloody long way behind, in my case," muttered Martin, *sotto voce* to Geoff who was walking rather nervously alongside him.

So they set off. Remembering how far from the forest the no-go line was, Sven set off at a good pace to where he judged it would be that soon had the others falling behind. Pat, too, was struggling to keep up.

"Hey, Sven, slow down a bit – we're not all superhuman like you!" Pat called out to the ever more distant figure in front of him.

Sven stopped and turned round to see the party straggling out behind him.

"Sorry," he called out, "I was concentrating on the onset of the fever symptoms as I don't want to go one step further into the zone than necessary. You'll remember why, I'm sure, Pat."

"Damn right I do, but we need to have every one near there at the same time," replied Pat.

When the group had caught up, Sven said:

"If it's the same as we found at Arbreville then it could start anywhere from here to the forest, so shout if you feel anything and do not go any further forward."

They all walked slowly forward again, with the Professor a few feet behind Pat and Sven, who continued to lead the group. John Fenwick walked alongside the Professor, the others a little further back still. All of them were more than somewhat nervous, wondering if the illness, so graphically described earlier by Pat and Sven would hit them suddenly and painfully. They were, in any case, also feeling distinctly uncomfortable in the very humid heat, which was all the more noticeable after the cooler conditions on board the boat.

When Sven was about fifty yards from the edge of the forest, he suddenly shouted out to Pat:

"My God, Pat, it's attacking me again! Quick, mark where I am now – I'm not going any further forward – I remember only too well what'll happen if I do."

Pat marked out a line in the earth with his boot while Sven stepped back a few paces, mopping his brow. The rest all halted in their tracks, frozen at the sight of this giant of a man struck down so suddenly.

The Professor, perhaps feeling the need to show his leadership and prevent a near panic in the others, said, in a slightly exaggeratedly calm manner:

"No doubt about the symptoms, I suppose, Sven?"

"Absolutely not!" replied Sven vehemently.

"Okay. I think I must experience the symptoms for myself – it may help my diagnosis of the fever if I have firsthand knowledge of them. John," he continued, "I'd appreciate you coming with me just in case of … well, just in case I fall over, when you should be able to pull me back without too much trouble, as it does seem to have a boundary, as Sven said. The rest of you stay where you are. Okay, John?"

"Yes," said John, putting on a brave front and stepping forward to be alongside the Professor. "Let's try it."

They walked very cautiously over to the mark Pat had made on the ground.

"Ready?" asked the Professor, and getting a nod from John, they both very tentatively took a step forward and were just about to take another, when John said:

"Bugger it, I think it's got me, too!"

He stepped back a couple of paces and sat down, when the others went over to him to help if they could. When they saw John was apparently okay and getting back onto his feet, they stopped talking and looked at the Professor, who had just stayed motionless where he'd been when it hit John.

"That's damned funny," the Professor said, "I don't feel anything. I'll try going a couple of steps further."

He did so, and then called to Pat: "Pat, will you try coming with me, please, I feel fine but I'd still like some company in case…"

Trying to sound nonchalant to hide his nervousness at the prospect, Pat replied "Sure" and walked to join him. When beside the Professor he added: "You're right, I don't feel anything either, so I'm game to go a bit further if you are. It's a very rum do, though because when Sven and I first got hit by it, it affected me far worse than it did him."

After they'd gone another ten yards, the Professor called back: "Anyone else, apart from you Sven and John, care to try and join us?"

Apart from the two lab assistants, who felt this was definitely outside their remit, the rest of the party walked slowly and very hesitantly up to the Professor and Pat, ready to turn and run at the slightest hint of ill-feeling.

Seeing them all safely there, John called out: "Wait! This is ridiculous! I'll give it another try."

This time he walked forward rather more quickly and discovered, as Sven had done previously, that the further in one went, the worse the symptoms. He turned and ran back as hard as he could, stopping a good ten yards behind where Sven was still standing.

Turning to Martin Airedale, his assistant, the Professor said: "Martin, make a clear mark here with a heap of stones or something so that we can find it again tomorrow while I see if I can help John. Then all of you get back to the dinghies – I think that's enough excitement for one day and it'll be getting dark soon. Remember, that happens very quickly at this latitude."

By the time he'd reached John he was sitting up, catching his breath and recovering slowly.

"Bloody hell, that was…"

"Just relax, John, you look to me to be on the mend, so let's get you back to the boat. When you feel up to it, describe to me in as much detail as you can what you experienced."

A rather subdued party made their way back to the landing beach. As they got there, dusk was starting to fall, and the first squadrons of mosquitoes were out looking for their evening meals.

"Let's hurry up and get aboard, or we'll get eaten alive if we're here for long," said Carol Spencer, Denise Carter's assistant, who knew from previous painful experience how they seemed to find her irresistible and apparently particularly flavoursome, as she'd been the first to see the beginnings of clouds of them congregating over the long grass beside the river.

"Well, we shouldn't be, not if those discs live up to their claimed efficacy against malaria," replied the Professor. "It'll be a good test, and one report we can get out of the way quickly."

Carol ran to the dingy, flailing her arms at the mosquitoes, clambered into the dinghy and sat down. It gradually dawned on her that the mosquitoes were not using her as a pin cushion to exercise their probosi, and that she hadn't had a single sting. Hardly able to believe they'd left her alone, she said: "That's amazing! I haven't been stung at all!"

"Glad to hear it," said Martin, "and it looks as though they have left us all alone."

They got back to the boat without further incident, and went to the lounge, where the Professor prescribed medicinal drinks all round, which offer was gladly accepted.

When they'd all settled down a bit, the Professor said:

"What bothers me most is why you two were affected and the rest of us weren't. Any one got any ideas?"

"I don't know about that, but I've just noticed that those bloody mosquitoes have given me a good going over. I'm glad I'm already up to my eyeballs with quinine from my time out here," said Sven.

"Me, too, and I didn't notice them earlier either. I suppose I was still a bit groggy from the fever," added John.

"I suppose you two forgot, or didn't bother to wear your discs, did you? If you didn't it serves you…" The Professor stopped short. "I wonder," he muttered more to himself than anyone else.

"Well, have you got them on, or not?" he demanded.

Somewhat shamefaced, both culprits had to admit that they had forgotten to put them on.

"Well, you'd better make damn sure you do tomorrow," continued the Professor sternly, "we're going to have enough problems on this trip, quinine notwithstanding, without one of you coming down with one of the many fevers out here looking for likely candidates. Also, we'll look like bloody idiots with the ministry back home if any of us gets ill after not using the means they gave us to avoid such an event, even if we don't know yet for sure that they work. So go and put them on now, under all your clothes, as instructed, and don't take them off again for any reason whatsoever, so that way you can't forget about them again. Is that clear?" he concluded in his most authoritative tone.

Suitably chastised, the pair went off to do as told, and returned to join the team for dinner. While waiting for it to be served, John described his fever symptoms to the Professor, which Sven confirmed were exactly as he remembered his first encounter with it.

After a convivial evening, they all retired to bed early, ready for an early start the next day.

The second day, the whole team set off again, this time primarily to check where the zone started. When they got near to the first mark where the pair had been hit by the fever, the Professor stopped them and said:

"I don't profess to have any rationale for what I am about to propose, and, of course, you can refuse, but I wondered if the fact that you two weren't wearing the discs yesterday may have had something to do why you were hit by the fever and the rest of us weren't. So, Sven and John, would you care to step forward and see if it hits you again?"

The pair looked at each other a bit apprehensively and then said they'd be prepared to give it a try. John, who was still feeling rather more guilty about not wearing his wretched disc than Sven was, volunteering to go first. Coming up to the line, John moved his foot forward for the first step across the line with all the enthusiasm of a captive about to walk a pirates' plank and tensing all his muscles as though waiting for a dentist to start drilling into a particularly sensitive tooth. He put his foot down. Nothing. No pain or fear. Another step. Still alright. "I think it's okay," he said sounding far from confident, but taking another step. By the time he was five paces in front of the line, the Professor told him to wait there and for Sven to move forward until he was level with him.

Denise Carter, who found herself suddenly feeling worried about Sven, said, almost despite herself: "Hope you're okay this time…"

Sven shot an appreciative glance at her and said, "thanks – I hope so too," and started walking forward somewhat hesitantly. Very quickly, he realised he was not being attacked, and his face broke into a big grin.

"Well I'll be…" Sven muttered, coming back to the Professor standing behind the line. "Looks like you were right about the discs, Professor, so I suggest we all go on to see how near to the forest we can get. Those of you who haven't experienced it yet will be in no doubt if it hits you. If it does, just run back to where we came from – fast!"

"Good idea, Sven, we'll do as you suggest," the Professor added, turning to the others. "However, before we do, I want to experience this fever thing for myself. Now, where's the start line you made? Ah! There it is. Right, Denise, would you please hold my disc for me for a minute or two."

"Don't do it, Professor! It could ki…" began Denise, only for the Professor to wave her into silence as he took his first cautious step forward. He managed three steps before the panic grabbed him and had him running back exactly as the others has done. However, Sven caught him as he came up to him, being concerned that the exertion might cause the Professor to have a heart attack. As soon as he thought the panic had subsided, he sat the Professor on the ground.

They all stood around rather nervously for a few minutes, waiting for the Professor to recover, and were very relieved when he'd recovered enough to speak.

"God in Heaven!" he managed to gasp, still catching his breath. A few moments later he had calmed down enough to get back on his feet, even if a little unsteadily and with Sven's help.

"Are you sure you're okay now?" asked Denise, "do you need any help?"

"Thank you, Denise, no – I'm feeling stronger by the minute. However, even in the pursuit of the highest traditions of scientific research, that is one experiment I will *never* repeat!" he said, smiling weakly at the others. He then went on, recovering his strength fairly quickly and putting his disc back on:

"I haven't a clue as to why it should be the discs, but I'm damn glad it is, or at least seems to be so far. It would make this expedition bloody difficult if we couldn't even get near the trees. Right, so let's keep close together and advance slowly in a line towards the trees and see if all is well."

They did as requested, and much to their collective surprise got right up to and just into the start of the trees without incident, though Sven and John were half expecting to be struck down any moment and the Professor also gave the impression of walking on eggshells.

"Well, that went okay," said a very relieved Professor when he got to the trees, "now that we've established that we can go into the forest we can start our study in earnest. I, and I expect Denise will need to return to the boat to collect our equipment to start our studies, so I suggest we all go back and treat ourselves to some morning coffee before we continue with our work. Also, and very importantly, remember to bring plenty of bottled water with you. We have enough to contend with out here without anyone succumbing to dehydration."

After coffee, they returned to their various tasks, the scientists surveying and taking samples that they took back with them to the labs for analysis. Pat and Sven reviewed the extensive damage that had been done to the part of the forest they could reach, as well as the state of the cleared ground. This was to form the basis of a report giving a layman's view of what had been done to the previously virgin forest, with photographs to illustrate the text. The state of the cleared ground was also to be part of the work by Denise Carter, so the pair of 'amateurs' could expect a bit of assistance from her and Carol, which Sven, for one felt would not be a hardship. Despite himself, he was beginning to feel quite protective about Denise.

For the rest of the day they did what they could from where they were, but as access to the forest was very restricted, the undergrowth being virtually impenetrable without hacking out every single step with a machete, it soon became apparent that they would have to go up river and access the forest from the river. Also, as there was no shade the heat from the sun was intense and added to the high humidity level ensured the conditions were stifling and debilitating so that the group could only work very slowly, pausing frequently to recover from their efforts. At about twelve o'clock the Professor decided they should retreat to the boat for a couple of hours to avoid the worst of the heat and someone going down with heat exhaustion.

Remembering the problems they had had – God, was it only a week ago? – Sven told the Professor that they may well find the boat's engine wouldn't work within the forest, to which the Professor replied that they would have to try it anyway, and that he'd speak to the Captain when they got back to the boat that evening.

They all had a pleasant meal and socialised for a while, getting to know each other a bit better all the time, then, having discussed their intended programme for the next day, went to bed early again.

After an early breakfast the next morning they were all ready to start their up-river trip before the heat of the day set in. It didn't take long for the captain to get the boat moving up river, and most of the team were on deck watching the activities of the crew. They had been going for a few minutes only when the steady throb of the engines fell silent.

"Looks like what we expected has happened, Pat," said Sven, watching as the boat slowly lost way, and then started drifting back down stream. A few moments later, the Captain had the engine restarted and was again heading up river when exactly the same thing happened. He turned to the Professor and began to apologise profusely for the engine failure, and said he would have his engineer work on it all day to try and cure the fault. The Professor, having assured the captain that this turn of events was not unknown in relation to the forest fever, even if he was completely unable to explain it, then asked him if he could drop anchor where they were, as they were not far from the location they were at when the engines stopped, and the expedition would try using the inflatables. It would mean they would have less time for their work, but as the boat obviously was unable to go any further upstream they had no other option.

So the party, including the guards, but not the lab technicians, who were going to work on yesterday's samples in the labs, collected what equipment they would need for their first foray further into the forest and loaded it into three of the available inflatables, then started up the outboards. The Professor decided that he, John, Sven and Pat and one of the guards would be in the first boat and would set off first. If their outboard motor stopped as the boat's engine had done, then they would have to abandon the trip and replan the whole expedition, possibly having to resort to paddling the inflatables, though that would obviously severely restrict the range of their expedition. If, however, the motor wasn't affected, then, on his signal, the other two boats should follow him.

Mentally keeping their fingers crossed, and more in hope than expectation, the first boat started up river, travelling fairly slowly. They were all hardly daring to breathe as they got to the point near where the ferry boat's engine had cut out. Little by little they edged up the river. After a few minutes John said: "I think it's going to be okay: open up the throttle a bit, Pat."

At that instant the guard gave a hoarse cry and apparently terrified, jumped out of the dinghy and started swimming frantically back to the ferry.

"Quick! After him, Pat!" shouted John. Pat had already started turning the boat back, and they quickly caught up with the guard and hauled him back into the dinghy.

"Poor sod, I hadn't thought of that, but of course, as he doesn't have a dog tag, the fever must have got him," said the Professor, surveying the guard who was slowly recovering, but was still fearfully looking around. "Let's get him back to the boat as quickly as we can, and I'll explain to the captain what's happened. One thing's certain: we are not going to be able to take the guards with us. I just hope their absence doesn't prove a problem."

They got the still shaken guard back on board and the Professor told the captain what had happened. The other guards were perforce also left behind, and after a little while they resumed their journey up the river.

They approached the point where John had thought they were going to be able to go on up the river, and this time Pat opened up the throttle at John's command.

The boat surged ahead as he did so, and a collective cry of 'Yes' rang out across the river, as the Professor turned round and waved his handkerchief at the other two boats, the signal for them to follow on.

They travelled for about half an hour before coming to a raw looking wide track hacked into the forest. It was obviously man-made and looked to have been in use until fairly recently. The track ran right down into the river, and had been used for logging operations, judging by the number of tree trunks stacked near the river, presumably waiting for a barge to take them down river.

"I haven't seen any crocs in the river so far, so I think we can safely land here," the Professor shouted over the noise of the outboard, so Pat turned the boat towards the bank. The other two boats followed suit, until all three were just off the muddy 'slipway' at the end of the track, their motors ticking over just enough to hold them against the sluggish river current in the bend in the river.

"Anyone seen any crocodiles yet?" asked the Professor. "No? Good, then lets pull the boats up the slipway a bit, tie them securely and then we can get on with our survey work."

When they got all the boats secured and were waiting to start, the Professor called them together and said:

"Try not to go too far off this track, and keep a sharp lookout for native tribes, as we believe there are some in this region, and they probably aren't very friendly, seeing what's been done to their environment," he said, looking at the destruction all around them. He then went on:

"Also, phone Pat every quarter of an hour or so if you're out of sight of any of the others, and indicate roughly where you are. The reason for this is if you have an accident or run into trouble we need to be able to find you quickly."

"Right, it's nearly ten o'clock now, so be back here for twelve, when we'll knock off for a two-hour lunch break to miss the worst of the heat. Pat and Sven have volunteered to rig up a tarpaulin shelter that will serve as our restaurant, and organise the packed meals that the boat's crew have put together for us."

"Everyone clear on what they are going to do and how? Right, so let's get on with it, and good hunting, everyone," the Professor concluded, as they all picked up their equipment and started up the track.

"How's your bush craft these days, Pat?" asked Sven.

"Nowhere near as good as it used to be when I was a boy scout, or as yours is now, so you'd better design how we're going to build the 'restaurant' that the Professor so kindly offered everyone for their lunch, courtesy of us!"

So they set about finding a suitable site in the shade of the few remaining trees, and cleared the ground to ensure there were no unexpected, unwelcome guests ready to join them. It was fairly easy to find suitable bits of wood that the loggers had left scattered about to build a makeshift table and benches with the tomahawks and thin rope they'd brought with them, even if it was hard and hot physical work collecting and assembling the pieces of wood and finally putting up the tarpaulin to give a bit more shade. The work was interrupted periodically by the others phoning in, as instructed, but fortunately, no-one had encountered any problems. When they had done, they both went to the edge of the river, and using the boats' bailers, scooped up water to pour over themselves to cool down after their exertions.

"God, what I'd give for a nice cold beer right now!" said Sven.

"Me too," came the reply, "beat you to the bar when we get back!"

They had a little time before twelve, so sat and relaxed for a while, before unpacking the lunch and putting it on the table they'd made.

The others all came back for lunch at about the same time, one or two opting for the 'river cool down' beforehand.

"Despite the superb woodcraft of your two builders oblique restauranteurs, please watch out for splinters from our imitation 'Chippendale' furniture!" said Pat, as they came back from the water's edge to relax in the shade.

Due to the heat and the morning's efforts, conversation was a bit desultory and mainly concerned particularly unusual items they'd seen. After lunch and a rest, they all resumed their survey for the rest of the afternoon.

At about four o'clock the Professor called them all back to return to the ferry boat, to ensure that they arrived back before dusk and the predations of the evening's ravening hordes of insects, just in case the discs did not give total protection against all the myriad insects thereabouts.

Over dinner it was decided to be worthwhile to return to the same place the next day, as both the Professor and Dr. Carter felt they hadn't investigated everything that was accessible there sufficiently.

"Great", said Sven, "if our table's still standing we'll have an easier morning – *n'est ce pas*, Pat."

"Don't bank on it, Sven," the Professor replied with a laugh, "there are plenty of other jobs that will need doing!"

So the next day's expedition was very similar to the one they'd just had, except this time, Pat and Sven explored the logging track for a lot further along its length. They collected a lot of data as to the extent of the destruction wrought by the indiscriminate logging activities that had been carried out. They found many more examples of the extensive destruction caused by the clearing of large areas of other trees and undergrowth in order to extract single large high value trees such as mahogany. They even came across a bulldozer that had evidently been abandoned.

"I'll bet it broke down and the fever got them before they could fix it," said Sven looking at the rather forlorn machine.

Pat's dossier and photographic record were increasing in size and scope daily, and its potential as a source of later income from the book of the journey he would write was not lost on him.

The third day they travelled a further two or three miles up river, where they found a natural beach situated by a long slow bend in the river, which for some reason the loggers had avoided. As they were thinking of landing, they saw a possible reason for this: the crocodiles enjoyed basking there. So, on a bit further, and they found yet another loggers' slipway, and the day's survey passed without incident as had the previous days'.

Over dinner that night, it was agreed that they'd probably got enough useful representative samples to check whether any of the vegetation or small fauna was responsible for the fever, and that they ought now to go on to the next phase of the expedition. This was to try to make contact with some of the primitive tribes that were known to inhabit areas fairly close to the river.

"One thing's been bothering me," said John, "how are we going to communicate with the people of any tribe we do find?"

The Professor replied: "Without wishing to appear boastful, I have had a few such encounters before on field trips I've been on. Plenty of smiling and a good display of gifts, the like of which we have brought with us, usually do the trick, though there was one trip when it did go decidedly pear-shaped and we retreated bloody quickly followed by a few arrows, though fortunately their aim was a bit off on that occasion. No, we'll just have to play it very cautiously and trust luck is on our side. As a last resort we'll have to be prepared to run like hell. However, as the tribes we're likely to come across are more likely to be scared of us rather than hostile, having been fairly close to the loggers with I suspect unpleasant outcomes. So don't let's worry about them now."

So that evening the party that would carry out this part of the work packed up what they would need for a two or three day stay away from the boat. The two assistants, Geoff and Carol would stay on the boat to help with the lab work, much to their disappointment, but as the Professor pointed out, not only was it vital to ensure that was all correctly done and documented, but there wasn't really enough room in the three inflatables for them to come too, bearing in mind the extra equipment that would have to be carried this time.

So on the morning of the fourth day the party, now consisting of the Professor, Martin, Denise, John, Pat and Sven, set off up-river again, this time looking for signs of the indigenous forest people. They went past their earlier landing sites without stopping, having already established that there had been no signs of habitation. Thereafter, they stopped at anything that looked like a small entry point into the jungle, but it was about mid-afternoon before they found an opening of any significant size that looked as though it might have been used by people as opposed to animals only.

"I think we'd better stop here, anyway, as it will take a while to set up a camp, and we haven't got too much daylight left," said the Professor, getting Pat to steer the boat towards the small opening into the forest and signalling the others to follow.

As they were getting out of the boat, John, pointing at the ground a little way in front of his dinghy, suddenly said:

"Bingo! Look! Footprints, unless I'm much mistaken, and fairly recent, I'd say."

"I'd agree," said Sven, being well experienced in such tracks.

"Well, if they're anywhere in the vicinity they must have heard us coming, so we'd better watch out for a hail of arrows," said Pat, half seriously. "Even if they are watching us, we're very unlikely to see them and certainly not hear them above the forest's own racket. Listen to those damned insects, squawking birds, and do I hear howler monkeys? Quite a welcome, either way!"

As they all remained fairly still, thinking about what Pat had just said, the Professor said:

"Sven, you and John come with me, and we'll check out this path for a little way. The rest of you stay here ready for a quick evacuation if we run into trouble."

The three of them walked carefully along the path, keeping a sharp lookout for any tribesmen. After about fifty yards they came upon a reasonably large clearing, that had obviously been an encampment up until fairly recently, though there was no sign of any occupation now. There was confirmation of its use in the shape of a well-used rock-encircled fire place in the middle, which John established was quite cold.

"I think this will do us very nicely as it looks as though it hasn't been used for a little while," said the Professor. "John, stay here just to make sure the previous occupants don't suddenly reappear, or if they do, let us know smartly as you beat a very speedy tactical withdrawal! We'll go back and help the others bring all the gear back here."

The others were relieved to see the Professor return, and it wasn't long before they had transferred all their equipment to the clearing.

As Sven had quickly been recognised as the one with the most bush craft skills, he was soon helping some of the less experienced among them to put up their hammocks under plastic sheeting covers, and storing the rest of the equipment off the ground to deter curious insects.

He said to them all generally: "I've heard it rains most nights in these parts, though not too heavily, so make sure your tarpaulins are well tucked in, otherwise you will wake up sloshing around in a pool of cold water. There are also very heavy thunderstorms from time to time, so we'll just have to hope for the best that we'll only get the lighter rains while we're here."

Denise seemed to be having more trouble than most putting up her hammock, not being very big physically, and Sven vaguely wondered why he felt pleased to have to spend a bit more time helping her. Against his better judgement he realised he was finding her disconcertingly attractive. When they were all reasonably settled in, Sven set up a couple of gas lanterns and got a fire going to heat up their evening meal.

CHAPTER 14

The Visitor

The group were just getting ready for their evening meal, which had involved most of them heating up the meals they had brought with them, provided by the ferry boat cook. They were making the most of it, as thereafter they would have to have reconstituted food, having no means to store fresh. The fire that Sven had started was going well in the middle of the clearing on the site that had obviously seen many previous fires, and they had set up their small collapsible table and chairs on the opposite side of the fire to where they had slung their hammocks.

Finally, they had got everything ready and were all sitting round the table when the Professor's phone rang. A voice he didn't recognise started speaking to him:

"It would be helpful if all the members of your party heard this important conversation, so could you please switch your speaker on?"

"Just a minute! Who are you and why are you calling me this late and what the hell's this all about, anyway?" the Professor replied, not recognising the voice, and not in the happiest frame of mind at having been disturbed just as he was sitting down rather uncomfortably to start eating his meal.

"Oh, forgive me," came the reply, "of course you don't know me and this call is obviously unexpected. My name is

Klaat, and in part it's about what you're doing out there in the jungle that I need to speak to you. I am sorry to disturb you at this time, but I have to speak to you all, and I wasn't sure you'd be together until about now. So if you would please make sure they can all hear our conversation…"

"Very well," he replied, "just a minute while I make sure we can all hear the speaker. I hope it is important as we're all pretty tired and just about to start a meal."

"Thank you. I'll keep this as short as I can, but the reason for wanting you all to hear this is that, in case of accidents, there's more chance of at least one of you being able to carry it back to your government."

"Carry it back to your government? What…who are you, who or what do you represent?" The Professor could contain his irritation at this seemingly senseless call no longer and was beginning to wonder if it was perhaps a hoax from someone back home.

"I've given you my name, but the organisation I represent you will never have heard of and I doubt would mean anything to you. I'm sorry to have caused you annoyance as well as disturbance, but please let me continue and I'll come back to my organisation later, when you'll be in a better position to judge its relevance to your expedition."

"Firstly, I'd like you all to look over to the side of the clearing away from your fire and directly in front of you, Professor. Even with only the light from your camping lights, you can see there is nothing there except a few stunted bushes, right?" Without waiting for a reply the voice went on:

"Now watch the space just in front of the two nearest little shrubs over there."

"What the…" a chorus of similar expletives emanated from the group as what looked like a smallish aluminium case, the sort used by photographers to carry their equipment, was suddenly sitting on the ground where, a second earlier, there had been nothing.

The voice from the phone continued: "Please, do not be alarmed. There is nothing to be afraid of in the case itself, and I have to apologise for its somewhat dramatic appearance in front of you like that. It is, in fact, merely a sort of compact disc player, albeit one with fairly advanced properties. If one of you would be kind enough to go over and open it, and press the large green button that you'll find inside, it will raise its viewing screen. I'll continue when you've done that."

Pat, never short of curiosity was on his feet first, and went over to the case, more cautiously the closer he got to it. The voice from the phone said: "You don't need to be worried; it will not harm you in any way."

Pat replied to no one in particular: "Maybe not, but the last time I saw someone open a box a bit smaller than this one they got a face full of ammonia, so you'll excuse me if I'm a bit nervous!"

Sven chipped in, "You're right, Pat – I remember how that phoney policeman got his!"

Eventually, Pat was close enough to see that it had a pair of simple latches on the outside, so bending down and turning his head away in a sort of reflex action, he undid the catches.

Nothing happened, so again, very cautiously, he lifted the lid of the box. Inside he saw what looked like a polished aluminium surface, with a couple of tiny green LEDs glowing in one corner, and a large green button in the middle. He hesitated a minute looking at it.

Again, the voice from the phone cut through the silence: "Go on; press the green button."

Very apprehensively, he pressed the button and retreated rapidly back to the group. After a second or two, what appeared to be a large projection screen arose from the box, expanding until it was about five feet wide and four feet high, standing just above the box.

"In a minute, I'd like all of you to go and have a look at the box. Firstly, you'll have to agree that you've never seen anything like it, particularly the screen. You will not know how it constructed, or indeed what it is made of or how it is supported, without apparent connection to the rest of the box. Oh, and you will also find that you cannot actually touch any of the box now. There is what you might call a "force field" protecting it. Now, I'll raise the box to a convenient height above the ground, say two feet."

They watched, astonished, as indeed the box rose a couple of feet above the ground and remained there, stationary, without any apparent means of support.

"Right, go and have a look at it now."

They all went over to it, each in their own way trying to fathom out what this was in front of them. "Well I'm buggered if I know what, or indeed how the hell this has happened, but I'll agree with the 'Mystery Voice' that I've never seen its equal before!" Pat voiced what they each were thinking, as evidenced by the muttered 'Me neithers' from the others.

"Tell you something else," broke in Sven, who being less technically minded than the others was perhaps not quite so awed by the thing in front of them. "Whoever's behind this little conjuring trick must be watching us. How else do you explain his various clear instructions about opening the damn thing?"

"Dammit, you're right, Sven," said the Professor pulling his phone out of his pocket. "Hey, Klaat, now that you've shown us your trick, how about coming forward to get your applause?"

"I'm sorry; I do not understand what you mean. Why should I get applause?"

This comment disturbed them all a bit as surely that slightly sarcastic remark had been clear enough for anyone to understand? Their apprehension started to return.

When no one bothered to enlighten him about the 'applause' he went on:

"Never mind. Go back to your seats, eat your meal and I will explain a little further. Please, let me finish everything I have to say, and then I will answer any questions, if I can.

The Professor, now getting a bit rattled at the anonymous voice said:

"Okay, we'll listen to you, but why the hell don't you just come out from wherever it is you're hiding and speak to us face-to-face? "I'm sorry I can't do that just now, but please listen carefully as though I was there with you. And just to be sure that there are no communication problems with your phone, such as its battery running out of charge, I'll speak through my projector box from now on. Just a minute and I'll bring it nearer so that you can hear it easily and I can show you some of the pictures as well."

They watched in amazement as the box and screen moved slowly over towards them, and stopped away from the fire and in front of them, where they could all see it easily.

"How does that sound?" the same voice asked, but this time from the box. "Okay? Good. What I have to say is this."

"Firstly, I think you must agree that what you have just seen and heard were completely outside anything any of you have ever experienced before. What I'm about to show you will also fall into that category, so before I go any further, please believe that this will be completely genuine and is not some trick or deception. I hope you will come to that conclusion when you have seen it all."

Without waiting for any response from his audience, who were still more than somewhat bemused by the events so far, he went on:

"We have been getting increasingly concerned at the destruction that human beings, your *'homo sapiens'* species, has been wreaking on this planet, but about which it doesn't seem to have either the ability or desire to do very much about. Unfortunately, though a lot of your people are concerned, there are a great number of others who couldn't give a damn about this destruction, particularly if they personally benefit from it. You will be familiar with the sort of thing I am referring to, such as clearing vast tracts of the rain forests, thereby removing the habitats of a great many of the species that rely on them for their existence. And this just to harvest a few high value trees or for agricultural use. Currently, the Amazon forest alone is being removed at a rate of more than twenty-five thousand square kilometres – an area the size of the whole of your country of Belgium – every year."

Then there is the killing of many other wild animals, as opposed to farmed domestic animals (including those in the oceans) for various reasons, particular as a consequence of habitat loss elsewhere in the world or their conflict with human interests by incursion on to farmland that was previously their habitat. Indeed, your own scientific researches have discovered the huge number of extinctions that early *homo sapiens* caused since the so-called 'Cognitive Revolution' about fifty thousand years ago, so it's far from a recent phenomenon and is still ongoing."

"Though as you, John, are doubtless well aware, the loss of species over the last forty odd years, as calculated and recorded in the 'Living Planet Index' gives a strong warning of the way it's going. And then, of course, there is the co-lateral damage to the ecosystems that these species belong to."

John, taken aback by being addressed personally like that, could only reply with a slightly startled, "Yes, that is absolutely correct but how did you…"

The rest of his reply was cut short as Klaat continued: "Other less obvious (but equally damaging) and longer term destructive effects are being brought about by water and air pollution."

In essence, what I have to tell you is that we are going to stop it. You see, despite there being an almost infinite number of them, there are very few planets with such a marvellous diversity of life forms on them as yours, which, as you know, all take many millions of years to evolve, and we are now in a position to prevent that diversity being obliterated on your planet due to the actions of just one of those millions of species, *'homo sapiens'*. You are the only one of all of them that is now no longer subject to the natural balances that control their populations."

He paused for a moment to let the import of what he had just said sink in to his audience. It obviously had done, particularly with John, who had a broader knowledge of ecology than the others, and had hardly been able to believe what he'd seen and heard. He spoke up, voicing thoughts that had been occurring to the others as well:

"You keep referring to 'we' in a way that says very clearly to me that you are not a human being and do not come from or belong to this planet. Either you've got a damn good hoax going on which we haven't been able to see through, or you are what I suspect. Would you please clarify that for us?"

"Yes, John, you are perfectly correct in your assessment of me – I can assure you that none of this is a hoax. I didn't want to start by telling you that I was what you popularly call an 'alien' in case it frightened you so much you all ran off to hide in the jungle. I would add that I am the representative of our civilisation, which for your convenience we have decided to call 'Servatur Gaiae'. We decided to follow the taxonomy practice of your scientific community – using Latin for the classification and naming of all living things. In our case this translates as 'Gaia's Saviour', Gaia being the Greek for earth and also the name coined by your famous Professor James Lovelock in his hypothesis relating to the earth's biosphere. Being Gaia's 'saviour' is what we will be, as I will explain shortly.

However, now that's out of the way, and you are all still here, I'll just show you a few satellite pictures to illustrate what the habitat destruction has done to one part of your planet, the Amazon rain forest. The actual total area of the forest is shown in the top right hand corner of each picture. When the picture is on the screen say 'closer', 'higher', 'left' or 'right' to move the view point, and 'next' followed by the time interval you want to jump, such as 'next ten years' or 'back five years' to move forward or backwards in time. We'll start this sequence six hundred years ago, long before any serious destruction took place. There were, of course, quite a few primitive tribes living in the forest at that time, and if you home in on a clearing you might see them. As the pictures show the normal passage of time (unless you jump to the next picture) you will be able to see them walking about. Professor, why don't you take on the job of 'driver' and take all your colleagues on an interesting trip around old Amazonia."

This time, when he'd finished speaking, the screen showed an amazingly clear three-dimensional picture of most of the north half of South America, including the entire Amazon basin, with a small white locating cross in the centre of the screen.

Though they were mentally dumbstruck by the enormity of the implications of what they had heard, no one had felt able to interrupt the speaker during the previous minute or two. However, the Professor managed to control his thoughts enough to say:

"If I understand it correctly, you have been watching the earth and have got a series of pictures showing us how the Amazon has developed over the last six hundred years, and you're about to show us some of those pictures."

"That is correct. Now if you'd like to start calling out the instructions you can see why we are so concerned."

They thus 'travelled' around the scenery on the screen. When they went in close enough, they did indeed find a clearing from six hundred years ago with people walking around, and by advancing in time were able to see the clearing being absorbed by reforestation and disappearing. They gradually moved towards the present time and were amazed to see just how much of the forest had indeed been cut down and fragmented.

After perhaps ten minutes, the Professor said 'end', the screen went blank and the familiar voice came back on.

"I'll now show you our best predictions of the forest's fate if it goes on as it is doing at present. Use the same commands as before. You will be starting from the present time, and, of course, the pictures you are going to see are simulations as opposed to the actual pictures you have just been looking at."

"Just a minute," said the Professor, finally managing to regain some sense of reality. "I'm having a difficult job absorbing what we've just been looking at. Are telling us that the pictures we have just been looking at were *real* pictures, (that is, they were *not* simulations) but taken from a satellite viewing platform or something similar, over the last six hundred years?"

"Yes, that is exactly what I'm telling you. We have indeed been watching and photographing the earth for at least the last six hundred years. By way of proof of what I am saying, home in on the picture on the screen now to see somewhere you'll probably currently recognise."

The Professor saw immediately that the area on the screen covered that part of the jungle where they were, so started going in closer, without changing the position of the white cross. They all watched with varying degrees of disbelief, as eventually a clearing became visible, and ultimately they could see themselves sitting near the fire watching the screen.

"So you see, the technology is pretty good at recording what is going on."

His remarks were greeted by a stunned silence that followed from what they'd seen.

"Ready to see the future of the Amazon simulation now?" came the voice.

Again, no one could think of a suitable response other than a sort of grunted 'yes'. The screen went back to the Amazon basin and they worked their way into the future. It did not take them many jumps into the future to find that the entire forest had become a desert, from the Atlantic Ocean right across to the Andes Mountains, and that the Amazon river itself had effectively vanished.

"My god, that can't be correct can it?" asked John. "I mean…" his voice tailed off as he looked again at the picture of the desert.

"Based on what we have seen happen on other planets previously (which was before we were able to influence what was happening there) and assuming your people continue to treat it as they have done up until now, our model of the demise of the Amazon forest is, I would say, about ninety-five percent accurate. The only thing that may be a bit out is the time scale. You can see the same simulation of the jungle you're in at the minute, if you like."

"No, thank you, I think we've seen enough," said Professor. "You said just then that you couldn't influence the earlier planetary destruction, with the clear implication that you can and will stop it happening here. Can you tell us how you intend to go about that?"

"Yes, certainly. One of the reasons for picking your little group for this meeting, is because this time we want to try to remedy the situation without causing too massive a disruption to your civilisation and…"

"Gee, thanks, you're all heart," came a muttered remark from Pat.

"Sorry, I didn't quite hear that; was it a question?"

"No, it's okay. Please go on."

"Right. I was saying in order to minimise the upset to your civilisation, we are going to spread the actions over a fairly long period, and in various locations, so none of the changes will be too sudden or too extensive initially. Some have already started to happen in some places, as I think Pat and Sven have already discovered, and John experienced slightly the other day, but has still to be implemented in others."

Just as those three looked at each other wondering what was being referred to, the voice continued:

"I was referring, of course, to the forest fever you two experienced a little while ago. We are in the course of enveloping all the major rain forests and a lot of smaller ones, particularly those that have been fragmented, in what I can best describe as a special shell shaped curtain that completely encloses them all round and over their treetops, (though it will not cover forests that have been planted for the purpose of harvesting timber, so you will not be cut off from all sources of wood). As you two found out, anyone trying to enter a rain forest experiences the sort of fever and terror that you did, which, I think you will agree, virtually guarantees they will leave as quickly as possible. If they don't, I fear they will not survive the experience."

In fact, one individual discovered this yesterday, though it will not make world-wide news. Along with several others he was going into a protected forest to hunt. When they experienced the terror they all ran out again. Unfortunately, this man ran into a tree in his panic, got totally disoriented and couldn't get out of the forest. He did not survive the experience and it is fairly certain the survivors will not try to hunt in the forest again."

This protection is, however, being implemented gradually and to protect those forests where it is not yet in place, there is also another type of protection to cover these areas. Again, I think you both experienced this: it prevents certain chemical reactions from occurring. One of these is the combustion in your petrol and diesel engines – they will not work inside the curtain. This will prevent the mechanised deforestation, particularly with chainsaws, that has been responsible for so much damage."

Another of the chemical reactions that will not function is the explosives in fire arms and other similar weapons, thereby greatly reducing the killing of the forest's indigenous species until we have all the forests protected. Some of this killing, particularly of large species already on the brink of extinction, is down to naïve belief in the magical power of 'traditional' medicines made from parts of these animals. These are sold to the gullible by those standing to accrue enormous profits from these 'remedies' which, as with all such 'placebos' are sometimes seen to provide some sort of cure. Hence the unfortunate rhinoceros is killed for its horn. For all the benefits obtained from the eventual 'medicine' made from it, they could just as well grind up their own toenail cuttings to obtain the keratin, this being the horn's main constituent."

He paused for a moment to let his audience appreciate what he had said and then went on:

"This protection also applies to the primitive tribes that still manage to eke out a living in the forest without disturbing its overall equilibrium. They do not use firearms and will be immune to the fever curtain, so that they can continue living as they have always done and cannot be attacked with firearms."

"Just a minute!" Professor cut in. "If this curtain is all you say it is, how come we managed to come into the forest as we have without falling prey to it?"

"Yes, I must apologise for the slight deception we subjected you to. Those necklace pendants, sort of ID Discs you could call them, supposedly sent to you from your minister to protect you from malaria and other diseases (that I'm pleased to see you've all been wearing), well they didn't come from the minister. We arranged for them to be delivered to you, and they are the reason you were able to pass through the curtain."

"I had supposed that to be the case but I'm pleased to have it confirmed," said the Professor.

Klaat resumed: "They also, incidentally, do actually protect you from all the jungle fevers and diseases, and have the added benefit of persuading all the other creatures, from the largest crocodiles, snakes and the like, to the smallest from ants to microbes that you are not to be approached, in very much the same way as the curtain affects human beings. Oh, and it also protects the small motors on your boats while you're in them and the motors are thus fairly near your discs, so that they will continue to work. This brings me back to what I was saying earlier, about why we arranged to have this meeting with you. We want you to go back and tell your government what we've told you here. As you are a party of well-respected scientists chosen by your government for this expedition, they will, we hope, pay heed to what you have to report, both the results of your expedition itself, and what you have experienced here tonight. We could, of course, have just broadcast the whole of this discussion we're having to the entire world's population, but that would have most probably caused an enormous panic and incalculable damage to your civilisation. By alerting your government who, in turn, can notify other governments and the United Nations, the message can be disseminated in a more acceptable way, as they will be aware of the consequences of starting a panic and will, we trust, act accordingly."

"To get over the initial credibility problem, you will take this projector box back with you. It will give you all the back-up you need, as apart from what we've shown you on it so far, it will also act as a video phone, and so we can answer directly any questions your government people may have."

Pat cut in as the voice paused slightly: "That sounds like a real bundle of laughs for one of us, but why should stopping access to the forests interest them unduly? I mean, it's not as though their position depends on timber, bush meat or the sale of endangered animal skins or parts, is it?"

"No, you're right it wouldn't," the voice continued, "so that brings me to the other measure we've taken that I haven't mentioned yet, and this most assuredly will interest them. It has in fact, already been noticed, but for obvious reasons not publicised nor explained. You see, there is one overriding cause of nearly all the problems that we've been talking about, and I'll come to that in a minute. But first a little digression to explain why we're going to have to do it.

Throughout the approximate eight hundred million year history of life on your planet, and indeed the very early primitive and simple bacterial type of life that existed earlier, that life has existed in one form of equilibrium or another. By that I mean if anything throws the equilibrium off balance, there will be an opposing force trying to correct the balance.

While I realise some of you are aware of this, it does no harm to stress its importance again.

Thus, while any life form will try to expand virtually indefinitely, this is usually kept in check by the food it can find to survive, or by it being eaten itself as the food of another life form. If for instance, there is a sudden increase in food one year, the animals (A) that eat a species (B) will increase in number dramatically, thereby reducing their food supply, that is, species B. Before long, species A will be starving to death because of the dearth of species B and their numbers reduce accordingly. In this fashion, A's numbers are decreased, thereby maintaining the overall equilibrium."

"There are, of course, other factors, disease or climate change, for instance, but in general, you could say that a life form's numbers will expand to the maximum permitted by the other environmental contra-factors."

"And, of course, there is one classic example of a life form that has managed to overcome nearly all the natural factors restraining its numbers, examples of which are listening to me here. I refer, of course, to you human beings."

The voice paused again for a moment, but this time no one felt inclined to comment, so it went on:

"So, many of the causes of the destruction of your planet are down to the sheer number of human beings. A prime example is the encroachment on the rain forests, being destroyed to provide farm land, but everywhere you look you can find other examples. Instead of trying to live in equilibrium with your finite environment, everything, particularly practically all sorts of businesses and industry, are geared to growth of one sort or another. They must always produce more merchandise, more crops, more timber, catch more fish or produce more food and more houses for the ever increasing population. Equilibrium and balance are never considered in the drive for increased production, which in turn, is supported by the fact that there are always more people needing these facilities or products."

"And then, of course, there is the problem of global warming, again mainly, though not entirely (as there are other significant factors at work contributing to it) caused by the sheer number of people using more and more energy all the time. So, until the population is controlled, the roller coaster to ultimate disaster will continue.

A simple analogy is to consider your earth as a lifeboat. After a ship sinks there is a defined number of survivors the lifeboat can hold. If more try to climb in when it is already full, it will sink, drowning all the occupants. In the same way, your earth is a finite entity, and can therefore only support a finite number of people.

Obviously, it is almost impossible for any government to even contemplate doing anything about everyone's assumed inalienable right to have children. Your Chinese and Indian nations have made some attempt at it, but without a great deal of success and with some unexpected consequences, such as the social effects arising from the imbalance of the sexes. Some parts of some countries are indeed experiencing a slight drop in birth rate, but this is more than off-set by others who are hell bent on increasing their numbers to ensure domination of other groups by sheer weight of numbers. Now, unfortunately, it is too late for simple control and the medicine has become very unpleasant to take. A reduction in numbers must be made to restore the planet as a habitat for all the species that remain, not just for *'homo sapiens'*. In any case, you would find out before too long, and when it was too late to remedy the situation, that it would not be possible for you to exist without the presence of many of the other species, bees for instance that pollinate nearly all vegetation, to take but one example."

"My God! They're going to wipe us out!" muttered Pat.

He started when the voice, which he had assumed could not hear his *sotto voce* remark, said:

"No. While that was an option we considered, we are going to try a more gradual approach. We have no reason to want to destroy a civilisation that has achieved so much, merely prevent it from continuing on its current path of self- and other life form destruction, as we have seen others do.

"We have decided to control your fertility in a gradual way that should give you time to adjust to a declining population. Initial estimates indicate that an annual decrease in the world's population of just over three percent will, after forty years, leave a total population of about two billion, a number that the planet can support without jeopardising all the other species' existence."

Initially, this will take the form of ensuring that no woman can ever have more than two children. It will also prevent innumerable casual matings resulting in children, which will, of course, also be of benefit to the children by ensuring a better chance of being born into a stable family. Then, to help cut down on a potential source of crime and strife caused by women with naturally strong maternal urges and men with drives to satisfy those urges, these will be partially suppressed artificially until they are in stable relationships, determined by the couple staying together for a period of, say, a year. Finally, there are areas prone to natural disasters where people can barely eke out a living just to survive and others where the damage they cause to the environment is so severe as to cause its complete destruction. In such areas they will find they cannot have children at all unless they move to another area."

"Of course, we will keep all these factors under constant review, and if the measures are seen to be causing more problems than they are solving, we will adjust them as necessary.

"Bloody hell, you can't do that!" exploded the Professor. "People won't ever agree to something like that!"

"Damn right," agreed Denise, who until now had been completely overwhelmed by what had happened, "no one will accept that! And besides," she continued, "it would cause great pain to all the women who could not fulfil their natural maternal desires."

"Yes, I appreciate that it will cause a lot of the sort of pain you describe, but I'm afraid you have no option," responded the voice. "You see, as John knows, the measures are already partly in place and starting to work. As I said …"

"But…but…you can't stop people having children – it's…it's…unethical and will cause great unhappiness," spluttered John, thinking of how upset Angela had been when she hadn't conceived their third child.

"I'm sorry, and I know why you and your wife are particularly concerned about that aspect…"

John looked at the screen in amazement: how could he possibly know about Angela not getting pregnant? Before John had time to say anything else, the voice went on:

"As I was saying, you have already experienced the 'forest fever'. This is now gradually being expanded to allow the forests to regenerate themselves by reclaiming the deforested areas, concentrating particularly on reconnecting fragmented areas of forest, thus allowing recolonisation by the previous fauna and flora, but where no one can now go to interfere with that process. There will also be a similar system to protect the life in the oceans by giving it areas where it can live without its populations being decimated by fishing, which, while not preventing the taking of some fish for food in certain areas, will restrict what can be caught and where (to protect species other than the target), and prevent collateral damage to the seabed and the lower life forms that inhabit it."

"There is one other operation that we are putting in place, and that is to modify the plants on which you and your livestock feed – rice, wheat, grain, maize, grass, vegetables and the like, so that they will produce up to one hundred fifty percent of their current yield from the same area. This will help you overcome the loss of 'new' farming land that were the forests, so with declining numbers and increased yields, the loss of 'wild' land for growing crops will not be too disadvantageous to you."

Denise, who had done a lot of work on increasing plant yields during her career, said:

"I think you'll find that very difficult. We have already done a huge amount of work on increasing plant yields and reckon we have gone as far as it is possible or practicable to go. Only very tiny further improvements *may* be possible, but it's very doubtful."

"While not wanting in any way to distract from the excellent work you and your colleagues have done in this field, I can assure you that we can achieve the increase I mentioned," the voice replied.

Martin Airedale, who up till now had left most of the talking to the others, had strong feelings about the fertility limitation that they were proposing, as he and his wife had been experiencing great difficulty in starting a family at all. He was fearful is to what it might mean to them, and, considering the practicalities asked: "And just how are you going to stop the women having babies – is it going to involve some sort of remote physical surgical procedure?"

"No, of course not – we are not barbarians! No, no one will be aware of any changes, and certainly there will be no physical 'assault' of the type you were imagining. I won't even begin to try to explain the technology involved, but you can envisage it, if you like, as a similar sort of curtain to that protecting the forests only in this case it simply controls the woman's fertility. There will be a similar sort of control on men's fertility as well. Initially, and to avert wholesale rape in an attempt to produce a child with any woman who might be fertile, men's desire to procreate will be reduced in a similar way to women's, it being restored in a stable relationship. However, I won't go into any more details now. You have enough general information to enable your government to start taking whatever action they deem appropriate."

I would add that we have not yet put all the measures in place, but are progressing with them as we think appropriate, taking all relevant factors into account. Thus there are some areas that are not yet being controlled but certainly will be before very long."

"The projector will reform itself as a small case that you can take back with you, though it will generally make its own travel arrangements, and will operate entirely automatically from now on. It will also become invisible unless you need to communicate with us, when it will reappear. However, it will come with you tomorrow on your hunt to find one of the tribes you're looking for, when it can act as your interpreter, as otherwise you won't be able to communicate with them at all. Oh, one final note: the projector has quite a few very effective self-defence mechanisms built in, so no one can do it or its keeper (who will be the Professor) any harm. And after you leave the jungle, it will only respond to commands from the Professor, unless we instruct it otherwise.

Goodnight."

As they watched, sure enough the screen retracted, the whole thing closed itself and returned to being a small case, still a couple of feet off the ground, which then moved under the Professor's hammock and settled onto the ground there.

"Has anyone else had the same nightmarish hallucination as I've just had," asked Pat of no one in particular, after a moment or two, "or did I have it all to myself?"

"Unfortunately, we all had it," said the Professor grimly, "and it doesn't look as though we can do anything except comply with the instructions."

"Yes, we can," said Sven, who had been rather quieter than usual, most of what was being discussed being outside his normal sphere of experience. "We could just chuck that damn thing in the river and go home when we've finished our survey here."

"That's my Sven," said Pat with a slight laugh, "always a rebel! Unfortunately, though, I very much doubt that would work. Firstly, such an expensive bit of kit (as that must undoubtedly be) has several protective measures built in, as the man said. Just for starters, why don't you try to move it now, Sven?"

"OK, I will," he replied purposefully, going over to the case. He reached for the handle but found he couldn't get his hand within about six inches of it – an invisible barrier prevented him from touching any of it.

"Goddam it, I can't even touch it!" he said.

"Rather as I thought," said Pat, "particularly bearing in mind his parting remark – 'It'll come with us tomorrow'. And besides, I think we ought to tell the government or at least somebody in authority, about this rather unusual meeting we've just had, and what's likely to happen. And you can easily imagine the reception we'd get if we tried recounting Klaat's message without the damn box to substantiate what we were saying."

"I agree," said Denise, "I'd also like to have a technical discussion with Mr Klaat along with some of our recognised world leaders in that field, always assuming he would co-operate. If so, it could have a profound effect on all the research being carried out world-wide on increasing plant productivity. So don't let's try dumping the box yet, please."

"Not much risk of that, apparently," added Martin.

"Well," Pat went on, gradually regaining his sense of humour "I don't know about you lot, but all this conversing with extra-terrestrials has made me quite hungry for the meals the cooks made for us though not a cold one. Anyone else want theirs heated?"

They were all so preoccupied by their thoughts during the meal that conversation was, at best, very fragmented.

Suddenly, Martin who had been rather quieter than the rest and seemed to have taken a bit longer than the others to absorb the enormity of what they'd just heard almost shouted:

"They can't bloody well do this! How dare they!"

Pat, the first to react to Martin's outburst, said:

"They dare, because they can, old chum, and there's not a damn thing we can do about it. Might as well calm down a bit and think how we can make the best for ourselves out of what's going to happen."

Martin started to reply, "I suppose…" but stopped short of any further comment.

Eventually, the Professor said: "I suggest we all sleep on what happened this evening, and we can discuss it over breakfast tomorrow, when we're all feeling a bit fresher."

After a general round of agreement, they all got into their hammocks and tried to sleep.

CHAPTER 15

Meeting Forest Tribes

They were all up early the next morning, no one having slept very well except Sven, who never let much bother him. He had the fire rekindled and the coffee brewing while the others were gradually waking up.

After a huge yawn, Denise said: "Oh, excuse me, but I don't think I slept for more than about half an hour at a time last night, what with never having slept (or even tried to sleep!) in a hammock before, the noises of the jungle and thinking through the implications of what Klaat effectively threatened for our future lives. Either way, I was glad when dawn broke."

"I was just the same," said Martin, "as I suppose we all were. Still, one bright side – Klaat's discs kept the bloody mosquitos (and for all I know lots of other unpleasant local inhabitants!) from eating me during the night."

After a slight pause he continued: "One of the things that helped keep me awake was the hope that the damn box doesn't let us down when we come to take the glad tidings back to the government and try to tell whoever our story – if it does they'll certainly shoot the messenger, or in our case entertain us in the funny farm for a considerable time."

"Considering the trouble they've gone to already to set up our meeting with Klaat, I doubt if they'd let the whole project just fizzle out because the box had blown a fuse. No, that I think is the least of our worries," Denise replied.

"Yes, I expect you're right about that, though it doesn't give me much comfort," added Martin, rather gloomily.

"I think the most important and useful thing to come from our friend Klaat and his projector is that it allows us to explain the origin and what we can, or rather can't do about the forest fever, the original reason why we find ourselves out here in the middle of this jungle. Without his visitation we would have to go home admitting we have no idea what has caused the fever or how to cure it," the Professor said.

After a few comments along the lines of 'You're right, of course,' no one had anything much different to offer to the discussion, so conversation petered out as everyone concentrated on their breakfast.

After a while, the Professor decided that they should complete their survey in the area they were in, even if the previous evening's visit purported to explain the reason for the forest fever. In general, this seemed to bear out what they had already found, that nothing, except human beings appeared to be affected by the fever. However, the Professor felt that in order to complete their original assignment, they still ought to check if indigenous forest people were susceptible to the fever even though Klaat had said they weren't. The particular river they were travelling on had been chosen because there were some primitive tribes living near it. Their landing site and clearing indicated that they were on the right track, so it was hoped it would not be too difficult to find them by following some of the clearer paths through the jungle.

It was decided that Sven should stay at their clearing site and look after it while the others set off on the quest, and that they should make sure they were back by about four o'clock. As a precaution, they made sure their mobiles had fresh batteries in them so that they could keep in touch with Sven while away, and, using the built-in GPS, he could come to their assistance, should the need arise. Similarly, they could return to base quickly if necessary.

Finally, when the survey party had got all their equipment and other items together, the Professor said:

"Well, Sven, I don't suppose you'll have any problems while we're away, but call us anyway so that we all know everyone's okay. Right then, advance the searching party!" he added to lighten the general mood.

Denise, being the botanist and less concerned with the anthropological details of the sought-for primitive tribe, said:

"I thought Clout, or whatever his name was, said that box thing was going to come with us. Who's going to volunteer to carry the damn thing?"

They all looked round at the projector, which was still under the Professor's hammock, where it had been all night, and just as Pat, having the least gear to carry, was thinking of volunteering, it rose a couple of feet off the ground and moved towards them.

"Well, that seems to be settled; I'm glad it has a sense of duty, and expects to pull its weight on our little expedition!" said Denise with a slightly sardonic laugh. "Let's see how good it is at playing 'Follow-My-Leader'!"

"How do we know it isn't just spying on us?" asked Pat of no one in particular.

"We don't," said John, "but as there's not a damn thing we can do about it, anyway, let's get on with our trip. If, as Klaat said, it'll interpret for us that'll certainly be a great help. So let's go."

"You're right, of course," said Pat. "I must be a little more upbeat. For one, it's not raining, and people back home pay ridiculous amounts of money to be subjected to the same sort of oppressive heat and stiflingly high levels of humidity in claustrophobic Sauna rooms that we're experiencing now for free!"

As they set off down the chosen track they saw that the box was indeed following them. As they were still looking at the Box, John said: "Good doggie, walkies!" to which everyone laughed, though the Box chose to ignore the remark.

Sven watched the party plus Box with a slightly bemused expression, then when they had gone out of sight and hearing, he had a look around the clearing to decide how to spend the day. Being someone who could not just sit and do nothing, he decided to have a scout round the immediate environs of the clearing. Arming himself with a heavy staff, cut from a small tree at the edge of the clearing, and his large sheath knife, he went a little way down each track to get a better idea of the layout of the place. Apart from the incessant noise of the insects and the occasional screech of some invisible monkeys and parrots, it all seemed (relatively) quiet and peaceful, even if still debilitatingly hot. Finally, he tried the track they'd all come along from the river the previous day, thinking to check that the inflatables were still securely moored to the tree roots where they'd left them. It was then that he thought he might be usefully employed by fishing and provide a decent meal for the party that evening.

Being proficient at bush craft, it didn't take him long to improvise a rod, and remembering that the survival pack they'd brought with them contained some hooks and line, soon had himself set up as the 'complete angler', even if the surroundings and basic equipment were a little different to those normally experienced by such people. He then sought out a rotten tree trunk and had soon dug out a few grubs for bait.

He had just settled himself in one of the inflatables as being the most suitable and comfortable place from which to fish when he saw the crocodile about twenty yards out in the river, nosing very purposefully towards him. Even though it only had its eyes and a bit of its snout above the water, he could see it was a very large animal. He started to move back carefully to avoid upsetting the inflatable while getting onto dry land, the while watching those eyes closing with him, surprisingly quickly. He realised his foot had got entangled with a rope in the bottom of the boat, and looked down to free himself. Though this only took a couple of seconds, the crocodile was now less than ten feet away and about to lunge at him. At the instant he was about to make a desperate leap to get out of the boat, there was a big splash, he had a fleeting glimpse of the greyish white belly of the crocodile as it turned tail and vanished under the water.

Sven stood stock still for a few seconds, not daring to move, and then as he calmed down, realised that the beast had indeed gone away. He got out of the boat and went back to the clearing, rather more shaken that he cared to admit, where he sat for a while, drinking a cup of cold coffee left over from breakfast. After a while, he thought to phone the search party to see if all was well with them and to tell them about his encounter.

Meanwhile, the survey team, with the Box still in tow, had explored a few tracks branching off from the main track they were following, but they all seemed to lead nowhere, with no indications of possible encounters with any primitive tribes. Then on one of them, where the track widened into a sort of clearing, they were suddenly confronted by a few chimpanzees that had an aggressive mien about them. The Professor, who was leading, held up his hand to stop the party, and said over his shoulder: "Go back onto the path very slowly while we see what these chimps are going to do. John, who was second from the front, was just thinking all was well as he reached the track, still moving slowly backwards, when all hell seemed to break loose in front of them, and with ear piercing shrieks the chimps charged towards the Professor. He turned to run, practically colliding with John who was also rushing to escape, tripped and fell quite heavily and winded himself. Terrified, he braced himself for the appalling injuries that would most certainly be inflicted by those terrible teeth that had been all too visible during the charge when the shrieking changed to a sort of whimpering and as the

Professor looked up, he was just in time to see them all running as fast as they had been when charging him but this time going back the way they had come and vanishing into the trees. In the space of a few seconds, all was quiet and peaceful again. Hearing the commotion stop, the rest of the party came slowly back to the clearing.

"Are you all right?" asked Denise seeing the Professor lying on the ground wincing in pain, while trying to breathe normally again.

"Yes...at least I think so," came the struggled reply. "I winded myself ...when...I fell."

She and Martin knelt by the Professor to help him sit up. Denise poured a little water onto a handkerchief and wiped the sweat from the Professor's brow to help him cool down a bit. After a few moments he had recovered enough to say:

"Phieeou! ...I thought we were in serious trouble then! Why the hell did they stop and then run off like that I wonder – they can't have been more than about ten feet from me when they backed off? Any ideas, John?"

"No, beats me. From what I know of their behaviour they occasionally go a bit Neanderthal when chasing small monkeys through the trees when they feel like augmenting a dull vegetarian diet with a bit of red meat, but they couldn't have had the same ideas about us, could they? Anyway, that wouldn't explain their change of heart. No, very odd behaviour, but I'm damn glad they've gone!"

As the Professor seemed to be recovering and not need any further help, Martin chipped in:

"I wonder, just wonder, mind, if what old Klaat, or whatever his name was, said was right about these ID discs. You remember he said they'd protect us from the fever and stuff, but he also mentioned animals would also be scared off. Do you remember?"

"Gosh, yes, you're right, he did say something to that effect. Maybe that's what scared them off," answered Denise.

"I'm fairly certain it couldn't have been the sight of my rather undignified scramble to get the hell away from them, so maybe that *was* it!" said the Professor. "Okay, then everybody, after that bit of entertainment and if everyone's ready, let's get under way again."

"I would suggest we go back and try another track," said John, "as apart from not wanting the opportunity to meet up with that bunch of distinctly uncuddly chimps, this path looks progressively more and more unused and doesn't look at all promising."

"I agree," said Denise.

"Okay, everyone, about turn! Backtrack again," the Professor called out.

They had just got back to the main track, when the Professor got Sven's call about his close encounter of the very uncomfortable kind with the crocodile.

"Funny thing, that," said the Professor, "we just had a similar apparently close call with a group of chimps that did not seem like a welcoming committee on behalf of the local wildlife – they looked like they were hell-bent on attacking us and then suddenly changed their minds and ran off. Martin remembered what Klaat had said about those anti-fever ID discs scaring off animals as well as preventing fevers and illnesses. We thought it might have been that, but if it was also that that decided the croc against having you for lunch – then it certainly fits in with what he said. Everything else he said seems to be turning out correctly, so why not that as well, though I wouldn't like to bet my life on it just yet, thank you!"

"Well, that makes me feel a whole lot happier," said Sven. "I was bloody sure I was in very serious trouble, then the damn thing suddenly turned tail and vanished. On the strength of what you've just said, I'll go back to the boats again. Actually I was hoping to give you all a surprise with some real fish to have for our meal tonight and was just about to start fishing when the croc turned up."

"Hey, that sounds like a great idea, but do keep a good watch out, just in case it wasn't the discs!" the Professor replied.

"I sure will!" said Sven as he switched his phone off, and decided to go and try his hand at fishing again. He resolved this time to make sure he could evacuate the boat a lot quicker if need be.

Even with his acknowledged lack of skill at fishing, he soon caught about a dozen fish, enough for a reasonable meal that evening, even allowing for not all of them being edible, which classification he knew would be easily resolved by the party on their return. As the heat and humidity was reaching its maximum and becoming almost intolerable, the river water, being clear and looking deliciously cool, became very tempting. He thought how nice it would be to go for a swim, but bearing in mind his recent close call with the crocodile, he opted to stay in the boat. He then stripped off and, using the boat's bailer, scooped water up from the river and poured it over himself, without creating too much of a commotion in the water, as he'd heard that that also tended to attract crocodiles. Having thoroughly enjoyed the ersatz shower, he then waited a few minutes hoping to dry off a bit. However, the humidity effectively prevented that, so he pulled his clothes on with a bit of difficulty (clothes being damp or wet with sweat, not slipping over wet bodies very easily) and then returned to the clearing to await the return of the others. Eventually, getting bored with the inactivity, he set off to collect some wood to build up the fire for the evening.

Being conscious of the hazards of the dense jungle floor with its leaf litter and other debris, though he had on thick jungle boots, he tied his trouser legs round them to prevent anything climbing up to attack him. Again armed with his knife, a machete and his staff he set off down one of the tracks, and soon saw a fallen tree off to one side. In classic manner, he started to hack away at the plants to clear a path through to the fallen tree. After a few moments of hard work, which had him sweating profusely again and promising himself a return to the river when he'd finished, he reached the fallen tree. Looking at it, he identified a few dead branches that would do for the fire wood, and was going towards it when his foot caught in a creeper that caused him to stumble. Instinctively he put out his hand to steady himself against the tree's trunk. What he had assumed was a dead liana wrapped around the trunk and on which his hand landed, suddenly sprang into life. He just had time to realise that it was quite a large snake that had adopted the classic pose of one about to strike, when with a quick movement, it fell to the forest floor and vanished.

"*Sacré blue*, I seem to be leading a charmed life!" he said out loud, getting over the fright it had given him. He stood quite still for a few minutes, machete at the ready, in case of further surprises, getting over the shock. Eventually, he decided that he had that part of the jungle to himself, and got on with hacking up the firewood, and placing it on the ground. When he thought he'd got enough for one trip, he bent down to collect the pieces of wood into a bundle he could carry. It was then that he saw the mess his boot had made of an ant's nest he'd been unknowingly standing on. He watched in amazement as the ants all seemed to be trying to get away, and contrary to all expectations, none had attempted to attack him. Grabbing the wood he went back to the clearing and sat for a while, cooling down then went back to collect the rest of the wood. By now, all the ants seemed to have vanished, and he gathered the last of the wood without further incident. The return to the boat for another cool down, as he'd promised himself, now seemed to him to be just reward for his efforts.

Feeling a bit better after his second 'shower', he went back to the clearing to await the return of the survey party. To help while away the time, he revisited the tracks occasionally, but other than the tail end of a snake beating a hasty retreat into the undergrowth, he saw little of interest. He also rigged up a sort of spit and made some skewers so that several of the fish could be cooked over the fire at the same time so that they could all eat at roughly the same time.

Shortly after Sven's call, the survey team's luck changed, and they saw a largish clearing in front of them with some rudimentary huts built in the centre, and thin wisps of smoke arising from a fireplace in the middle of the clearing. The Professor held up his hand again to stop the party, and went back, calling them together a little way back down the track.

"It looks like we've struck lucky at last," he said. "There are huts in a clearing up front, and smoke coming from a fire place, but no immediate sign of any people. We'll go forward slowly, and stand in a group just inside the clearing and wait for a few minutes to see if there's anyone home. If that doesn't produce any inhabitants, I'll call out. You all stay close together behind me. We don't want to give them too many targets if they decide to welcome us with bows and arrows in a similar friendly fashion to our last encounter with the local residents!"

A few minutes passed and there was still no sign of life.

"Hall-oooo," called the Professor.

There was a slight rustling about thirty yards away at the side of the clearing, and a man appeared, holding a spear in the launch position.

"Bingo!" said John quietly, "our first tribesman, and from this distance, my first impressions are that he is definitely one of the primitive ones we're looking for. Keep very still and let's see what he does."

After a few seconds pause, the man called something out to them.

Without thinking and in the excitement of the encounter, John called out:

"Don't be worried! We mean you no harm – we just want to talk to you. We…"

He stopped abruptly and got quite a fright when a loud voice close behind him said a few words that were completely unintelligible to him. Spinning round he saw the fairly comical sight of all the party staring open-mouthed at the Box that had moved silently up to just alongside the group, and out of which had come the words John had heard.

As they looked at the Box, they heard the man say something, and as they turned to look at him, the projector said "He asks what you want."

"Well, I'll be... Tell him we would like to talk to him and his elders and want to ask if any of his people have had any serious illness lately. Also tell him we bring him some gifts from outside the forest," John added, remembering that they had packed a few items for just such an occasion.

The Box then spoke again, presumably translating John's words. It seemed to John that it was rather more than he'd said, and was about to ask what else the Box had said when it started speaking again.

"The man said as we spoke his language we must be from a friendly tribe, though he had never seen anyone like us before – we looked very strange to him. However, he was keen to see our gifts and learn from us, though as we seemed to be white men would we not get too close as they didn't want to get any sickness from us, and no, they hadn't had any sickness in their tribe recently. Please, to come nearer."

"Okay, everyone, let's go over slowly, but be prepared to leg it if it isn't as cosy as it seems," said John quietly, leading the way towards the man.

While these exchanges had been progressing, Pat had been unostentatiously taking photos, hoping that he had got some absolutely unique shots of a hitherto unknown people.

When they got to within about ten yards of the man, they stopped and stood still.

"Won't you come out of the trees a little so that we can see you?" John asked, the request being duly translated by the Box.

The man did, and stood a few feet in front of the trees, saying nothing.

Pat said quietly, "I can see a few of his mates still hiding in the trees. Aren't you supposed to start handing out beads or some such to get their trust?"

"Look, we have some beautiful gifts for you," said John, slowly slipping his haversack off his back, but being careful not to take his eyes off the man in front. As the man heard the words from the Box, he looked at the haversack and took a couple of tentative steps forward. At the same time another two men came out from the trees and joined him.

"What gifts?" asked one of the new comers.

"We have brought you metal cooking pots and knives, also some beautiful beads and decorations for your head-dresses. Look, I'll put them on the ground here for you to come and have a look at." After he had spoken, and while the Box was translating, he laid out the items on a small sheet of plastic, and then stood up, saying to the others, "move back a bit" and at the same time, moving back himself and gesturing to the three men to come and have a look at the gifts.

They didn't need a second invitation, and were clearly delighted with the articles, posturing with the plastic beads and other decorations, and quite in awe at the saucepans and knives, being of a quality far superior to anything they had ever seen before.

To gain their confidence, John started talking to them about the items, gradually moving nearer so that conversation was easier, even allowing for the continuing need for the Box's interpretation.

Eventually, John was able to confirm that none of this tribe, or, as far as they knew, none of the other tribes they came into contact with had been ill with anything unusual for quite some time, which was certainly longer than the 'fever-curtain' had been in place. Further, they hadn't noticed any sick animals, confirming the fever's specificity to human beings.

"Right," he said over his shoulder to the others, "that confirms what we needed to find out about whether this forest fever affects any of the indigenous peoples or the animals in the forest – it doesn't. So let's say friendly goodbyes and get back to our base.

Having said a few friendly words through the Box, they backed off for a few paces, and then turned and walked away, with many a backward glance just to make sure their apparently friendly reception didn't suddenly turn into a hostile confrontation. However, the men were still intrigued with the gifts and hardly spared a glance at their departing visitors.

Back on the track, they made their way back without further incident to their temporary camp, the Box again following the Professor, dog-like. After their earlier amusement at this aspect of the Box's behaviour, they had accepted it and didn't comment on it further. On arriving at their clearing, the Professor saw Sven sitting at one of the tables, reading.

"Hi!" he called out. "Everything okay back here on the ranch?"

Sven got up and went over to meet them, saying:

"Yeah – beat off an attack by hostile natives, had a fight with a croc, nearly got bitten by a snake – just a normal day in the jungle really, I guess. How about you?"

Denise said: "You did what..." then stopped short, realising that the others were all tittering a bit. "Oh, I see. Well, we had a few frightening moments too," she finished a bit lamely.

"But you're okay, I hope," said Sven, now quite serious.

His change of tone was not lost on Denise, who replied with a smile: "Yes, I'm fine thanks," and then started to take off her back pack.

"Here, let me help you with that," offered Sven, taking the weight of the pack.

"Oh, thanks – it has got a bit heavy."

They all sat round the table, glad to unload their knapsacks and rest after a fairly long time on their feet, and discussed the day's events. Pat and John went to have a look at Sven's wood gathering site and brought back some more wood, and then they all took it in turns to have a 'Sven-shower' as they called it. Eventually, as the afternoon passed, the fire was lit, all bar two of the fish being identified by John as edible, and Denise, displaying culinary skills they hadn't suspected, managed to cook them on the skewers Sven had made in a way that was much appreciated.

"A vote of thanks to our newly discovered chef," said Pat. "They were some of the best fish I have ever tasted, even if I haven't a clue what they were!"

This was greeted by general assent and 'Yes, thanks' from the others.

"Well, I'm glad you all enjoyed them," said Denise, almost blushing at receiving such praise in such unusual circumstances. Feeling a bit encouraged and smiling at Sven she went on: "and if Sven can catch, rather than just fight off the next croc, I'll cook crock steaks for the party!"

"I'll see if I can manage it, just to please the cook," responded Sven, laughing, and noticing a strong feeling of attraction to Denise, that he hadn't felt for any woman for a long time.

"And let's have another vote of thanks for the fisherman, even if his croc got away!" joined in John, to a chorus of muttered 'here-heres' and laughter.

After a while when they'd finished eating and rerun some of the day's more amusing moments, as well as more discussion on the discs apparent power to ward off animal attacks, as witnessed by Sven's later experiences, they decided to turn in, as an early start was called for again in the morning, in order to pack up and return to their ferry back down the river.

CHAPTER 16

Out of the Jungle

It didn't take them long to pack up all their equipment and get ready to carry it back to the inflatables. It was Sven who noticed it first. He had offered to take the Professor's tarpaulin down for him as he was busy checking the packing of some of his equipment.

"Where's the damn Box gone to now?" Sven asked, looking around. The others all stopped what they were doing, and looked at the spot where it had last been seen, under the Professor's tarpaulin.

"Well, I'll be...it was certainly there last night," offered Pat. "Maybe Klaat, or whatever his name was, has decided his toy wasn't safe with us and has taken it back. Easy come easy go, you might say."

"Remember that Klaat said it could disappear at times," said Martin. "Maybe it just felt shy."

"I'll not lose any sleep over its disappearance, anyway," said Sven. "One less thing to worry about."

"That's as maybe," said the Professor, "but the whole point of the thing was to ensure we got Klaat's message back to our government. You can imagine the reception, not to mention the ridicule, we'd get if we try telling our story without the damn box to back us up. Why on earth would Klaat take it away?"

"Why on planet X might be more appropriate, Professor," said Pat, "but maybe he had to take it back for new batteries or some such. Either way, there doesn't seem to be much point in hanging around here looking for the damn thing. If it's gone, it's gone and nothing we can do about it. We'll just have to miss that little episode out of our expedition report. Shouldn't affect it all that much really..." he finished, leaving the slightly sarcastic comment hanging.

"I guess you're right," answered the Professor. "Right then, let's get under way!"

Leaving the mystery unsolved, they started to carry their things along the path to the dinghies.

Martin then returned to the clearing to make sure they hadn't left any equipment or rubbish behind and that the fire was completely extinguished.

When they had packed all the equipment safely in the boats, they set off downstream to return to the ferry boat. The journey proved uneventful, and they arrived back in time for a late lunch. The crew helped them unload the dinghies, and they were about to return to their respective cabins, when there was a tremendous clap of thunder and a very intense rainstorm started, followed by much more loud thunder and numerous brilliant lightning flashes, the ferocity of the storm being new to all of them except Sven who'd already experienced similar downpours while logging in Arbreville. Sheltering on the boat and watching the curtains of rain descend, Denise said, "I'm damn glad that lot didn't drop on us while we were in the jungle, or even worse, in the dinghies!"

To general murmurs of assent, they all watched for a little while and then went to their cabins.

Just as they were all getting there, there was a call from the Professor, standing in his cabin doorway:

"Could everyone please come here for a moment?"

When they were all standing in the corridor, he went on:

"Do you all see what I see, on the floor by my wash basin?"

They all peered in through the doorway and there was a collective expression of amazement. There, sitting on the floor, as though it were part of the Professor's luggage was the aluminium Box.

"How the hell did that get here, I wonder," mused the Professor.

"I was obviously right," said Martin, "it was just shy and didn't want us to see it swimming in the river."

"Either that or it obviously didn't fancy our company in the dinghies," said Pat, "or then again, maybe it was just worried about Sven's threat yesterday to chuck it in the river!"

The Professor went on: "As you're all here, after lunch let's get any outstanding lab work done, as we'll be returning to Djambaville. Going downstream won't take as long as it did to get here, so we'll be there fairly early in the afternoon. We must be ready to disembark with all our equipment and personal belongings as soon as we arrive, as I understand they've managed to organise the same Navy frigate to take us back to Douala. They are on a tight schedule, and so want to get us on board as quickly as possible."

.

They spent the rest of the day seeing to their respective tasks. In the evening, they had all gravitated to the bar when the Captain came in and said that he and the other officers would like the team to join them for dinner. This turned out to be a splendid meal, given as a sort of farewell gesture from the crew, which they all thoroughly enjoyed. Afterwards, as the drink started to flow fairly freely, everyone started to unwind and get more and more relaxed until an impromptu party developed. One of the barmen started some music playing and fairly shortly thereafter, the First Officer of the crew rather formally asked Diane Johnson to dance. After a moment's hesitation she accepted, and was quickly followed onto the floor by John Fenwick who persuaded Carol Spencer, rather against her better judgement but not wishing to appear churlish, also started to dance. Encouraged by the sight of the other couples, Sven asked Denise if she would like to join the dancers. Not wishing to appear standoffish and letting her usual self defensive emotional shield drop a little due to the happy atmosphere and a few drinks, she agreed and thoroughly enjoyed herself. However, her inner control made sure she did not let herself get too involved physically with Sven as even while letting herself go a little, she realised there could be no future to such a romance, if for no other reason than the total incompatibility of their two careers, hers with her academic future and Sven's with…what, she wondered?. For his part, Sven had come to much the same conclusion and so just enjoyed the evening as it was, dismissing any thoughts of a future relationship with Denise.

The next morning, despite a few slightly sore heads, they set about their packing up, and effectively had it all done by lunch time. No sooner had they finished their lunch than the boat was being readied for docking, which the team stood on deck watching.

"Oh no!" groaned the Professor, as he spotted a white clad figure walking rapidly along the dock towards their boat. "It's our good friend and organiser, Mr Claude Kindusa come to meet us."

The Professor thanked the Captain and his officers who had come to see them off the boat, saying how much the team appreciated all that they had done to make the expedition a success, and he would personally make sure that message was relayed back to the government of Nimeroon.

He then led the party down on to the quay. Mr Kindusa greeted the Professor like a favoured uncle from whom an inheritance was expected. A string of rapid fire questions assailed the Professor: Had everything been alright, was the boat satisfactory, and was there anything more he, Kindusa could do personally to help the team. Before the Professor could get in a word, he went on to say that he already had the dockhands unloading all the team's equipment and taking it down the dock to the frigate.

The team started walking toward the frigate, with Kindusa still apparently trying to impress the Professor with the amount he'd done to ensure the success of the expedition. As they got to the gangplank of the frigate, the Professor turned to thank Kindusa and shook his hand. As he was turning away to embark, Kindusa finally said what had been on his mind the whole time:

"I hope you have a nice journey home and that you'll put in a good report to the president of the arrangements I have made for your expedition here in Djambaville. Goodbye, goodbye," the latter addressed to the team in general with a genial wave of his arm, intended to include them all.

The team, having all arrived on board, were delighted to be invited by the Captain into the wardroom for a welcoming drink. They all sank gratefully into comfortable chairs, delighting in the cool air-conditioned room as much as the drinks they were offered.

As soon as all their equipment had been loaded, they set sail back to Douala, expecting to arrive early the next morning. They spent the afternoon writing up their individual reports of their findings, most of which merely confirmed that they had found nothing unusual in the flora or fauna that could possibly have caused the fever. The Professor had instructed them not to mention the appearance of the 'Box' or anything that had happened as a result of its presence, as this would be the subject of a separate report that he would write himself.

The Professor called the team together in the bar just before they went in to dinner with the captain.

"I just wanted to tell you how much I have appreciated how all of you pulled together to make our expedition such a success, even if we exclude the intervention of Klaat with his, shall we say, rather unwelcome message of how they intended to amend our planet's ways. At very short notice and I don't doubt, considerable personal difficulties you have all contributed magnificently to the success of our expedition. I for one, could not have asked for a better team, so thank you all."

They all burst into spontaneous applause when the Professor had finished, and a few toasts were drunk, so that the party was in very high spirits when they went in to dinner.

CHAPTER 17

Back to England

The return journey to Brize Norton was uneventful, and transport had been arranged to take them from there to a local hotel for an overnight stay, where they were all very conscious of the drop in temperature from their previous few days. The next morning they were taken to John's office for the initial debriefing. As a result of the phone call the Professor had made after arriving at Brize Norton, the minister from the Foreign Office, Henry Cowley, who had arranged the expedition, as well as the Environment minister, George Bentley were present. To try to stress the importance of what he had to say, the Professor had asked that the Prime Minister also be present, but was told that would not be possible.

Due to traffic delays, the party was a bit late arriving at the Ecowotsit's offices, to find the two ministers annoyed at being kept waiting and about to call the whole meeting off. The Professor managed to calm them down enough to agree to stay a bit longer, while the rest of the party settled themselves around the large meeting table.

"I'm sorry you've been kept waiting, but the traffic was particularly congested everywhere this morning," the Professor began. "However, the importance of deciding what to do next as a result of our expedition cannot be delayed. Our findings can be divided into two sections: the first, the detailed analyses carried out on the flora and fauna will be described in detail by my colleagues, but in summary, nothing out of the ordinary was found that could have caused the fever. The second…"

"Do you mean to say that this entire expensive charade has discovered nothing untoward and you dragged us here and kept us waiting all this time just to tell us that?" the Foreign Office Minister practically shouted, rising in his chair.

The Professor fixed him with a withering stare for a second before continuing:

"If you had had the courtesy to let me finish my sentence, you would have realised that was not the entire outcome of our 'expensive charade' as you so tellingly described it. Now, if you'll kindly sit down again I'll continue."

The minister realised he'd made a complete fool of himself in front of all these people who were now staring at him, at least one of whom was trying, partially successfully, to suppress a snigger. However, he was not used to being spoken to like that and was on the point of storming out of the meeting altogether. A warning voice in his head stopped him. Suppose that this bloody academic *had* found out something of importance that subsequently came to light and that he, the minister hadn't acted on it immediately, well, it wouldn't improve his image as a thoroughly competent, tough acting minister. So with bad grace he sat down again.

"Thank you. As I was about to say, the second, fully explains what has been going on, and I am extremely glad that there were six of my team there to witness what happened, as well as the aluminium box by the wall there that is evidence that all seven of us were not hallucinating. Just a minute and I'll show you."

He went over to the Box, and opened it, pressing the green button as Pat had done the first time the Box appeared.

"Hello, Professor, you had a comfortable journey back home, I trust?" came Klaat's voice from the Box, which the forest party remembered very well.

"Thank you, yes," replied the Professor. "You will remember you said you would repeat the demonstration you gave us in the forest should we need it. Well if you could do it now, it would be a good way to start spreading your message to the wider world. It would also help if you could answer questions when you've completed the demonstration."

"Certainly."

The minister, seeing a possible chance to save a bit of face in what he saw as a continuing charade now apparently involving a bloody tape recorder, was about to get up and ask a stingingly sarcastic question. He stopped halfway to the standing position as he saw the Box move apparently entirely on its own to a position a bit above one end of the table and raise its screen, on which appeared an amazingly clear three-dimensional picture of a jungle and river system. At the same time the voice continued:

"I showed you the history of the destruction of the Amazon Jungle, which I will do again, but for the benefit of those who were not present when I introduced myself last time, I will repeat what I said on that occasion."

The minister dropped back into his seat, his face a picture of astonishment. Even he realised that what he had just seen in those few seconds could not have been an elaborate conjuring trick, designed merely to fool the two ministers. The Environment minister, even if he had been beginning to share his colleague's feelings earlier, was also now completely entranced by the scenes being displayed in front of them.

"Klaat, just before you begin, I'd better give our visitors here a brief outline of the circumstances of our first meeting," the Professor interrupted.

"Of, course," came the reply from the Box, "go ahead, and I'll start whenever you've finished.

The Professor then sketched out the events of that first night in the forest clearing, keeping it very brief, as he could see that the visitors' attention was almost entirely on the Box and not on what he was saying. When he had finished, he turned to the Box and said:

"Right, Klaat, if you'd like to begin…"

The earlier lecture from the Box was repeated almost verbatim, as far as those who heard it the first time around could tell, and the scenes of the Amazon's transformation to a desert repeated. However, instead of showing them the jungle clearing where they had first encountered the machine, this time (was there a hint of devilment about it?) it homed in on the Foreign Office minister's house, where a woman in a floral print dress could be seen gardening. "You no doubt recognise those pictures Mr. Cowley, which show you your wife gardening at this very minute, which, of course, you can verify when you get home. I hope that finally convinces you that what you have just seen is absolutely real and not just a trick from a new super tape recorder." The minister appeared to be about to say something, but decided against it, and slumped back into his chair, slightly shocked, his mouth half open.

"Well, there you have the explanation for what's been happening to the rain forests," the Professor said, standing up again and looking pointedly at the Foreign office minister. "Perhaps you see now why I wanted the prime Minister to hear that, as we obviously have to take it and present it to the United Nations, this being a world-wide problem that all governments should know about as soon as possible. What will they do with the information? Well, who knows?"

"One thing is absolutely certain: we must not let the information about Klaat or the real reason behind the forest fever become public before they have all had a chance to decide what to do about it. So that applies stringently for everyone in this room. It must remain strictly confidential until further notice."

Looking around the room, his eye lighted on Pat O'Hanlon, who had been sitting quietly listening and secretly recording all that was said.

"I'm afraid that goes particularly for you Pat, and what you write up about the expedition. The gist of it has to be that the expedition was a success, and that we came back with many samples which are going to require detailed analysis back here in our laboratories, all of which will take time before we can identify the causes of the fever. Skip any mention of the birth rate at present, as it hasn't yet, as far as I know, been linked to the forest fever. We'll cross that particular bridge when we get to it. Also could you join us in Mark's office afterwards, there are a few details about the report you're writing that I'd like to discuss with you."

"Certainly, Professor. Glad to help. You gave me the opportunity to take part in one of the most sensational enquiries anyone has ever undertaken, I would guess, so anything I can do to help…"

"Thank you, Pat."

Mark then spoke up for the first time:

"That comment about them controlling the birth rate has certainly happened in this country, and so has presumably happened everywhere else as well. Your research confirmed that, didn't it, John?" he finished, looking at John.

"Yes," replied John. "I checked several clinics around the country a little while ago, and the reduction in numbers, compared to a similar period last year, bears out what Klaat said."

"Thanks, John, but as I said, absolutely no mention of that aspect yet. Well, I think that concludes all we have to report from our 'expensive charade' or expedition, as I prefer to think of it," the Professor said (pointedly looking at the minister from the Foreign Office), in closing the meeting. "We have answered the original question as to what caused the forest fever, though I must admit I never could have imagined such a result. I'm glad it's not up to my team to advise what must be done next. That's over to you, ministers. So, thank you, every one."

"Oh one thing, Mark," the Professor continued, "they may not have put the birth rate controls in everywhere yet. Klaat mentioned that there were still areas that they hadn't dealt with yet, so this may be one of them."

"So we still have some nice surprises to look forward to, I suppose," replied Mark, as they were getting up to leave.

"Professor, could you spare me a few minutes?" asked the Environment minister, as they were leaving the meeting room. The Professor eyed him slightly quizzically before replying: "Yes, certainly," and allowing himself to be guided back to head of the table by the minister, by which time all the others had left the room. "How can I help you?"

Before there was time for an answer, the minister from the Foreign Office felt it would be advantageous to try to recover the damage done to his image by his earlier outburst, so forestalled the other's answer by bestowing on him his most ingratiating smile and saying:

"Oh, Professor, I'm sorry if I was a little short with you earlier, but I'd just come from a very unsettling meeting that requires some urgent action on my part, which taken with your delayed appearance had I fear rather coloured my demeanour."

The Professor looked at him for a second as though examining a particularly unpleasant growth on a slide under his microscope before replying in an offhand manner: "Apology accepted," and then, turning immediately to the Environment minister, continued in a markedly more friendly tone: "Now, how can I help you?"

"It's like this. As I mentioned earlier, the Prime Minister didn't have time to attend this meeting this morning, and so I have to report back to him on what transpired. As I'm sure you realise, there is no way I could stand in front of him and baldly relate what occurred in the meeting. I'd be – well, I think you can imagine what my reception would be. No, what I was going to ask was would you be kind enough to come with me and bring that, er, box thing with you to demonstrate that I wasn't suffering from some form of hallucination."

The Professor gave a short laugh and said: "Yes, I know *exactly* what you mean, and of course I would be happy to accompany you to your meeting. When is it?"

"I'm afraid it's not until nine o'clock tonight."

"That's no problem," the Professor replied. "Where shall I meet you?"

The minister from the Foreign Office chipped in with:

"I think I should come with you both to hear the PM's views on what we should do next."

"You'll have to clear that with his personal secretary first. I am instructed to bring him up to date on the matter with the Professor – he didn't say anything about you coming along as well," replied the Environment minister.

"Oh. Right. Yes. Of course," came the mumbled reply, and feeling humiliated for the second time in a few minutes, he picked up his brief case and left.

Once he'd left the room, the Environment minister said slightly conspiratorially:

"I didn't want to tell you while Henry was in the room, but the reason the meeting has to be so late is that officially, he is attending a special ministerial meeting, unofficially, he wants to watch the football match on TV that's scheduled to finish then, though, of course, I didn't tell you that."

"Of course not," said the Professor smiling. He was warming to this man who still seemed not to be a ministerial apparatchik, whereas the recently departed 'Henry' undoubtedly was.

"And of course," he went on, "in the way these matches sometimes run into extra time, no doubt our meeting will be late starting."

"Very probably," replied the minister, gloomily. "God knows what time I'll get home. Do you have far to go?"

"No, I've got a room in a hotel for the night. I expected to be tied up with this matter for a while."

Thinking ahead to the coming meeting with the PM and then back to what he had heard earlier, the minister said:

"That must have been the most amazing encounter you had out in the jungle with that Box. Just to suddenly appear like that – must have been a bit unnerving, to say the least!"

"Yes, it was. At first I thought it must be some hoaxer on the phone to me, but when that thing was suddenly there on the other side of the clearing… Well, let's just say it gave us considerable pause for thought!"

They chatted on for a few minutes, and arranged to meet later for the meeting with the Prime Minister, after which the minister left. The Professor went along to Mark's office to discuss the meeting and what, if anything, they should do next, and then phoned his wife to confirm he wouldn't be home until tomorrow evening. Other than a tidying up exercise of completing their reports on the expedition's findings which the Professor would include in his overall report to the minister, it was agreed there was nothing else to be done for the minute.

At five minutes to nine that night, the Environment minister and the Professor presented themselves at the main gate through into Downing Street. The policeman on guard recognised the minister, and with a cheery 'Good Evening, sir' to the minister and a nod to the Professor, let them in. Just afterwards, the minister looked at the Professor and said:

"Where the hell's the Box thing – we'll never get the PM to believe a word we say without it!"

"Don't worry! Sorry, I forgot to tell you, but it has a very useful habit of becoming invisible when I'm travelling and going through any sort of check. It saved no end of questions at the various Customs and Immigration posts we've been through. The first time it happened I wondered where the hell it had got to as well, as in most respects it behaves a bit like a dog, trotting alongside me – I don't even have to carry it as it will just float along at my side, but to avoid funny looks if it's visible, I make a point of holding its handle – otherwise once past the officials, it reappears as though it had never been anywhere other than by my side. Somewhat disconcerting the first couple of times, but now I seem to have got used to it. You'll see, as soon as we're in the PM's house it'll be there."

"I bloody well hope you're right, as we're going to look like a couple of effing loonies trying to tell that story without the damn Box," replied the minister, uneasily.

Five minutes later they were being ushered into the study to await the PM's arrival. As the door was closed behind them, the minister gave a sudden jump as he saw the Box reappear alongside the Professor.

"Well I'll be bug..." he began, but was cut short by another door in the study opening and the PM entering.

"Hello, George. Good of you to come at this late hour, but I didn't want to delay seeing you any longer than necessary and I had to have the meeting that's just finished."

As he walked round the small coffee table between the visitors' chairs, the Professor caught George's eye and gave just the hint of a smile at the PM's remark.

"Ah, and you must be Professor Kowalski," he continued, walking over to him and shaking him by the hand. "Please take a seat," he added, indicating a settee and couple of arm chairs round the table in front of his desk, "and I suppose you both wouldn't be averse to a little refreshment?" This last as he went over to a cupboard, built into the wall.

"George?"

"That splendid single malt I believe you hold in reserve for special occasions would fit the bill very nicely, thank you, Prime Minister."

"Professor?"

"With such a recommendation I'd like the same, please"

"Good. I think I'll join you both in that choice."

The PM was feeling particularly expansive, as not only had he had several notable successes with the day's business in the House but his team had won the match he had been watching.

"So, what have you got to tell me?" he asked, when they were all settled in their chairs with their drinks.

George started the conversation:

"What we have to tell you is very probably the most unbelievable series of events that you have ever had presented to you in your political career. Fortunately, we have absolute proof that it is the truth, no matter how difficult it is to believe or unfortunate it may turn out to be for all of us. So…"

"Come on, George, you make it sound like Armageddon and I was led to believe it was just an hitherto unidentified jungle fever or some such!" said the PM with a slight laugh.

"Would that it were just that. I'm afraid it isn't, and it may well be nearer the former. But please, listen to what Andrew here has to tell us about his expedition, and then say how serious you think it is."

"Okay, Andrew, let's hear the worst," said the PM.

So Andrew recited his abbreviated account of their expedition, and when he got to the appearance of the Box in the jungle clearing, the PM said:

"And I suppose this Box thing is your proof, which I can quite see you will need to lend any credence at all to your story. Where is it and can you get it to re-do the picture show?"

"It's here, beside my chair, and yes it will rerun the show for you. If you could be patient for a couple more minutes while I complete my account of the expedition, I will demonstrate it to you."

There was just a hint of cynicism in his voice as he replied:

"Okay, go ahead. I'm prepared either to be astounded or laugh if it doesn't work!"

The Professor finished his account and then said: "Now, I'll show you the proof."

He lent over the arm of his chair, opened the Box and pressed the green button. Immediately Klaat's voice came from the Box: "Good evening, Professor, I take it you want another run of our Amazon scenario?"

"Yes, please," replied the Professor. "We have our prime minister with us now, and it is obvious he will have a very large part to play in convincing other governments of what you have to say. So please go ahead."

The PM was just about to make some slightly scathing remark about the new wonders of a tape recorder, when he saw the Box move by itself a little distance in front of him, and produce its screen. The voice then continued:

"Good evening, Prime Minister Cranham, the Professor has given you the necessary introduction to my presence here, so it just remains for me to tell you what I told him in the jungle a few days ago and show you the pictures to back up what I said. So, if you're ready..."

The PM had sat rigid with amazement as the Box moved and introduced itself. He just managed a stifled 'Yes' in reply, before the voice repeated the account it had given to the expedition in the jungle explaining its presence.

When the exposition was completed with the usual 'Do you have any questions?' the PM could only sit staring at the screen as it slowly disappeared back into the Box, which then resumed its position alongside the Professor's chair. It was left to the Professor to say:

"Thank you, Klaat. I don't think there are any questions just at this minute, but if you could be there for a few more minutes, there might be when the PM has had time to appreciate the enormity of what you've just told him."

After a few moments the PM shook himself slightly, and said:

"George, tell me I fell asleep and I've just had a nightmare, can you?"

"'Fraid not, Prime Minister, what you have just seen bears out exactly what Andrew found during his expedition, and what my department found on a recent survey of doctors' surgeries around the country. I'm afraid there's absolutely no doubt that what Klaat there said is true. We are going to have to adjust our entire economy, and come to think of it, way of life to accommodate a declining population and restrictions on such things as hardwoods, some fishing and anything else caught in the net of these areas from which people are to be excluded."

The PM, following the habit of a lifetime spent in politics, was about to start advancing some counter argument when a thought struck him. Seeing the Box still there, he spoke to it:

"Thank you for your clear account, Mr. Klaat, but just at the minute I don't have any questions. I may well do so tomorrow after I've had a chance to mull over what you have told us, in which case I will get the Professor to open up his communication channel with you, but in the meantime, thank you and goodnight."

Seeing the other two about to say something, the PM put his finger to his lips, pointed at the Box and shook his head. He then said:

"Thank you for that very interesting demonstration. I have had a long and tiring day, and would like to sleep on the matter before discussing it further. George, can you put up in a hotel near here for the night and come round again at nine tomorrow morning. I will cancel my other arrangements while we discuss what we are to do next on this matter. Professor, we won't need you immediately, but if you could be available on the phone, we may well have some questions for you."

Leading the way to the door, the PM said: Goodnight, thank you both very much and see you in the morning, George.

Once back in the Mall, George phoned a hotel that always had a room for ministers in such eventualities and then called his wife to apologise for yet another unexpected night away from home. The two of them then hailed a taxi to go to their respective beds for the night.

On the way, George said:

"I think that went quite well. One thing's certain – it's given the PM a great deal to think about."

"It surely has," replied the Professor. "I'm damn glad deciding how to handle this matter isn't my responsibility. I wonder what he'll do about it."

They chatted a bit more about this aspect until arriving at the minister's hotel.

"Well, goodnight Andrew, I'll be in touch again very soon."

"Goodnight," replied the Professor, who was very glad to get into his hotel bed a little later. It had been one hell of a long day.

CHAPTER 18

The Prime Ministerial Plan

Meanwhile, back in the PM's study, he had poured himself another drink and was mulling over the events of the past couple of hours. What were the implications of what he had heard? He'd decided, initially against his better judgement, not to dismiss the whole matter as some wildly elaborate hoax, as he couldn't see how any of his enemies, of which he knew he had plenty, could hope to gain from such a ploy or indeed make a box that could perform as that one had. No, it must be genuine, even if he hadn't the remotest idea by whom or how the whole thing was being orchestrated. After a few more moments' thought, the natural cunning and ruthlessness that had taken him to the top of the political tree began to assert itself. Okay, assuming it was genuine, how might he personally turn the whole thing to his personal advantage? He thought long and hard on this matter, and was just beginning to see some possibilities when his wife came in to enquire if he was coming to bed at all that night. He restored domestic harmony, as he had so often in the past that his wife no longer questioned what it was that was so important, by saying he just had a few more important things to complete before turning in. On his own again, he started thinking his plan through, and with growing excitement, could see the possibility of success.

In essence he would keep the real reason for reduction in birth rate secret for the time being. After all, there weren't many people who knew what was really happening, and it should be possible to keep them quiet, one way or another. Then he'd get in touch with that Kart fellow, or whatever his name was, and do some sort of deal with him to get the birth rate restored, for which he could then work out some way of taking all the credit personally for preventing a national catastrophe and indeed effectively saving the world. Just as he was congratulating himself on the start of a beautiful scheme, he realised he'd have to get hold of that Box thing as soon as possible. Right. He'd get George to bring it round tomorrow under the guise of national security, and then he could start working on Bart or Kart or whoever it was. Then another thought struck him. Even if he couldn't get Kart to agree to his scheme, the use of the Box for spying on his enemies, even his friends, come to that, would be a very powerful and useful weapon to have. Yes, he must definitely get his hands on that Box and find out from the Professor how to operate it.

He finished his drink and went up to bed. However, the excitement at the prospect of the grand schemes he had just envisioned, and turning over the details in his mind, prevented him from getting to sleep for a long time.

Feeling somewhat jaded the next morning due to lack of sleep, the PM, none the less, was ready for his meeting with George.

"Morning, George, glad to see you're right on time as I've got a great deal to do today. But first things first. Could you get hold of Professor Kowalski and get him back here as soon as possible with that Box thing of his. Use the phone on the desk there. I'm just going to get some more coffee – would you like some?"

"Yes, please."

The Professor was none too pleased to be woken by the bedside phone in his hotel room. He had taken a sleeping pill the night before, as he knew from past experience that after all the travelling and activities of the previous day he would have trouble falling asleep, and its effects were just wearing off when the phone rang. However, he agreed to get round to Downing Street as quickly as he could, but explained that it would take at least an hour or two. Eventually, the PM agreed that they would meet at eleven that morning, telling the Professor via George to be sure to bring his Box with him. When the call was concluded, he told George to come back at a quarter to eleven, as he needed to speak to him privately before the Professor arrived.

When George returned, the PM outlined his 'public' plan to him, which, of course, contained no clue as to his real intentions. He said he would embark on a series of meetings with the ambassadors of our main friendly countries to see what could be done to minimise the effects of this apparent takeover of the world. While it might have been better to have done it with a single meeting, unfortunately, due to their various commitments this was impossible to arrange at such necessarily very short notice. Also, of course, it had to be done with the utmost secrecy, so he intended to handle this himself. To this end he intended to take ownership of the Box from the Professor, who could then get back to his normal work, and should be discouraged from making any further reference to his work or the results of his recent expedition. They would also have to ensure the silence of anyone else who witnessed the events in the jungle, in the interests not just of national security, but also of preventing a world panic, as Mart himself had said via the Box last night.

On the face of it, George could see nothing wrong with the PM's comments, except probably for his intention to exclude the Professor from any further involvement in the matter.

The Professor was shown into the study just as they were finishing their discussions. The first thing the PM noticed was that he hadn't brought the Box with him.

"George, I distinctly remember telling you to make sure the Professor brought that damn box thing with him," the PM said angrily.

"I did, I…"

Before he could continue the Professor, somewhat surprised at the PM's tone said:

"Don't worry, as I told you yesterday, George, it usually makes itself invisible when travelling with me through any sort of security barrier, otherwise I usually carry it like a suitcase, as it obviously attracts less attention than floating alongside me. It'll reappear any… There! As I said," he finished, looking at the Box, in the same position beside the chair that it had been the previous night.

George gave a big sigh of relief and the PM tried to conceal his delight and amazement at the thing, by uttering a curt 'Good' and then offering the Professor some coffee.

When they had settled down with the coffee, the Professor sensed a very different mood in the PM from that prevailing the night before, but couldn't be sure just what it was.

"I'll be blunt. There isn't much time, and I've got to make a lot of difficult arrangements to make," the PM began, in a tone that brooked no comment, and was a long way from the friendly discussions of the previous night. "George here, will fill you in on some of the details, but I'm sure you appreciate just how serious a matter this is and that, as a matter of national security, indeed world security, the whole thing must be treated as top secret while the nations' leaders work out what to do and what to tell the public. Accordingly, you will hand over the Box to me and have nothing further to do with this whole matter. Go back to your research, or whatever it was you were doing, and forget all about this. It is absolutely forbidden for either you or any of you team, under pain of imprisonment, to speak to anyone, anyone at all about any aspect of it. Is that clear?"

For a second or two, the Professor felt he was back being a schoolboy up in front of the headmaster, having been caught perpetrating some terrible misdemeanour, then he started to feel anger rising at the way he had been spoken to. Realising, however, that there was not much he could do about it said:

"As you wish. I have nothing further to contribute, anyway, so I'll gladly leave you with it," the Professor said, getting to his feet and making for the door.

"George, go with him and explain to him what I told you earlier. Goodbye."

His last remarks were nearly lost as George followed the Professor out of the room. The PM went to the window to make sure they had left the building, and while watching them leave phoned his secretary to instruct that on no account was he to be disturbed until he called back. Rubbing his hands at the success of his scheme so far, he turned to tackle the Box.

It wasn't bloody well there!

Goddamnit, he could have sworn the Professor hadn't taken it with him. Then he remembered something about him saying it became invisible, so he started flailing about beside the chair where he'd last seen it.

Nothing. Not a damn thing!

Shit! It must have gone out with the Professor. Nothing else for it but to try and catch up with them. So thinking, he ran out into the street in a state of some agitation to try to follow them. He was just in time to see them disappear behind the buildings in the Mall. The policeman on duty at the door looked at him quizzically and said:

"Everything alright, Sir?"

"Er, yes, I just remembered something important I'd forgotten to tell the minister, but as I've missed him, I'll have to call him. Thank you, officer," he said, going back into number ten with rather more dignity than he'd left it a few moments earlier.

Back in his study, he called his secretary.

"Get me George Bentley on his mobile immediately!"

A few moments later, George answered.

"Get that bloody Professor back here immediately and bring that damn Box with you, d'you hear? He deliberately walked out with it after I'd said to leave it with me. I'll have a few words to say to him when you get back here."

"I didn't see him take it, I…" began George, but the PM cut across his reply:

"Of course you didn't, you bloody idiot, didn't he say he could make it invisible? Now bring him back here immediately!"

"I can't he's …" George started again, before he realised the PM was no longer on the line.

"Hell! I'd better call him back and tell him the Professor took off in a taxi and I don't know where he's gone," George said to himself, "more bloody trouble. I wonder why the PM was so upset about the whole thing."

The PM for his part, still seething at not spotting the loss of the Box until too late, told his secretary not to put any calls through to him until he called back, and then sat down to await the arrival of George and the Professor and tried to reformulate his plan to recover from this temporary glitch.

George, meanwhile, having tried unsuccessfully to call the PM tried to find the Professor, but was unable to do so, as he was neither in his hotel nor at the office with Mark Bedford.

The Professor, still simmering from his treatment at the hands of the PM, had decided that there was nothing much else he could do in London for a day or two, and so might as well go home. And to ensure there was no further disruption to prevent him doing so, he switched off his phone. He directed his taxi to wait while he checked out of the hotel and then went to Euston to catch the next Birmingham train on the first leg of his journey. He had forgotten all about the invisible Box accompanying him, having vaguely assumed it had stayed on in the PM's study when he left, as per the PM's instruction.

After ten minutes or so spent pacing up and down, the PM had his secretary call George again. As luck would have it, at that moment George was on his phone trying to find the Professor. It was thus another ten minutes before the PM, by now thoroughly irate, finally got through to George.

"Where the bloody hell are you?" the PM started out, practically shouting into the phone, but before he could continue came a reply:

"What the bloody hell's it got to do with you where I am, and who the hell are you anyway, you loud-mouthed bastard?"

The PM slammed down his phone, and then spoke to his secretary, in an excessively calm and polite voice:

"That was a wrong number. Now, do you think you could possibly dial the right number," and continued almost at a shout: "and get me George bloody Bentley, NOW!"

This time he checked he had got through to George before ranting at him for his nonappearance.

George explained that they'd gone their separate ways in taxis on leaving him, and that he had been unable to raise the Professor.

"Well keep at it until you find him. I don't want to see you or hear anything from you until you arrive here with the Professor and that damn Box. I don't have any use for a minister who can't even find one of the people working for him, so you know what to do if you want to keep your present job."

Phew! thought George, I know it's important but he seems to have fallen off his trolley over this. Eventually, he did manage to arrange to contact the Professor as he arrived at Birmingham, and told him to come straight back to London, and to make damn sure he brought the bloody Box with him.

"I'm not sure where it is. I told you it usually becomes invisible when I travel with it, so it is probably with me somewhere, but I can't see it. However, I'll come back and hope it is with me. Quite honestly, after our last meeting with your boss, I'd be quite happy not to meet him again, and I'll certainly not be voting for his party next time, not that that will make a blind bit of difference, of course. See you at Euston in about an hour or so," he finished.

Five o'clock saw them back in the PM's study. Controlling himself with an effort, the PM managed to sound nearly civil as he asked if they'd brought the Box with them as it still wasn't visible. Without waiting to be asked, the Professor sat down in the same arm chair he'd used previously, and looking down beside him, saw the Box there.

"Yes, there it is," said the Professor, coldly. "So now if you'd like to take control of it I'd like to resume my journey home."

"Right," said the PM, managing to conceal his delight at the future prospects about to open to him when his plan was put into operation. He bent down to lift it by its handle, and found he couldn't get his hand within about six inches of it. He tried other approaches, but there seemed to be this invisible barrier around it.

"Alright you clever bastard," snarled the PM, "what clever fucking trick have you pulled this time? I can't get within six inches of it!"

The Professor looked at him contemptuously. "I have observed that phenomenon before. It seems to be some sort of built-in self-defence mechanism about which I know nothing and over which I have absolutely no control. Why don't you try swearing at the 'fucking' Box – maybe you'll frighten it into doing what you want."

With a great effort, the PM pulled himself together, and realising that his prize might be slipping away, tried another approach.

"Please forgive me, Professor, I've had a very trying week and am a bit overwrought. I do apologise for swearing at you like that."

"That's all right, I'm getting used to being sworn at by politicians. However, in the wider interest of enabling you to have convincing meetings with other governments, I'll try something else to hand this over to you."

He leant over the arm of the chair and opened the Box without any trouble. Ignoring the PM's muttered, "Well, I'll be…" he pressed the green button.

"Hello, Professor, sorry to see you haven't got home yet, you must be pretty tired after all the travelling and meetings of the last few days."

"Yes, I am a bit. Anyway, the reason for calling you is to request that control of this Box of yours be transferred to my Prime Minister, so that he can start meetings with the other governments, in line with your original plan. At the minute, no one other than I can operate it, which, apart from anything else, would jeopardise your plan if I am taken ill or something."

"Don't worry about your personal health in that regard – control would automatically pass to John Fenwick. No, I'm sorry, but it cannot be passed to your Prime Minister, for reasons that he will appreciate. It will remain with you, and you will have to be present at any meetings where its presence is required."

"What the bloody hell does he mean, 'reasons I will appreciate'," spluttered the PM. "I demand to have control of that damn Box!"

"If you really want the reasons spelt out, watch the screen, and I'll take you back to this study last night, after the other two had left. Perhaps they would be interested in your real reasons for wanting to control my Box. Are you sure you want me to replay that? I should warn you that your thoughts will be replayed as a normal sound track."

A moment or two of deathly silence.

The looks that crossed the prime minister's face in quick succession were a study: incredulity, guilt, cunning then fear at exposure, finally his famous smiling charm expression trying to mask everything that had gone before.

"No, of course that won't be necessary. When I think about it a bit further, I think it would be very beneficial to have the Professor at all the meetings with your Box. I don't know what I was thinking about in trying to run them without his expertise in the first place.

"A wise decision. I will connect with his computer and download all the calculations and predictions we have made about the developments on your planet with and without our intervention that can then be printed out and distributed to the other governments during your meetings. We will, of course, monitor your progress during these meetings, as well as the effects our controls are having on your environment.

One other thing. The Professor was quite correct in saying that my Box has a built-in self-defence mechanism. This is normally totally passive, as you found just now, but be assured that that is not its only defence measure; there are many others of far greater severity that can be deployed should the need arise. It would, therefore, be extremely unwise for anyone to try to interfere with it, or indeed with the Professor come to that, who, as its keeper, is also afforded similar protection."

At this last remark the Professor raised his eyebrows slightly in surprise. "First I knew of that," he muttered to no one in particular, then went on: "Anyway, thank you, Klaat, we won't take up any more of your valuable time just now. Goodbye."

"Goodbye," came the reply, as the Box closed itself up again and resumed its position beside the Professor's chair.

The Professor, feeling rather as though he had just won game, set and match stood up.

"I will obviously make myself and Fido here," the Professor said, bending to pat the Box as though it were indeed a dog, "available as you need for these inter-governmental meetings. I would just ask that you give me as much notice as possible. In the meantime, I bid you goodnight."

The PM, feeling for the first time in a long time, thoroughly beaten, could do nothing other than watch as the Professor walked to the door.

"Goodnight," he called rather weakly to the retreating figure, then glancing back at the Box, saw it had indeed vanished again.

"God, I need a drink – care to join me?" the PM said to George.

"Yes, thanks," replied George. He was still aware of the danger to his career prospects of the earlier contretemps with the PM and enough of a politician to swallow his pride when he saw the chance to regain something of the PM's favour. He was also wondering what scheme the PM could possibly have been dreaming up after they left last night, and thought he might get a clue by staying for a drink with him.

However, in this he was to be disappointed.

After George had left, the PM thought it might be worth a last try to get hold of the Box without the Professor. Another drink and it seemed like definitely worth a try.

A few phone calls to ex-directory numbers and his rapidly devised plan B was set up. He sat back to await a phone call telling him that the plan to retrieve important government documents contained in an aluminium box currently in the unauthorised possession of a person who would be approaching a certain address a little later that night had been successfully completed.

CHAPTER 19

The Prime Minister's Plan 'B'

The Professor, leaving his usual station after most of the other passengers, saw that all the taxis had been taken, and there was a fairly long queue. He decided to take a bus, as it wouldn't take much longer, and the short walk he had from the bus stop to his home would be refreshing. As he started walking towards his home from the bus stop, he was vaguely aware of footsteps behind him that seemed to have started rather suddenly. Glancing round he saw there was indeed a man walking quickly in the same direction as he was. Looking back he saw two more men coming towards him from the opposite direction. Having heard that muggings were not entirely unknown in his area, and trying unsuccessfully to rid himself of a feeling of unease at these three unknown figures, he crossed the road. The unease turned into cold fear when the three figures also crossed, and within a few seconds were within feet of him. He was about to shout for help when one of the men said:

"Andrew Kowalski, I think you've got something that doesn't belong to you, so if you'll just hand over that metal case you're carrying you won't get hurt. Otherwise…"

Momentarily non-plussed by their use of his name, he said:

"Who the hell are you? This is my case, now if you'll kindly get out of my way…"

"Oooh, I *do* like it when they don't do what they're told, I *dooo* so like to teach them a lesson!"

So saying the figure stepped forward, swinging a punch at Andrew's head.

What happened next surprised Andrew as much as the three thugs who had accosted him. The man was thrown back about six feet, landing heavily on the pavement, holding his arm and moaning in great pain.

"Clever, bugger, are you?" he managed to gasp, "Fred, grab him, and Len, teach him a lesson he'll not forget in a hurry!"

This time Andrew saw what looked like small flashes of lightning streak from the Box to the arms that were about to grab him from behind, as something he didn't see caught the fist that was all set to smash into his face.

The man in front of him was also now on the ground, eight or ten feet away, also holding his arm and groaning softly. The one behind lay on the ground, very still, while a curious smell, a mix of ozone and roast pork hung in the air.

Andrew was momentarily transfixed, looking at the bodies on the ground. He looked around. No sign of anyone in the road, no cars and no one peering round curtains from nearby houses. Evidently, no one had seen or heard the attack. So thinking it would be very difficult to explain what had happened, and it might look as though he were the guilty party if found surrounded by three apparently fairly severely injured men, he started to walk away fairly rapidly, restraining the urge to run as fast as he could. As he turned into his road, he looked back to see the men still lying on the pavement, and still no sign that anyone had seen what happened.

A few moments later, a motorcyclist came out of a side turning further back down the road, and went slowly up to the three men still lying on the pavement and groaning softly. As his instructions had been to collect a small aluminium box from the three, and there was no sign of the box, but every likelihood of a lot of trouble if he was associated in any way with the bodies on the ground, he drove on past as quietly as he could, and well clear, made a phone call to explain why he would not be delivering the box. No, he hadn't seen what happened to the men, but they looked in a bad way and needed as ambulance quickly, though he wasn't prepared to get involved. Ringing off, he disappeared into the night.

Andrew, who had not seen the motorcyclist as he hurried up his road, entered his house, and leant against the front door, breathing heavily for a moment. Then his wife called to him: "That you, Andy?"

He put the Box and small suitcase down behind the front door and went in to the sitting room, where his wife had been waiting for him.

As he entered the room, she came over to him and kissing him lightly, said:

"How was the trip?" and then giving him an extra hug went on, "I'm very glad you're back safely – I must admit I worried quite a bit about what was happening to you out in the jungle."

Returning her hug he said: "It was fine, and though there were one or two hairy moments, as you would expect on a trip of that nature, I escaped unscathed, and am very happy to be back home with you again."

The irony of the failed attack on him in a street just around the corner from his house some five minutes previously, compared to the hazards of the jungle expedition was not lost on him, but he decided not to mention it for the moment.

Later, in bed after a pleasant evening relaxing over dinner and giving his wife Myra an abbreviated account of the trip, though deciding not to mention anything about Klaat just then as he just wanted to go to bed. He could tell her all about that aspect tomorrow. In bed, he couldn't get to sleep immediately thinking about the attack. It couldn't have been a straightforward mugging attempt – what was it the first man

207

had said 'you've got something that doesn't belong to you' – they must have known about the Box. After all, it looked just like the sort of small aluminium case used by photographers, so 'doesn't belong to you'? And, he suddenly remembered, they had used his name. His usual quickness of mind slightly blunted by the events of the evening and tiredness, it nonetheless dawned on him that he must have been set up, but by whom?

Tiredness was obliterated and he sat up suddenly in bed. The bloody prime minister! he thought, it has to have been him! No one had expressed an interest in or wanted to control the Box in the way he had.

Myra, feeling him sit up suddenly, assumed it was a reaction of some sort to his tiring journey, and said in a sleepy voice:

"Are you all right, dear?"

"Yes, Myra, I'm fine. Go back to sleep. I guess I'm just a bit overtired and had a bad dream."

He lay back, turning the whole matter over in his mind, and trying to decide what he should do about it. After a while, he began to feel better about the whole thing, primarily because of the way the Box had dealt with the three thugs. Klaat had said he would also be part of the Box's self-defence mechanism, and it had certainly demonstrated that this evening, in spades! With this comforting thought, he eventually drifted off to sleep.

Meanwhile, at about ten o'clock that evening, back in Downing Street the Prime Minister called the same ex-directory number again.

"Has the package been recovered yet?"

"No," came the reply, "and curiously I haven't heard from my agent yet; can't even raise him on his mobile. I'll let you know as soon as it's been delivered."

The PM put the phone down. Why had it taken them so long? His contact had always delivered his various requests on time and with no trouble before. Had something gone wrong this time?

He realised he could only wait, which, as many before him had found, is often the hardest part of any enterprise.

An hour later he could contain his patience no longer and rang again.

"Something seems to have gone wrong. There has been some sort of serious accident that my agent seems to have inadvertently become involved with, so delivery will inevitably be delayed. I'll call you in the morning when I know more, so there's no point in calling me again tonight."

As soon as he awoke the next morning, the Professor thought that a bit more information on his encounter the previous evening might be useful, so phoned Pat O'Hanlon. After explaining why he was calling him and giving him a brief run down on the encounter he finished with:

"So I thought you might like to do a little investigative journalism and see if you can find out anything about what happened."

Pat thanked him for the tip off, and said he'd follow it up right away, and would like to meet up with the Professor at Birmingham New Street station at about ten that morning. Pat's first thought was that it would be useful if John, with his environment ministry credentials, could accompany him, so he rang him. After a short talk with Mark, his boss, John had got permission to go, and in a very short time, the two of them were on their way to Birmingham. They met the Professor as planned, and went into the cafeteria.

"I don't want to sound too melodramatic, but it's just possible any or all of us are being followed, also our phones may be being tapped. So a quick run down, Professor, if you please, for John's benefit, and then you'd better go out and catch the next train to London and continue your meetings with the politicos. We'll catch up with you in Mark's office later today. Meanwhile, John and I will slip out through the kitchens and start our investigations."

They did as suggested, and were soon going their separate ways, apparently undetected. Pat and John decided to try hospitals local to the Professor's home, with John posing as a man whose had been expecting to visit a work colleague (the Professor who lived locally, if pushed for a name) with another colleague the previous evening, but this colleague hadn't arrived nor had he phoned, and so John was wondering if the missing colleague had maybe met with an accident. They struck lucky with the second hospital they tried. Pulling a bit of rank by showing his ministry ID card he managed to have a meeting with the A& E consultant.

"Nasty accident, by the looks of it, and their injuries were very unusual. I'm sorry to have to tell you that two of them have had their right arms severely damaged, with tibia, fibia, and a large number of both wrist and hand bones badly shattered − almost as though they had tried to stop a fast moving train by punching its front buffers − extraordinary amount of damage − never seen its like before, in fact. They are currently being operated on to try and put some semblance of order back into their arm bones − they'll be lucky not to have to have them amputated. The other had some very nasty burns to both his arms. It appears it was probably a hit and run, though I don't see that accounting for the burns. Someone out walking their dog found them all lying on the pavement, so called an ambulance. They were obviously in extreme pain when they were brought in late last night, and have been under heavy sedation since. The police were called, but as they were effectively anaesthetised even before they went into the operating theatre, have not been able to ascertain any details about what happened. I would suggest you phone this evening, and if they're conscious, you could come round and see if one of them is your colleague, Mr. Fenwick. The police will be glad if you are able to identify him and his two friends, as apparently they didn't have any means of identification on them, just some money. Having a night out, I wouldn't wonder, though funnily enough there was practically no alcohol present in any of their blood samples. Still, with the muggers about these days, it's best not to carry credit cards or other documents with you, just cash for the drinks."

"Thank you very much, Dr Hawkins, it's very kind of you to spare us your valuable time and let me know what's happened, though I can't say I like the sound of what happened to my colleague, always supposing he is one of the three. As you suggest, I'll call this evening and see how things are. Thanks again. Goodbye."

Once back in a taxi on their way to the station, Pat said:

"I guess we might as well go back to London, there's nothing else for us to do here now. That certainly sounds like our three heroes from last night's go at the Professor, but wow! That Box sure packs a punch! Punching a train's buffer! Brings tears to my eyes just thinking about it. One thing's for sure, though; I doubt they'll ever be in a position, or even have any desire to mug anyone again."

"Bloody right," replied John. "But what is still bugging me is who could have wanted to get the Box off the Professor, as from what he told us, that sounds definitely to be the motive for the attack. Surely, it couldn't possibly have been the PM as he suggested, could it?"

"Yes, I've been wondering about that. As you say, it's hardly credible that the PM could be behind it. Still, let's see what comes of your phone call this evening."

Back in Downing Street, the PM had given up waiting for the phone call telling about progress on acquiring the Box for the moment, and had spent the morning arranging the meetings he had to hold with various ambassadors. This had assumed top priority in his agenda, as with or without the Box, he saw this as a superb opportunity to appear as a world statesman *par excellence.* It would be an absolutely monumental chance for personal aggrandisement on the world stage. Imagine the kudos if he, personally, could take the credit for beating off this threat to the world!

He allowed himself to fantasise for some time about this golden future stretching out before him, finally standing before the United Nations and able to say that he, Paul Cranham, had saved the World!

Then he realised that he'd better arrange for the Professor to come round for a dry run of the meeting he'd managed to set up with several of the ambassadors. That would be a suitable opportunity for the Professor to admit he'd lost the Box and could be safely dismissed from the proceedings. The slight worry that he hadn't had another call yet telling him that the difficulties in obtaining the box had been overcome and that it was on its way was put to the back of his mind for the moment.

His enjoyable reveries were rudely interrupted by a call on his special private phone.

"Yes?"

"Something seems to have gone wrong. I've just found out that my agent was actually personally involved in the accident, and so has not been able to arrange for delivery of the equipment. I haven't been able to speak to him, but I'm afraid you'll have to assume delivery won't take place with this shipment, and it may be delayed indefinitely."

"Well, due to the commercially sensitive nature of the goods, you have to make damn sure your agent doesn't speak to anyone about it. Absolutely no one, under any circumstances whatsoever. Do I make myself clear? Good, and let me know when the matter has been concluded."

He put the phone down and cursed. How the hell had they managed to bungle such a simple operation? He'd have to make a few changes in his 'Special Operations' squad, but that could wait a few days. In the meantime, he must arrange the dry run meeting with the Professor and George Bentley. Accordingly, he phoned George, and told him to bring the Professor round for a meeting early the following morning, as the first meeting with the ambassadors was scheduled for eleven o'clock that morning.

Back in Mark's office later that afternoon, the Professor had joined Pat and John to catch up on what they had found out about the attack. Having brought him up to date, John said:

"It's about time to phone the hospital again and ask about my 'colleague'. I'll tell them that I am sorry to have bothered them this morning, as he turned up safe this afternoon, full of apologies for not letting me know why he didn't come round last night."

He dialled the hospital and asked to speak to Dr. Hawkins.

"I'm sorry, Dr. Hawkins has been called to an emergency in the operating theatre. I'll put you through to Dr. Perkins, who is due to take over the next shift in A & E."

"Thank you. Hello, Dr. Perkins? Hello, my name is John Fenwick and I came to see your colleague Dr. Hawkins this morning about my missing colleague. Dr. Hawkins said he may have been one of the three men seriously injured in a hit and run accident last night, and I said I'd call again this evening to see if there was any further news."

The others stood watching John silently as he listened to the response.

"I see. Well, do you know to which private hospital they were taken?"

"Very well, if you can't help me, I'll have to phone Dr. Hawkins tomorrow. If you see him you might be kind enough to tell him that my colleague turned up safe and well this afternoon, so I won't be able to help him with the identification in any case."

He put the phone down. "Now, that's rather mysterious. All three have been transferred to a private hospital, collected by ambulance this afternoon apparently, but that bloke didn't know which hospital they'd been taken to. I got the impression that he was just fobbing me off. Wonder what's happened to them. They must have been the three that attacked you, Professor, so what's going on?"

"I've had a bit of time to think this through," he replied. "There's only been one person who has expressed any interest in the Box, I mean other than something to be amazed about as you all have been, and that, I regret to say, is none other than our prime minister. His behaviour when I couldn't hand it over to him, and comments by Klaat in the ensuing remarks between them make me absolutely convinced that he must be the one behind the attacks. Why he should be so desperate to get it that he'd organise something like that, I don't know. But he's the only one who fits all the facts about it. And ominous as it sounds, if it was indeed he, then 'disappearing' the three thugs in case they spoke about the business would make sense. Also, it needs someone with a lot of power and facilities at their command to pull off a thing like that."

"I think you have to be right, Professor," said Pat. "Do you think we should leak a few hints to the press? Also, do you think he's likely to try again?"

"In answer to the first, hold fire for the minute – the local paper may have picked up on the story, anyway. As for the second point, so long as I have the Box with me and based on last night's performance, I could say I'm not worried either way. You should have seen the speed with which those three very unpleasant specimens were dealt with. I get the impression that it would have made no difference to the outcome if it had been a gang of ten rather than three."

Anything further he may have said was interrupted by Mark's phone.

"Hello, Mark, is the Professor with you? George Bentley here."

When the Professor picked up the phone, he was told about the meeting the next morning.

"Funny," mused the Professor as he put the phone down, "but I'm glad to say, I don't think he knew a thing about the attack last night."

CHAPTER 20

Start Spreading the News...

At five past nine the next morning, George and the Professor were again seated in the prime minister's study. The Professor had decided not to give the slightest hint to either of them about the attack, and even felt a slight grudging admiration for the PM that he could be quite so brazenly two-faced, enquiring solicitously after the Professor's health and hoping he felt a bit more rested after his night's rest. For his part, the Professor maintained his impersonal, almost cold, aloof manner when speaking to the PM, which he did to the minimum required for the work in hand. The upshot of their dry run was that the PM would make all the introductions then leave all the exposition to the Professor. The PM did not offer to run through his introduction, and having already heard what the Professor would be saying, dismissed them at about nine thirty and told them to return at eleven sharp. Once they'd gone, he sat down to carefully construct his introduction. This was aimed to steal as much credit and kudos for himself from the Professor's lecture as possible, and leave the Professor just to fill in a few gaps and drive that damn Box of his. He was still inwardly furious at the bungling of his 'Special Operations' squad – how much better if he could have done the whole thing without having to have that damn Professor present. Still, just have to make the best of it this time, and think of a way to get the Box for himself later.

George and the Professor duly returned at the appointed time, and were shown to a couple of seats at the back of a room used for small conferences, where they sat awaiting the arrival of the PM and the ambassadors. Half a dozen or so leather arm chairs were set in a slight curve in front of a beautiful mahogany table, behind which were two chairs, the one in the centre for the PM and a small chair to one side for his secretary and note-taker. The furnishings were completed by a lectern placed a little to one side of the table.

The PM was welcoming his guests in a reception room, where they were also being served coffee and biscuits while awaiting the arrival of all those invited.

The party eventually wandered into the conference room at about quarter past eleven. As they came in and not knowing or recognising either the Professor or George, after a cursory glance at them, they sat themselves down. The PM came in last, chatting and laughing with the American ambassador, the one he most hoped to impress with this presentation. When they'd all settled into their seats, the PM stood behind the lectern to officially open the meeting. He talked at some length, paraphrasing as best he could remember the account of the expedition the Professor had given him two days before. When he felt he had wrung as much kudos as he could for his part in the whole affair, he rather off-handedly introduced the Professor and mentioned who George was. The Professor, who had listened with mounting annoyance to the PM's diatribe, had been tempted to walk out of the meeting and leave the PM floundering. However, his sense of responsibility in getting Klaat's message across prevailed and he sat waiting for the PM to finish. When he finally started speaking, the first thing he did, while smiling condescendingly at the PM, was to correct several glaring errors he'd made in describing the expedition, and add a few important details that the former had omitted.

When he came to introducing the Box, the gasps of astonishment as it moved and opened its screen had almost become routine to the Professor, who carried on as though it were the most normal lecture aid that anyone might use.

As soon as Klaat had finished with his usual 'Any questions?' the PM was on his feet.

"Well, thank you, Professor; I don't think we need detain you any more as we now have important matters of state to attend to. I'll answer any questions our guests may have with the aid of your er, box thing here."

Before the Professor had time to give vent to his anger, fortunately, the American ambassador spoke up:

"Just a cotton-picking moment, Paul! I've got a few questions I'd like to have the Professor here answer before he goes, as I'm sure some of the others must have," he continued, looking at the others, to be greeted by a few murmurs of assent.

"Yes, of course," replied the PM, inwardly seething at having lost the initiative for the moment. "Please, fire away!"

The Professor then answered several questions, none of which was particularly taxing, and was able to get a little more information from Klaat, though nothing that was in any way specific, such as how the birth restrictions would affect a certain area, or when access would be permitted again to the forests or indeed how long was it intended to control the world's environment in this way. Klaat gave reasons for being unable to answer such questions, somewhat to the frustration of the enquirers.

"Could I have a look at that box thing you've got, Professor?" asked the American ambassador.

"Of course," the Professor replied, "but I think you'll find you can't touch it. I think the people that made this value it pretty highly and have built a lot of very sophisticated self-defence mechanisms into it. I get the impression that it would be impossible for anyone to take it from me as I seem to have been assigned by them as its keeper, for my sins," he finished with a slight laugh. "Also, it doesn't appear to respond to anyone else's commands, as we found the other night, didn't we prime minister?"

"Er, yes, it did appear that way," the PM replied with a forced laugh that completely belied his true feelings.

They all came up to have a closer look at the Box, with one or two tentative attempts to touch it, which were found not to be possible. Various muttered comments accompanied these efforts, until the PM cut in again:

"Well, if that is all the questions for the Professor, we can let him go now, and carry on with the larger questions of what we can do about the situation that has arisen. Oh, and thank you, George, I'll be in touch later if we need any more work done this end."

Having dismissed the two effective stars of the presentation, he was about to start talking again when he saw no one was paying any attention to him. They were all watching the Box pack itself up and move to the Professor's side, then, as he went to open the door, vanish.

"Neat little box of tricks, isn't it?" joked the PM, hoping thereby to imply his far greater mastery of affairs than this little gadget, but no one was listening to him. After a moment or two when they'd all regained something of their composure, it was the American ambassador, who seemed to have been silently elected leader of the group, who spoke out again:

"I see that little thing as the source of one *b-i-g* heap of trouble for everyone, and I don't see as how we can do a goddamn thing about it. Also, I'd like that Professor guy's number – I'd like to have another talk with him when we've done here, and eventually have him over to the States to meet with a few of our top flight committees. We're going to have to do a lot of heavy duty thinking about this one. Now, what were those bright ideas you were going to share with us, Paul?"

The best the PM could reply, rather weakly, was: "Why don't we go through to the other room and discuss it over a drink and lunch?"

"Normally, I would be delighted to do just that, but I feel I must appraise my President of what I've heard this morning as soon as possible. So, thank you, Paul, but I'll have to take a rain check on that lunch. Oh, before I go. The Professor's number, please."

The PM signalled his secretary, who looked up the number, wrote it down, and gave it to the ambassador.

"Thank you and good day, lady and gentlemen," he said, glancing at the others as he made his way to the door.

The others, expressing similar sentiments, followed suit fairly rapidly, until the PM was left standing in the room on his own with the secretary.

"Damn! Damn! Damn!" said the PM smacking his hand hard on the table to emphasise each expletive. The secretary wisely said nothing and quietly left the room to start writing up notes on the meeting.

The American ambassador's official limousine pulled out of the gates to Downing Street, and turned into the Mall. Suddenly, he felt his luck had changed, as there was the Professor standing at the edge of the pavement, waiting for a taxi. The ambassador had his driver pull up alongside the Professor, lowering his window as he did so.

"Professor Kowalski," he called out.

The Professor, having seen the car approach was just beginning to wonder if he was about to be attacked again, when he recognised the ambassador.

"Here, let me give you a lift. I'd like a few more words with you, anyway," he said, opening his car door.

"Thank you, that's very kind of you, Mr Ambassador. There appears to be a dearth of taxis hereabouts at this time of day."

As soon as they were under way again, the ambassador said:

"I'm glad I caught you, as I was going to phone you a little later, anyway, after I have spoken to the White House. Unless I'm very much mistaken, our president is going to want to speak with you as soon as possible. How are you fixed for coming to the States at short notice?"

After a slight pause while he raced over his coming commitments for the next couple of days in his mind, he replied:

"I reckon I could be ready to go after a few phone calls and going home to pack a bag. How long do you think it would be for, Mr. Ambassador?"

"A couple of days or so initially, and the name's Jake. I think I caught your name as Andrew from what your Prime Minister was pleased to call an introduction to you in his office. Sorry to be undiplomatic, but his manner annoys me more every time I have to have any dealings with him. He reminds me of a common sight in London when I was here as a student in the late fifties. Then you had large advert hoardings promising all sorts of delights, but behind them were the weed-covered remains of bombed out buildings! All headline promises for effect and no substance behind any of them."

"Anyway (sorry if I let my annoyance carry me away!), depending on how this situation develops, we may need to call you back to the States. Where's that box thing of yours, by the way?"

"In the car with me, I imagine; it's never far from me, even when it's invisible."

As though to confirm what Andrew said, the Box appeared, sitting on the floor beside him.

"Well, I'll be goddamned...I can quite see why an awful lot of people would give more than just their eye teeth to get their hands on it – your Prime Minister for one."

"Yes, I think you're right with that one."

"It's a bit early for me to phone the president yet, so why don't I drop you wherever you want, maybe make some of those calls to clear your diary for the next couple of days and go home to pack. Where do you live, by the way?"

The Professor asked to be dropped at Euston and gave the ambassador his address. While waiting for a train, he phoned Mark and George to bring them up to date. He also called his wife, Myra to say he was on his way home, but might have to leave again shortly.

"Really, Andrew, I do think it's a bit much. They might at least let you get over your last trip before having to start another."

"Yes, but don't worry. This one's different. I'll tell you about it when I get home. Bye now."

He'd been home about an hour when his phone went.

"Hi, Andrew, Jake. I've arranged for one of our cars to pick you up at eight o'clock tomorrow morning. The driver will have a few notes for you about the meeting. Oh and if Mrs Kowalski would like to come along for the ride, my boss says she'll be very welcome. Sorry to be brief, but we have to worry more than usual about security. Can you attend as we discussed earlier today and be ready for tomorrow morning – a straight yes or no, please."

"Yes, certainly, and thank you very much. I shall look forward to our meeting," he replied, putting the phone down.

"Myra! How would you like a two or three day visit to the States? That call was to confirm it's all on, but the good news is you're invited as well!"

"But I haven't got anything to wear and there isn't time to go out and get something now. I…"

"Well, if you want to miss out on a chance like this for the sake of some clothes, you're not the go-getter I always thought you were."

"What the hell! You're right. I'll sort something out, and maybe I can buy something classy over there. Yes, maybe in Bloomingdale's or Macey's or perhaps even Tiffany's," she added, brightening visibly.

"I don't think there's time to take out a mortgage on the house before we go, so you may have to be content with something a little more down market," he said, laughing, and delighted to see how happy she was at the whole idea of the sudden trip. He just hoped the whole damn thing wouldn't be cancelled just as quickly.

They both were ready by seven-thirty the next morning, with Myra in a high state of excitement. It had been quite a long time since she had had the chance to accompany Andrew on any of his expeditions, and this one sounded very much better than his usual trips into hostile jungles.

Promptly at eight a car which, except for its tinted windows, looked much like any executive-type taxi, the like of which Andrew had used on many previous occasions, drew up outside their house. The driver, in chauffeur's uniform, got out and rang their doorbell.

"Good morning. You are Professor and Mrs Kowalski I believe?"

"Yes, that's right."

"Good. I've come from Jake," he said, handing over a folded page, which had the US Embassy's crest at the top, and a handwritten note from Jake. "May I carry your luggage to the car?"

A few moments later, as they were driving away, the driver handed a buff envelope over to the Professor.

"I think you'll find all you need to know immediately in this. It'll take us about an hour, depending on traffic, to reach the Hadley Base.

"That'll be the USAF Base?"

"Yep." Further conversation was obviously not going to be welcomed, so the Professor opened the envelope to see what they had let themselves in for.

As predicted, just over an hour later, they were being waved through the gates to the base, after what seemed like a pretty thorough check on the car and driver, eventually being dropped off at the side entrance of what looked like the main admin building of the base. They were shown into a small waiting room, where a moment or two later, the ambassador and three other people entered the room.

"Andrew! Good to see you," and holding out his hand, turned to his wife, "and you must be Myra. Very pleased to meet you and that you were able to come at such short notice. Oh, and I'd like to introduce my wife Mary Lou, who is also coming to Washington with us, so you won't be bored rigid by us men talking shop all the time," he finished, smiling broadly.

After they'd spent a few moments getting through the introductions, and the ambassador had introduced the two aides who were evidently going with them, he went on:

"We're lucky that we have one of the large executive Lear jets here to fly us directly to Washington, so we don't have to worry about going through Heathrow with all the usual security delays. Which reminds me, I trust you have your box of tricks with you, Andrew?"

"Yes, just there beside that chair. As you know, I always make sure of that."

Andrew saw his wife was about to ask a question about the Box, but caught her eye and gave a slight shake of his head. Then to distract any further attention to the Box he asked:

"What time do we fly out?"

"Any minute – Ah, I think we're ready to go now, is that right?" he asked of a uniformed man who entered the room at that minute.

"Yes, Sir, whenever you're ready."

"Good. Let's roll!" the ambassador finished jovially.

They were led out to a small bus, the driver loading the luggage, and then out to the apron, where their plane was waiting.

Myra, for all her appearance of outward calm, was very excited at the whole experience. She'd never been on a similar plane before, and was amazed at the luxurious way it was fitted out – comfortable armchairs instead of the usual aircraft seats just the first of many things she noted, as a stewardess showed them to their seats.

"Hello, this is your captain speaking. Welcome on board our special flight to Washington. Please make yourselves at home, as we're going to be about seven hours on the trip. We'll be serving lunch in about an hours' time, there's a call button in the arm of your chair for a bar service or anything else you need, and the television screen to help while away the time. I hope you enjoy the flight."

Once they were airborne, the ambassador and his wife came over to Andrew and Myra, and looking at her, he said:

"I'm afraid I've got to discuss a few things with Andrew, so why don't you two ladies get acquainted?"

When they were seated with a coffee, the ambassador said:

"Andrew, I'd like to have a general discussion with you and hear your thoughts on this whole business from 'a' to 'zee'. Anything from the way they approached you to what you think their real motives are, and, of course, the sixty-four thousand dollar question, what the hell, if anything we can do about it."

Their discussion lasted until pre-lunch drinks, by which time the ambassador knew just about everything that he needed to. They then joined the others for lunch, and the rest of the flight became just like any other long haul flight, except for the levels of comfort and facilities on board.

Late that afternoon they arrived at a small private airport near Washington and found special diplomatic 'limos' waiting for them at the foot of the aircraft's steps.

"We've arranged for you to be accommodated at one of our ambassadorial visitors' suites, where I think you'll be very comfortable. It's known in the business as the 'Crow's Nest' as it's where all the 'high flyers' roost! I've stayed there a few times myself. It's just like a small country hotel really, but with a few well worthwhile extras including really excellent food, so I hope you enjoy your stay there. However, first we're going to the White House as the President has said he wants to meet Andrew right away, so while we're doing that, Myra, you and Mary Lou can do the special visitors' tour of the place. Then when we're all done there, we'll take you to the Crow's Nest."

On arriving at the White House they were met at the door by a presidential Aide, who took them inside, and showed Myra and Mary Lou to a small reception room, where there was an official guide waiting for them.

"Hello and welcome to the White House tour. My name's Helen," the guide said by way of introduction, smiling warmly at her two visitors. "I would suggest we all have a coffee while I give you a brief introduction to the tour and some background information that I hope you'll find interesting."

The Ambassador and Andrew were then lead down a corridor into the famous oval office. As they entered, the President rose from his desk and came forward to greet them, holding out his hand to the Ambassador.

"Hiya, Jake, good to see you again, and you must be the famous Professor Kowalski, about who I've heard quite a bit lately. Glad to meet you. Won't you sit down?"

Just as they sat down on the comfortable sofas on either side of a low coffee table in front of the president's desk, a maid came in and set a silver tray with coffee and biscuits on the table in front of them. When they'd settled down the president began:

"Well, I think I've heard a lot of the main details of what's been happening, but I'd like to hear a few more details from you at first hand, Professor. After all, it's not every day that the president has to decide what to do in the face of what amounts to a partial world takeover by aliens. The one good feature seems to be that they didn't want to create a world panic by just announcing their plans to the whole world, but doing it through the United Nations leaders. I understand you have some sort of phone thing by which they speak to us, is that so?"

"Yes, it's here," said Andrew, patting the Box that had appeared beside him on the floor.

"Christ, how the hell did you get that bloody thing in here past the security? My security chief is going to have some explaining to do!" So saying, the President got up quickly to go to the phone on his desk.

"Just one minute, Sir," said Andrew, "the Box makes itself invisible when travelling, and moves itself without any help from me, so your security people wouldn't have had the slightest idea of its presence."

The president stopped and looked at the Box.

"Well I'll be goddamned! You mean it just, er, *vanishes* when you travel and travels with you of its own accord and then, sort of reappears when it feels like it?"

"Yes, that's the way it seems to be," answered Andrew. "Sorry, but I sort of take it for granted now, and tend not to mention it. So don't be too hard on your security people – no security system yet has picked it up. It's quite some piece of technology is this little Box, as you'll see."

The president slowly resumed his seat, not taking his eyes off the Box, as though it might spring up unexpectedly and attack him.

"You don't say," he muttered, half to himself as he lowered himself into the settee again.

About an hour later they'd been through the communication routine with Klaat, seen the pictures from the Amazon and the President had had some uncompromising answers to his questions. He sat in silence for a few moments as the Box closed itself down, and then said:

"Well, in a fairly long and I think, very successful political career, that's the first time I have ever been completely at a loss for an answer. Yes, obviously, we'll go through the same routine at the UN as all the others have to know what's going on, but speaking for the US, we're going to have to do a hellova lot of hard thinking about how we handle the huge problems these two changes are going to have on us. Business will have to adopt a whole new mind-set and the demographic effects will require some pretty serious planning, otherwise everything could collapse around us."

The other two nodded their agreement to these sentiments, and then the president went on:

"Anyway, the best the UN can do is convene a meeting of most of its delegates for the morning after tomorrow, so I'm going to make a start on what I've got to do right away. I think I'll have to have you back for the first high level meeting I'll hold late this afternoon or this evening, as without your Box thing, Professor, I suspect they'd carry me off in a strait jacket! I'll let you know what time it is, but in the meantime please make yourself at home in the Crow's Nest. Take this special phone with you wherever you go, and I'll be able to reach you and bring you here in about a quarter of an hour, so if you feel like it, go do a bit of sightseeing. The official car and chauffeur will take you wherever you want to go."

"Oh, and one other thing. As I understand from Jake, you've already been of great assistance to us. One of the privileges of my office is that I can get to appoint you as a special adviser to the USA. So you'll find a contract I've had drawn up for you in this envelope, together with a cheque cashable in any bank in Washington (or the US Embassy in London) for your services on a per diem basis. It covers the first two weeks and an ex-gratia payment for the time you've had to take away from your work at very short notice. I hope you find it all acceptable. If you have any queries on the contract, there's the phone number of the head of the legal department that drew it up who will be happy to discuss it with you. Glad to have met you," concluded the President, holding out his hand to Andrew.

A very surprised Andrew, who had certainly not been expecting anything of the sort replied, "Well, thank you very much indeed, sir, and of course I will be very happy to continue to assist in any way I can," shaking the President's hand firmly.

He and the ambassador were only half way to the door before the president was on the phone arranging his top level meeting. Once outside, the ambassador took the Professor to the tour reception room where Myra was waiting for him, and then on to the car to take them to the Crow's Nest.

The driver took them on a slightly circuitous route to see some of the sights of Washington, and then helped them up to their suite with the luggage. As soon as they had driven away from the White House, Andrew told Myra about his new temporary appointment, and opened the envelope.

Looking at the cheque, he let out a low whistle of surprise.

"Wow! You won't need that second mortgage now to buy a special dress! Look at this. Serious shopping is now definitely on the agenda. This is more than I earn in six months at home."

He relapsed into silence, astonished at the amount on the cheque, particularly as it had never occurred to him to ask for anything for what he had done, or was likely to have to do. He put it back in his pocket, deciding to peruse the contract next morning. He was still thinking about this unexpected turn of events when the car stopped.

"Should you need me or the car at any time press that button on the phone the president gave you," the driver said, indicating a button on the phone's keypad, "and I'll be right with you."

"Thank you very much, but I think a bit of rest is called for first," said the Professor, laughing, "we've been on the go for, what's it now, some twenty hours."

Having had a good look round the superbly appointed suite, both of them amazed at the opulence and features that seemed to belong more to a luxurious fictitious film set than a 'real-life' residence, albeit even one for Ambassadors visiting the President of the USA, Andrew suddenly felt rather tired. Being one of those lucky people who can go to sleep in a matter of minutes and then sleep for an hour or so and wake up refreshed, he took off his shoes and jacket, lay on the bed, and within a few minutes was fast asleep.

Myra, not having the same facility, decided to have a bath and then rest awhile. She was fascinated by the astonishingly wide selection of toiletries that were laid out in the bathroom and the bath itself, which had underwater jets and air bubble nozzles. She spent some time looking at the toiletries and eventually selected an extremely exotic sounding foam bath perfumed oil. Having then had to spend a little time working out which of the fairly extensive set of controls to use (and in the process doused herself unexpectedly with two of the shower heads), she immersed herself in the bath.

"The hell with asses milk," she said half aloud to herself, "I'll bet Cleopatra would have chosen this set-up if she could have done!" She lay back and luxuriated in the scented warm waters, with water jets massaging her gently and air bubbles caressing her very pleasantly in all sorts of unexpected places. She felt thoroughly self-indulgent and loved every minute of it.

Eventually and reluctantly, she finished her bath and dressed and had just done that when the special phone rang. The Professor was asked if he would kindly be at the White House in two hours' time. She called the driver to find out how long it would take to get back to the White House, and found that there would be plenty of time to have dinner from the room service that she had found out about in the 'Welcome Pack' on the entrance hall table. Having spent a little time looking through the amazing range of meals on offer, she decided what would be a suitably celebratory meal for their first night in Washington and made a mental note to have it the next night, but for tonight it would have to be a fairly light and quick meal, which she ordered up, then woke Andrew.

He showered and changed and was equally amazed at the 'ablution's experience' as he dubbed the bathroom, saying it would be like calling a billionaire's luxury yacht a sailing boat just to call it a bathroom. However, knowing he didn't have time to indulge himself there just now, he hurried through a shower, dressed and then they sat down to their meal, served with all ceremony by properly uniformed waiters with a *maître d'* in attendance to ensure that everything was to their satisfaction.

"I had better be on my way – can't keep the president waiting," he joked. "I must say, that meal was superb, and indeed I think the whole place is entirely up to and indeed surpassed how good Jake said it was. In fact, I feel like a new man!"

"So do I," Myra said with a suggestive grin, "so you'd better come back and show me that maybe I don't need one, just yet!"

Smiling at her he replied: "My, you are feeling skittish tonight, but don't go out looking for one until I get back. You might find one and I wouldn't like that one little bit!"

He called the car, and at the knock on the door, kissed Myra goodbye, saying: "I hope this doesn't take too long – I don't want to waste a skittish young wench," then added, "well, youngish, anyway!" and dodged the pretend punch she threw at him.

Once he'd gone she decided that a rest would be a good idea, and then if it wasn't too late when he got back they could maybe go and see some of the city by night. She was still thinking about the possibilities when she fell asleep.

She was still asleep when Andrew returned about an hour and a half later. As the president had said he wouldn't be needed until the UN meeting the following day, they decided to try and catch up on some sleep and beat the jet lag that was waiting to hold them in its wakeful arms. They could then start the next morning fairly early and spend the next day doing some serious tourism.

They went to bed, but Myra found, having been woken up by Andrew's return, she couldn't get back to sleep. Andrew, his mind racing from the meetings he'd had that day, was also finding sleep a bit difficult, and put his arm round Myra, cuddling up behind her. Myra wriggled a little to get into a more comfortable position, and much to both of their amazements, both found themselves sexually aroused in a way that hadn't happened to them in a long time.

Quite a long and very passionate time later, they both lay back feeling they'd regained a bit of long past youth, and he said:

"I hope you don't still feel like a new man, darling."

"No, I'm more than satisfied with the one I've got now thank you very much, but I think I'll have to send you to the White House again from time to time – it seems to have a marvellous effect on you!"

CHAPTER 21

Becoming Tourists

They slept well and woke with the feeling that so many cosmetic products promise but unfortunately cannot deliver: that of rejuvenation. With the unfamiliar surroundings and the memory of their new found passion from the night before, both felt a new lightness of spirit, and *joie-de-vivre* that they hadn't felt for a long time. So after a playful shower together and a 'to-hell-with-the-diet' breakfast served in their apartment, they set out to 'do' Washington.

The day was a wild success. Everyone seemed to be smiling at them as though reflecting the happiness that seemed to radiate from them. They covered most of the major sites, had an excellent lunch chosen from the list of restaurants included in the Welcome Pack in their suite, did a small amount of shopping, Myra having seen a dress that she felt was 'just her', and thoroughly enjoyed every minute of the day. At Andrew's insistence, she bought far more than she had originally intended to, he saying that she had earned her part of the generous payment he had received. As he fell asleep that night in preparation for his attendance at the UN, Andrew felt that the visit to Washington had turned out to be one of the great moments in his life.

They set out for the UN building the next morning in good time for the meeting, scheduled for ten thirty. However, on arriving, though Andrew was allowed in on presentation of his delegate's pass, given to him during his last visit to the President, Myra was told that none of the public or the press were being admitted today as this was a special closed meeting. Rather disappointed, she opted for some more sight-seeing instead, while Andrew found his way to the US delegation's office. When the President heard that Myra had been refused admission, he quickly arranged for her to be brought back to the UN, be given a pass and join the US delegation.

After the initial introductions, Andrew had taken a seat at the back of the office to await the start of the meeting. He suddenly had a terrible nightmare of a thought: suppose the damn Box decided not to put in an appearance! What would he, what *could* he do? In panic he reached down outside the arm of his chair, patting around wildly feeling for the Box. To his intense relief, it suddenly appeared, and for the first time spoke quietly to him directly:

"You didn't think, after the trouble we've taken to arrange this meeting that we'd suddenly decide not to bother to attend, did you?"

"Well, it did cross my mind that if you weren't here I'd be in a most invidious position."

He was going to say something else when he saw one of the delegates looking at him in a rather suspicious way, so decided against it, but took comfort from holding the handle on the Box, as though to prevent it from going away.

Eventually, they all moved into the great hall as did all the delegates from the other countries. Myra was given a seat next to Andrew. After a few minutes the meeting was called to order by the Secretary General, who made all the introductory remarks as to why the meeting had been called and the events leading up to it. He, in turn, had been briefed by the President, so was pretty well up to date with the situation. When he had completed his remarks, he introduced Andrew, who was invited up to the rostrum to address the gathering. Myra gave his hand a reassuring squeeze as he got up, this time carrying the Box with him. As he stood for a second or two surveying the large number waiting to hear what he had to say, he was suddenly assailed by an attack of nerves the like of which he had never experienced before: he was about to speak to representatives of the whole world! Swallowing hard, he glanced down at the Box, from which came Klaat's voice: "Go on, you can do it. We couldn't want a better person to get our message across."

Thus encouraged, he smiled briefly and began his address. Once he had started, his nervousness disappeared and he got into his stride describing his foray into the jungle, the appearance of the Box and a brief resume of everything that had happened since. The audience's interest in the Box was short lived: after all, it looked just like any other small aluminium case, and what this man was saying was beginning to sound more than a little farfetched. So after he'd mentioned the arrival of the Box, Andrew was careful to say as little as necessary before setting up the demonstration of the Box as he had done several times now. This time, though, things turned out slightly differently. Yes, the Box performed as usual, moving to a position some distance above Andrew's head and producing its screen. This time, however, the screen was enormous compared to previous appearances, though still showing three dimensional images, so that everyone could see it clearly from anywhere in the large hall. Also, the speech began differently:

"Hello. This meeting has been arranged to impart some very important information to all the rulers of all the world's countries, and will be given in confidence, for reasons that will become apparent. So all press reports and broadcasts have been prohibited and will in any case be prevented. No one outside this hall will hear what is being said, so the first thing is that the interpreters will be disconnected, and you will hear this speech directly in your own language, so, please remove your headphones as you will not need them."

There was a pause, and the delegates started looking at their headphones and then at one another a little mystified. This was totally outside the normal procedure, but most did as requested. Those that didn't heard a click in their headphones as they went dead. After a few moments, even these people removed them and stared at the screen as the speech went on, as promised, each hearing it in his own language, simultaneously.

Klaat then went through a fairly similar programme to the one Andrew and the others had heard in the jungle originally, though he spent a bit more time on other areas of the world where forests had been decimated, and describing in painful detail, for some of the delegates at least, what their various regimes had done to their particular areas. When he had finished, he again asked for any questions.

Most were too astonished by what they had heard and seen to have any coherent thoughts for a few moments, but one delegate from a Middle Eastern country felt he had seen through the whole charade and was not going to be cowed like the other delegates into saying nothing. He got to his feet, looked squarely at the US delegation and in fairly broken English said:

"So the great Satan seeks to destroy our civilizations by some new devilish technology. I am not taken in by all these conjuring tricks, these so-called historical pictures. We will not let the devils inflict this on us – Allah will help protect us from, and damn, these Satanists! Allah Akbar!"

He looked round expecting applause from other similar minded States, but on hearing none, and seeing no one looking at him, looked back at what they were all now staring. The screen had practically retracted into the Box, and it was moving in his direction, very quickly.

Before he had time to do anything, it was beside him.

"So, this man believes his dogma more than the evidence of his eyes and simple reasoning. Perhaps something a little more personal might persuade and enlighten him."

The man suddenly found himself suspended eight feet above his seat, while the Box went back above Andrew and reproduced its screen.

"You might like to consider how the 'Great Satan' has managed to suspend you in the air and how it obtained this information and these pictures of you from the time you were born, also how it manages to speak in some hundred different languages simultaneously but you only hear your own in this large hall."

For a minute or two the screen showed a series of pictures of the delegate growing up, (starting at the present time and going back in time so that there was no doubt it was the same man) with a commentary describing some of the major events in his life, particularly those that could not be got from official records. It was pretty obvious, even to the most sceptical, that the information related to the official concerned, and some of the details of his early affairs with girls, whom he later castigated for their immoral ways, were downright embarrassing and fitted with rumours one or two of them had already heard.

"Right, I'll put you back in your seat. We do not expect you to lose face by admitting you were wrong. I think everyone here will have come to their own conclusions about that."

The man sat silent, baffled, humiliated, angry and terrified by turns, but could not bring himself to say or do anything. Being suspended and completely powerless like that while aspects of his earlier life, that he had thought were well buried, now shown to the whole world in clinical detail...

"So to conclude: you will all have to decide how best to inform your people about what is going to happen so that there is not widespread panic with all the death and destruction that that would entail. One suggestion that the good Professor here has made refers back to a book written by one of your great astronomers, Professor Fred Hoyle, some fifty years ago. It was entitled 'The Black Cloud'. For those of you unfamiliar with this fictional work, it supposed that the solar system was travelling through a large black cloud of interstellar dust, causing worldwide problems."

"So you could use this idea to explain that both the forest fever and falling birth rate are due to the Solar System passing through an interstellar cloud, which astronomers have seen but are as yet unable to say either what it is or when it will pass. The cloud is extremely difficult to detect and indeed was only found when testing the very latest Quantum MASER sensors at Mouna Loa in Hawaii. Of course, all professional astronomers would have to be persuaded to co-operate, but I'm sure that when it's explained to them and the fact that they don't have the equipment to check the statement anyway, they will confirm the theory. It is up to you how you tell your people, but our approach, as I said, was to tell the world leaders and leave them to work out the best approach. It would also be better if you all made your announcements at the same time, or as near as you can manage it and as soon as possible, before damaging wild rumours start leaking out. I would suggest you try to agree a time with the UN Secretary immediately after this meeting."

"One last word: We are not prepared to see this world destroyed by overpopulation with humans and the consequent decimation of all its natural flora, fauna and other natural resources. So, it is up to you to make it work to avoid us having to take more drastic measures."

With that unspecified but barely concealed threat left hanging in his audience's mind, Klaat finished his speech, the screen returned to the Box, and to general surprise, the Box then disappeared.

For a few seconds, no one moved or said anything, and then the whole place erupted at once: everyone trying to speak to their neighbours or allies, and general confusion reigned. The UN Secretary tried unsuccessfully to call for order, but eventually gave up though not before getting an instruction through that the meeting would reconvene at two o'clock that afternoon. The US delegation retreated quickly and quietly to their office. There, the president thanked Andrew for his speech, and said he might well want to consult with him again in the next day or so, but in any case he'd be very welcome to stay on as a guest of the US government for a few days, which invitation Andrew was very happy to accept.

By about two thirty that afternoon, the general hubbub had abated enough for the Secretary to finally agree a window of eight hours in two days' time when all the countries would make their announcements, it obviously not being possible to have a single worldwide time for this event.

The next summons to the White House came rather more quickly than Andrew might have liked: the next morning, when he joined the President and some of his advisers.

"Morning, Andrew, thanks for coming at such short notice, but a couple of things have come up on which we'd like to hear your views. Firstly, however, some introductions: I think you all know Professor Andrew Kowalski here," he said, turning slightly and smiling at Andrew, "even if you haven't met him yet. Jim, would you start and then everyone else please introduce yourselves."

When the introductions were over, the President continued:

"Well, Andrew, as you will appreciate, we have a hell of a lot of things to consider, none of which can be resolved in half an hour at this meeting. However, there are a couple of points that only you can answer, and could well influence our further deliberations. The first and most important is how do we get hold of that Klaat character, and do you think he will listen to any requests we have?"

"Answering the last part first, my impression is that they're going to go ahead with their plan and nothing we can do or say will prevent it. However, if we were looking for minor changes or slight delays, they might, and I stress might, listen and if the request didn't seriously impact their objectives, *might* agree. However, I can hardly claim to be a *confidante* of Klaat so I can't be any more specific than that."

"With regard to the first part, it seems that I am the only means of communication with Klaat as I seem to be the *de facto* keeper of the Box. I might add in that connection, it has some very persuasive powers to ensure I remain its keeper, as some would-be thieves found out very painfully a few days ago. Three of them planned to take it from me on my way home. All three survived, I believe, but were hospitalised, very seriously injured without, I hasten to add, any action whatsoever on my part. So I guess if you need to get a message or question to Klaat, you'll have to do it through me."

"Okay, thank you for that. Now the other question: How come your party managed to get into the forest without getting hit by the fever?"

"That's quite straightforward, in a way. I don't know how, but Klaat had managed to get what I can only describe as some special ID discs issued to us by a ministry official beforehand, which we had to wear next to the skin. They were quite some piece of kit, I can tell you. Not only kept the fever off us but even prevented a crocodile and a group of angry chimpanzees from attacking us. Also they kept all the insects away. However, they were apparently custom designed for each of us, and would not work with anyone else, we were told, though come to think of it we didn't try swapping them around. Having experienced the fever, believe me, it's not something you ever want to take the slightest risk with."

One of the military generals at the table said:

"Gee! I sure wish we could get hold of dog tags like that. Would make jungle warfare a breeze!"

"Somehow, I think that'll have to stay on your wish list for quite a while yet, Hank," said the President, laughing.

"Andrew, thanks very much for your information. Incidentally, did the Box accompany you here?"

"I think so," he said, reaching down and patting his hand in the usual position the Box adopted beside him. "Yes, here it is." As he touched it, the Box reappeared.

"I thought it useful for these guys to see it, just in case they were beginning to think I was ready for the funny farm. Hey! One thing I just thought of. Could you call up Klaat and ask him when he expects to have all his measures in place?"

"Sure," said Andrew, opening the Box and hitting the green button.

"Hello, Professor, how can I help you?"

"Two things, please. Firstly, can you tell us when all your measures to control the population will be in place, and secondly, could you please show the people here those pictures you took of us in the jungle last week, starting from your space platform and zooming in."

"Certainly, Professor. We have most of the major measures in place, but still have some of the smaller areas to analyse and cover. Now just watch the screen for those pictures you wanted to see again."

As before, the audience was astonished at the way the Box rose, produced its screen and then showed the pictures, the razor sharp clarity of which were still a source of wonder to Andrew and were almost unbelievable to the others. When it had all finished, the Box closed up and resumed its place beside Andrew.

"Well, thank you again, Andrew, I feel I have a rather less sceptical audience that I did before that demonstration," said the President, with a slight laugh and glancing at one or two of the participants in his meeting, who had suddenly found the condition of their hands in need of close scrutiny. "I don't think we need keep you from your sightseeing any more. However, please keep the phone I gave you with you at all times, so that we can get through to you and hence Klaat with the minimum of delay should the need arise. Lieutenant Robson here will take you back to the car. Goodbye and thanks again."

With a collective wave to the meeting he said goodbye and left.

Andrew and Myra were told that if they could postpone their return to England for three more days, they could return with the Ambassador on the same private jet. They didn't need any further arm twisting, and planned to spend the next three days having what promised to be one of the best holidays of their life, particularly as they seemed to have rediscovered some of the magic in their marriage since that first night of passion in the 'Crows' Nest'.

On his way back to collect Myra, Andrew noticed the splash sheet by a news vendor –"Mars Invaders Arrived!" Thinking that it had been too much to hope that none of the UN delegates would abide by the ruling and not use the opportunity to cash in on possibly the biggest story ever, he asked the driver to stop while he bought a paper. Predictably, there was a lot of hyped-up speculation, and very little hard information, so Andrew hoped that it wouldn't start a panic, though obviously there would be a lot of trouble for politicians trying to keep the lid on the whole matter until the official announcement.

However, there was a slight delay before they could continue their holiday – a message waiting for Andrew when they got back to the 'Crows' Nest' asking him to please call the British Ambassador to the UN as soon as possible, which he did as soon as they were back in their room.

"Ah hello, Professor Kowalski, thank you for calling back so promptly. Sorry to intrude on your holiday but I wonder if you would be so kind as to spare me an hour or so here at the British Embassy. I need to talk to you about the special meeting yesterday. I've been speaking to my US counterpart, and he tells me you're the expert on all this, so if it would be convenient I'd like to see you as soon as you can get here."

Though couched in official politeness, there was no mistaking the nature of the conversation – it was more an order than a request, so Andrew left Myra to get ready for their next foray as tourists, hoping to be back to join her within an hour or so.

Andrew was given the VIP treatment and shown into the Ambassador's office without any delay.

The ambassador rose to meet him, holding out his hand and said:

"Thanks for coming round so quickly, Professor. I am Sir John Battle, our ambassador to the UN, and was very impressed with the speech you gave there yesterday, and somewhat overwhelmed by your co-presenter, I must admit," he added, with a slight laugh.

"Please take a seat," he continued, indicating an armchair by a low table in front of the desk where he'd been working when Andrew entered. The ambassador then asked if Andrew would like a coffee and ordered it before he sat down opposite Andrew.

"Right then Professor, my reason for wanting to talk to you is to get some background on how you seem to be almost part of the American team, and apparently haven't been talking to our government to give us any advantage that may accrue from your apparent close association with that, er, person that spoke through that phone or projector thing."

His manner had become rather more brusque as he spoke, and Andrew realised he'd need to tread very carefully to avoid upsetting this man, and possibly get into trouble back home.

Before he could answer a tray of coffee and biscuits was brought in and laid on the table in between the two men. This slight interruption gave Andrew a chance to think about his answer, the manner in which the question had been put being markedly different from the friendly atmosphere he'd encountered in his meetings with his American hosts, and had momentarily thrown him a bit.

Andrew took his coffee and looking straight at the ambassador said:

"You seem to have been singularly misinformed, though from my experience of the meetings I had with the Prime Minister before coming over here at the American ambassador's personal request, I can't say I'm unduly surprised."

Andrew saw that his opening remark had got home to the Ambassador. Though he could not have known it, his low opinion of the PM was shared by the Ambassador.

"Oh, I'm sorry – I didn't know about any meetings you'd had with the PM, but if you had, why weren't you brought over to our office here for the UN meeting?"

"I'm afraid I can't answer that – you'd need to ask the PM. What I can tell you is a summary of what happened when I tried to inform him about the whole business."

Twenty minutes later the Ambassador had heard all the salient points.

"Well, thank you for that, Professor. I can now quite see why you took up the Americans' offer, and I must say I'm glad you did. What are your immediate plans?"

"My wife and I have accepted the President's offer to stay on at the 'Crow's Nest' as his guest for the next couple of days and continue to enjoy a holiday, though to be on call should he need any further information, after which we'll be flying home. I presume you'll be informing HM Government of what you've heard here, and probably joining them to debate what course of action to take in the light of the UN meeting. It goes without saying that if you need any further information during the next two or three days, before we fly back home with the US Ambassador, please feel free to call me. The President has given me this special phone, so I can be contacted at any time through his office if I'm not in the 'Crow's Nest'. Obviously, I will again be available back home at the Ecowotsit office should you need to contact me later on.

As he left the Ambassador's office, Andrew felt he'd made a useful acquaintance of the man, who had obviously been miffed at not being informed by Downing Street earlier about the whole business. So he returned to the 'Crow's Nest' to collect Myra and continue their holiday. On his way back he had a sudden thought: he did not want to be lumbered with some one hundred and fifty countries' governments all individually calling him with assorted requests. Someone, definitely not him, would have to co-ordinate and review the requests so that his involvement was minimal. He decided it warranted a call to the president to see what could be arranged.

Five minutes later, he was very glad he had done so: the president appreciated the problem fully, and said he would personally arrange a co-ordinating office with the UN Secretariat through which all such queries would be routed. Though he didn't make any mention of it to Andrew, it occurred to him while speaking that having some of his own people in such an office would provide a lot of very useful information of the effects of Klaat's actions on all the other countries.

When they got up the next morning, the early news on the television was still full of speculation about the 'invasion' and a variety of pundits was wheeled on to voice their respective opinions. After listening for a few minutes, Andrew decided there didn't seem to be much of an air of panic, so they should get on and enjoy the rest of their time on holiday in Washington

The next morning the news bulletins contained the official announcement. Andrew felt they had done a good job of down-playing the whole scenario so as to avoid any sort of panic, by acknowledging those aspects which were becoming generally known, such as the no-go areas of rain forest, but not mentioning the maximum two child restriction yet. However, the door was left open to add that a little later by saying that strenuous efforts were being made to identify the threat posed by this cloud of interstellar gas that was seen as the source of the problem. Further information would be issued as soon as the nature of the problem was established. In the meantime, there was no need for any alarm, as the problem would be of relatively short duration.

"I'm darned glad I didn't have to put that announcement together," Andrew said to Myra, "but I don't see how they can keep the lid on it for very long."

"Surely, the fall in the birthrate will become apparent very soon," Myra replied, "then, as they used to say, it'll really hit the fan!"

"Yes, you're very probably right, but by reporting results of the 'research' in dribs and drabs, interspersed with items that will not be affected, I suppose is the best that could be done".

"Well, there's nothing we can do about it just now. Look on the bright side – civilisation may implode shortly, so let's not waste another second of our holiday and enjoy our last day here while we can!"

"Spoken like a true optimist!" she said, laughing. "You're right. C'mon – let's get on with it!"

They had just started on their journey when the special phone rang.

Andrew gave a little start and for a second was afraid that their day's fun was about to be curtailed. However, the President was simply asking how he thought the announcement had gone, and whether Andrew had any thoughts on what should be included in the next one to help reduce any general unease.

So they had the day to enjoy themselves, which they did with gusto and unusually for them, being wildly extravagant with some shopping and as Myra remarked, enjoying one of his 'fifty horsepower' lunches. A midday walk in a park helped to settle the lunch and provide a bit of needed exercise and fresh air.

They returned to the Crow's Nest somewhat tired by their activities but feeling very happy. After a bit of a rest and shower they ordered up another splendid dinner. Both were a little surprised and delighted to find that on going to bed, their tiredness left them and they regained a bit more of their passion and youthful enjoyment of each other.

CHAPTER 22

Back Home

The next day, Andrew and Myra had to get ready to return home, and while packing up their few bits and pieces, Myra had looked around the beautiful 'crow's nest' and said a little ruefully:

"I think it's just as well we're leaving now, as I could very easily become accustomed to living in this superb style, a magnificent apartment, five star restaurant meals at the end of a phone, a chauffeured limo to go where and whenever we want…Yes, I could definitely get used to this!"

"So could I," replied Andrew with a short laugh, "but very shortly it will all seem like a dream, anyway, rather than reality, so let's think of it like that. Come on, we'd better hurry up – don't want to keep the Ambassador's plane waiting, or even worse, miss the damn flight altogether!"

On their drive back to the airport, Andrew noticed some of the placards by the newsstands, some of the more lurid referring to invaders from Mars and other extra-terrestrial potential disasters.

"Looks like we'll get home just in time to miss a major panic, unless we have the same at home," said Andrew. "I hope they manage to calm it all down. It shouldn't be too difficult, as there will be nothing to see or feel for the vast majority of the people."

"I hope you're right," replied Myra.

The rest of their journey passed without incident, and they enjoyed the luxury of the Ambassador's plane back to England. On arrival at the US Air base where their trip had started, they were taken home in the rather mysterious car that had collected them at the start.

Gosh! Was it really only just about a week ago? Andrew found himself thinking as they drew up outside their house. Neither felt like doing anything such as unpacking, and were still in a bit of a daze, as well as being very tired. Hence after a bit of aimlessly looking round the house and putting together a light meal collected from the deep freeze, they sat down to have it. So much had happened to them in the previous two weeks for which they had been totally unprepared, that they were almost in a state of shock, scarcely able to believe it. Coming back to their everyday previous normality was going to require some considerable adjustment, and take a little time. They were still reminding each other of little incidents, rather as children still chattering excitedly amongst themselves about a film they'd just seen – "D'you remember when…" and "I liked that bit when…" – when the phone rang.

It was John, who, after a few pleasantries about their trip asked if Andrew had had time to catch up on the news about the Prime Minister.

"No, what's happened to him – nothing too trivial, I hope," Andrew answered, remembering rather too vividly for comfort how he had been treated by the man, and the suspicion they had that he was behind the attack on him to acquire the Box.

"He's resigned," replied John, "and the official version of events is that it was due to ill health. However, you-know-who with a nose for news, has discovered that he was caught arranging to permanently remove one of his 'fixers' who was blackmailing him over the incident with the Box (which apparently resulted in three heavies being found dead somewhere – almost certainly the ones that tried to relieve you of Klaat's little toy). The second fixer he approached to do the deed evidently had a greater loyalty to the first one, so the pair of them shopped him. Don't know much else as, of course, it is being spun like a gyroscope with *delirium tremens*, but either way, the PM is definitely an ex-PM. Not sure who the new one is to be yet, but he can't be any worse than the last, can he?"

"God, I hope not. Anyway, could you tell them I'll be in your office the day after tomorrow? I have a few things to clear up as a result of my trip to the states and I could use a bit of a rest, too! See you then. Bye."

"Well I'm damned," muttered Andrew turning to Myra, and then telling her what had happened.

His intention to take a couple of days rest was soon just wishful thinking. So having lazed about a bit on the first morning after getting home, he phoned Norton University and found himself spending a lot of time discussing outstanding matters with them, which stretched into the next day.

On the third day back he was in the Ecowotsit office early to catch up on other events arising from the 'Klaat Regime', as they had christened it. At the end of the day, he had just about finished these discussions and was preparing to go home, when he received a totally unexpected phone call.

"Hello, Professor Kowalski?" enquired an unknown voice. On receiving his acknowledgement it went on:

"I am Secretary to the Prime Minister, the Right Honourable Roger Johnston, and he would very much like to meet with you at number ten tomorrow morning at either eight or eleven o'clock."

As the latter meant he could go home for the night, he agreed it, and then made his way home.

The next morning at a few minutes to eleven, Andrew was shown into the new Prime Minister's office by an aide. "Professor Kowalski, sir," she said, introducing the visitor, and then left.

"Good morning, Professor, I'm glad you were able to come at such short notice," said the PM, shaking Andrew's hand. "I've heard quite a bit about you and your involvement with this business from John here, our UN Ambassador," he said nodding towards Sir John Battle, who was seated at the small table, "following your meeting with him in Washington."

"Hello, Andrew, good to see you again. I trust you managed to get in a bit of a holiday in your time off over there."

"Certainly did, thank you, Sir John, we had a marvellous time!" said Andrew with a broad smile as he thought back to those few days he and Myra had spent so enjoyably.

"Well, let me tell you why I wanted to speak to you, Professor," said the PM, after the trio had exchanged a few more pleasantries, which the PM used to assess his visitor. "Apart from a few clarifications I'd like to hear from you, there are one or two questions I'd like to put to this Klaat friend of yours. Can that be arranged?"

Andrew was surprised how different this visit to the PM's office was from his last one. The man himself was so different, that in the space of the few minutes he'd been there, he already felt he was a man who he could trust, and indeed like. He felt completely at ease, and answered all the questions he could in a frank and friendly manner.

"Good," replied the PM when Andrew had finished his last answer. "Thank you for those very helpful answers. I now feel I am getting a good grasp of where we're likely to be heading. So we come to the questions I'd like you to put to the Klaat person. In a way, I'd like to ask him for his advice. Do you think it would be forth coming?"

"It's not something we've tried in the past, but I'll certainly give it a try," said Andrew. "Have you got the questions ready yet?"

"Yes. There aren't many – don't want to put the man off answering before we start."

"John," he said, turning back to the UK's Ambassador to the UN, "any further thoughts on questions we should put to Klaat, other than those we were discussing a little earlier?"

"No, Roger, I can't think of anything other than the generalities we've already spoken about," replied Sir John.

"Good," said the PM, and turning to Andrew added: "Okay, so, how do we set about it, Andrew?"

"Like this," said Andrew, reaching down for the Box which duly appeared.

As it had been invisible when he entered the room, its presence had not been remarked on, and so caused both the PM and the Ambassador quite a fright, the former with particular concern as to the security aspect. Andrew went through his usual explanation, having got used to the commotion the first appearance of the Box caused, and set about opening up communication with Klaat.

"Hello, Professor, how can I help you today?" came the voice from the Box.

Andrew explained the reasons and finished by handing over to the PM.

"Hello, er, Klaat is it, excuse my hesitancy but I find talking to someone I don't know and can't see like this a little disorientating."

Before he could continue, Klaat replied: "No need to apologise, I fully understand. Firstly, I would like to congratulate you on being appointed the Prime Minister so recently. I would like to wish you every success in what has something of a reputation for being an extremely difficult job. So, what is it you wanted to ask me?"

Having an excellent ability to think rapidly, the PM quickly recovered his composure and started with his questions.

"Thank you for your good wishes with my job, but I fear your intervention in our world has made it that much more difficult for me," he replied with a slight laugh. "So, I hoped that you may be able to offer some advice from your previous experience (as I understand this is not the first time you have acted like this) as to how we should set about coping with the huge imminent changes to our established order."

"It was never our intention to take over the running of your planet, so I can't tell you how to do it now," came the reply from the Box. "What I can do is give you a few thoughts on where you should concentrate your efforts. There are no quick fixes, and you will have to be prepared to change policies quickly if something is seen not to be working. I have noticed in the past an almost unwritten rule in your governments never ever to admit that any legislation you brought in could ever be wrong, and so you virtually never back track or cancel it. You should face up to having to correct a policy that isn't seen to work as soon as possible.

"You will also have to undertake longer term planning than is your usual practice. I've seen how expedient short-term fixes (even though these are not the proper solutions for the long-term) are often employed to get the Administration out of their current troubles. This has the obvious advantage that they are seen by the voters to have done something to resolve the problems immediately, though in reality it is their successors who will have to provide a proper and probably more difficult resolution later on, and deal with unexpected consequences of the quick fix.

"You will also have to imbue a culture of equilibrium, and initially even decrease, into every aspect of life where growth is currently the only measure of success. Your industries will have to readjust to be able to continue in existence and develop their futures without the need continually to increase the size of their enterprises. Very difficult to change the culture that has existed for so long, I know, but something I'm afraid you will have to learn to live with.

"The loss of areas of the planet, such as the rain forests, which we have cordoned off (to give them and their indigenous inhabitants a chance to recover from the wholesale decimation that has been your practice up until now), will require some ingenuity to overcome. As a typical example of the sort of approach you should adopt to overcome these losses, perhaps you should look at ways of mechanically reconstituting the huge amount of wood you currently waste or devising better ways of recycling scrap metals that recovers more of them. These are currently dictated nearly entirely by financial considerations, which will need to be adjusted to take into account the increasingly reduced availability of the raw materials due to the decline in output from the producers. More effort must be made to eliminate the current disregard paid to wasting finite resources, typically precious metals and, to take a single example of another material, helium.

"The decreasing population will help in reducing the demand for all the raw materials, thereby ameliorating the loss of these resources. However, this will, in turn, require some changes as to how much of the population can be supported by those generating the wealth required for that support.

"None of this will be easy, and we very much regret this. It will, however, and you should bear this in mind when contemplating these difficulties, be a great deal easier than trying to cope with the ultimate disaster the planet will experience if you carry on as you are going now. This, in turn, will require that your policies can be made to work despite those who say: 'It's not our problem what happens in the future, people alive then will have to deal with it. I'm going to enjoy my life now and they can worry about it then'.

"With regard to the longer term solutions I referred to earlier, it seems that you have just started making efforts to try and reduce the carbon dioxide concentration in your atmosphere, the need for which seems to have near general acceptance. It is a good start, but on its own will not prove to be sufficient.

"One suggestion I would offer that will help: Put as much effort as you can afford into developing nuclear energy as your primary source of electricity generation and hence other sources of power.

Consider building many small plants around the country rather than a few very large ones, as this could prove a quicker and cheaper alternative. Extensive research into the so-called problem of nuclear waste will pay handsome dividends as you will find that the radioactivity can be removed completely, the waste rendered harmless and plenty of useful electrical energy generated from the process. It will not be easy to solve the problems, but given your track record you will crack it if you persevere. Unfortunately, we are not allowed to tell you (or indeed any other civilisations) how to do this; you will have to work it out for yourselves, but it is possible.

"And on that topic, don't waste your soon-to-be-declining resources on trying to develop dead-end technologies purely for ideological motives, such as trying to harness horrendously expensive and intermittent wind energy, only viable with the payment of huge subsidies. Your research efforts will be far better rewarded with other systems, such as I've just mentioned – nuclear energy and its waste.

"I think that is about all the advice I can give you now. I hope you find it useful. Goodbye."

There was a moment or two of silence in the office, then the PM said:

"Doubtless good advice, but not very easy to convince the world of it, as a great number of them are going to be a lot worse off in the future. Well, thank you, Professor, for bringing those words of wisdom to us. Should we wish to consult that particular Oracle again, I assume you'll be able to help?"

"Yes, of course, Prime Minister, though I think we all got the message that answers to specifics are not part of the agenda as far as they are concerned."

"Yes, I think you're right there. Now, a couple of other matters before you go: Firstly, how did you get on with Pat O'Hanlon during your expedition to Nimeroon a few weeks ago?"

"Very well. He struck me as a very dependable character who fitted in very well with the team, and from what I've seen so far, has written an excellent record of our experiences. I would be very happy for him to accompany me on any future expeditions of a similar nature."

"Good," replied the PM, "because we are thinking of offering him a worldwide roving reporting role to keep us informed of how other countries are coping with the problems we are all going to have to face. While there will obviously be official discussions between various countries to do what we can to minimise problems, the unofficial accounts, of the sort someone like O'Hanlon could provide would be very useful. Actual observations on the ground as opposed to the official line describing the success of government agendas, if you catch my drift."

"Now, the second thing: He will be part of a team I want to set up at the Ecowotsit department to monitor as much as possible of the effects the new regime will be having around the world, and I'd like you to head up this team. If you're in agreement with this we will square it with the Norton University. Oh, and one other thing: please don't mention any of this until you hear it officially."

Somewhat taken aback by this development, the Professor replied:

"Prime Minister, I am very honoured to be offered this appointment. But, as it's all quite unexpected, could I please have a day to consider it, discuss the ramifications with my two universities and also my wife before accepting? However, please be assured that I will try damned hard to clear it with them (without explaining why) so that I can take it on. I will let you know by noon tomorrow, at the latest."

"However, there is one other aspect I would like to have agreed before accepting, and it is this: While this new appointment will be my top priority, I would like to be able to keep in touch with, and do some further work with my university, when time and other commitments allow. Will that be acceptable?

"Yes, I don't see why not, just so long as your new job is your main area of work. Otherwise, good – I'll look forward to hearing from you and I sincerely hope it will be to accept the job," replied the PM, getting up to signal the end of the interview. Holding out his hand to Andrew, he went on:

"Thank you again for your visit, Professor. When, if ever, I have a bit more time I would like to hear a bit more about that Box of yours and its capabilities. I'm glad it's not my responsibility!"

As Andrew and the Ambassador walked out of Downing Street, Andrew could not restrain himself any longer, and said:

"I don't suppose I should say so, but what a difference between this PM and the last. One has to wonder how on earth the previous character ever got voted into office!"

"Yes, my sentiments entirely, and I shouldn't say so either!"

Then both of them laughed a little remembering their earlier experiences as they walked out into the main road to catch a taxi. A sudden downpour of rain had them struggling with umbrellas and trying to avoid getting a soaking.

"A pity we didn't ask Klaat if he could do something about our weather while he's at it!" said Sir John, laughing.

Andrew had a fairly traumatic few hours on the phone as soon as he got back to the Ecowotsit office. Having told Myra, who was very pleased for him, as long as it didn't mean him spending all his time travelling, he then had the difficult task of extracting himself from his university commitments. At the end of the day, he had managed to satisfy all the relevant parties, and the following morning phoned the PM to accept the job.

Not surprisingly, a period of considerable upheaval followed the start of what was to become known as the 'Declining Age', this being a more accurate and longer lasting description than the 'Klaat Regime', more favoured by the Ecowotsit team.

Two days after Andrew's visit to the PM the start of re-arrangements became apparent to the members of the Ecowotsit department. A rapidly expanding team was set up under Professor Kowalski with direct access to the Prime Minister with a brief to monitor as much as possible of the effects the new regime was having around the world. Part of the thinking behind this was to get warning, where at all possible, of detrimental developments taking place around the world with a view to preventing their occurrence, or at the very least, to minimise the effect they would have in the UK. Similarly, if anyone came up with a useful strategy for easing the transformation into the reduced economies now forced on the world, it could be followed up.

As may have been expected, John Fenwick was promoted to be his second in command, with Pat O'Hanlon offered the post of head of Data Assimilation. John went home that evening to tell Angela how delighted he was at the prospect of the new job and insisted they go out that night to celebrate. Fortunately, her mother was able to babysit for them at virtually no notice, and they had a memorable evening.

As they went into their bedroom, Angela, smirking rather archly, said:

"I'm afraid I haven't had time to get any gooey cream deserts…"

He pulled her to him and kissed her passionately then said:

"Somehow, I don't think we'll miss them tonight, I can barely wait to get you to bed... Hold on a mo' – I've just had a thought."

He reached into the drawer beside the bed and retrieved the dog tag from the Jungle expedition and put it on. Seeing her looking at him curiously, he said, with a conspiratorial wink:

"Works just like 'Viagra' – now get onto that bed quick before I ravish you on the floor!"

Quite some time later, as they lay recovering from their passionate lovemaking, she remarked sleepily:

"That Viagra substitute seems to work almost as well as cream cakes. We must try it more often."

"If I'm right, I think you'll find it surprising how well it worked," he murmured.

A bit puzzled by his remark, but too tired to ask about it further, she was soon asleep.

John had hoped that the disc might overcome the pregnancy barrier that Klaat had said would be imposed worldwide, but in this he was to be disappointed. Though Klaat had not specifically mentioned it to the team, the discs were deactivated when their expedition was completed.

Not surprisingly, details and wild rumours began to leak out about the team's expedition to the Nimeroon jungle, and the part played by these 'magic' dog tags in allowing them to enter the jungles. This, in turn, led to fairly extensive criminal plans to get hold of one of these tags, when it was thought they would then have sole control of the logging operations, which due to the greatly reduced access to the forests, had now become even more lucrative. An elaborate plan eventually homed in on John Fenwick as probably the easiest one of the team to find and burgle.

The raid on John's home was very carefully carried out and it was two days before John realised that his dog tag had gone missing while looking for something else in the drawer.

He decided to mention it to the Professor only, as nothing else had apparently gone missing so he didn't think it worthwhile to report it to the police.

The Professor thought to tell Klaat that the disc had been stolen. The response he got was the nearest they'd heard from Klaat that could be described as slightly sardonically humourous.

"Well, they're in for a nasty shock if they try to use them to enter any of the areas we've protected. Not only will they not work as they did for you, but it's possible that the tabs may have a negative effect and they may not get out alive. However, should you ever need to go back in, we will arrange for your personal tags to be reactivated or provide new ones.

Reports eventually circulated that a gang of loggers, who had apparently decided that they knew how to bypass the invisible barriers around the jungles, set off into one prepared to collect some hardwood trees. The news was that very few of the gang survived and they lost virtually all their equipment, as the few survivors had been totally focused on getting as far away and as quickly as possible from the jungle.

The Professor told John that he'd heard from Klaat that it was his stolen tab the gang had tried to use, with such disastrous results. The news of the gang's fate helped reduce the number of attempts made by others to mount similar expeditions.

Spurred on by this event, the Professor contacted Klaat to ask how they could arrange scientific research into forests or how they could mount a rescue operation if a plane crashed into the jungle.

The outcome of this discussion was that the UN would set up an office to deal with all such requests which would be passed electronically to Prof Kowalski for automatic transmission on to Klaat. Klaat confirmed that ID Discs will be provided for the research team individuals and rescue teams and that the barrier would be deactivated around the crash site, though he didn't say how any of this would be done. As with the Professor's expedition's tags, they would only be activated by contact with the designated person, and de-activated when the particular purpose for which they had been issued was completed. This fact would be advised to all those issued with tags, and a general announcement covering their use and specific function made, to avoid too many attempts to steal or reuse such tags being made. There would, therefore, be no problems with anyone trying to reuse them for any reason whatsoever.

CHAPTER 23

The Plan

It did not take the Americans long to set up a 'Central Contact Point' for all the various country leaders to put questions to Klaat, as the President had said he would just after the UN meeting. On being told this was all set up and 'ready to roll', Andrew wondered how he could get all these questions to Klaat without spending most of his day on his computer, and told Klaat about his concern. He was told not to worry, and that the matter would be dealt with very shortly.

Later that evening, he was astonished to see another small aluminium box sitting alongside the original one in his study, which must have made its own way into the house at some stage without his knowledge.

"Come and have a look at this," he called through to Myra. "We now have 'Son-of-box' as a lodger!"

"Well I'll be…" was Myra's comment on seeing the new box, "…I just hope they don't keep breeding at that rate or you'll have to move out of your study!"

A message from Klaat shortly thereafter advised that the new box would handle all the questions from the Central Contact Point, and that Andrew needn't worry about it at all. Klaat did add that obviously not all questions would be answered, as Andrew had already found out during earlier discussions with Klaat, but that they would at least all be acknowledged.

A week later, Andrew was just thinking that he was getting on top of all the administration required to set up his new department, which had driven him nearly to distraction and he was wondering if he could take a day or two off when he had a phone call from the Prime Minister's personal private secretary, asking him to attend a cabinet meeting at ten o'clock the next morning. As the PM hadn't made any specific requests as to what he was required for, he felt he was just about on top of his new appointment to be able to answer any questions relating to the progress he had made. However, to be on the safe side, he made sure he had all the information relating to his new Ecowotsit organisation on his laptop, which he took with him to the meeting.

Being a bit nervous about attending a Cabinet meeting for the first time, he got there a bit early and was shown to his seat. As the rest of the ministers came in, he recognised a few of them from newsreel pictures, though, of course, they didn't know him, but he then felt better when George Bentley, the Environment Minister came in and greeted him personally.

Finally, the Prime Minister took his seat and began the meeting by saying:

"I think you all know why I've called this meeting, but before I start, I'd like to introduce Professor Kowalski, who probably knows more about this whole environmental catastrophe, and I use the word advisedly, than anyone. As there are several of you here who will not have had the latest accurate information about the situation, I will ask the Professor to go through the same introduction to it as he gave me a couple of days ago. That way, I think we can dispense with any doubts some of you may have as to the seriousness and indeed authenticity of what is happening to our planet, and you realise we have to deal with a *fait accompli.*"

"Right, Professor, go ahead," added the PM, resuming his seat.

Still feeling a bit nervous, and not sure whether protocol had it that he should stand to address the Cabinet meeting or remain seated, Andrew decided to stand. This would be the better to see everyone around the long table, and for them to see him. So looking around the table, he began:

"Good morning, everyone. Firstly, I must give you a brief account of how I come to be speaking to you here today, after which I will hand over to the star of the show."

He then repeated most of his talk to the UN and finished with the box giving its usual demonstration. The air of astonishment bordering on disbelief was familiar to the Professor when the box appeared, started and then vanished when it was done. This time it produced some comical expressions on the faces of some of the audience, though none was about to comment.

"Thank you, Andrew, and also Mr Klatt, if you're still listening," said the PM in the slightly stunned silence that followed when Andrew sat down.

"Right," continued the PM when everyone had settled down a bit. "That is the future we face, and what we have to do is come up with methods of dealing with it that prevents a possible wholesale breakdown of our society, as has been starting to happen in some countries apparently."

"I'll give you a few pointers as to the main areas we need to address first. The decrease in birthrate can be put on one side for now, though I understand there is already a move by quite a large proportion of the immigrant population to return to their countries of origin in response to urgent appeals from their families there to come home to help them survive the crisis.

Though it is difficult to see how this can help either the immigrants or their distant families, they believe it will and so are leaving here. One of the non-work related aspects of this is apparently that in certain countries the men have decided that their manhood is being threatened by not being able to father children at all, and blame the women, which, depending on the prevailing culture often results in dire consequences for the women. Typically, they are forcing many lone women, whose husbands are working abroad, to submit and often with the approval of the 'elders', in order that they may become fathers. From this, it would appear that the reduction in mens' desire for any sort of sexual congress that Klaat said would be put in place, either isn't as effective as he'd thought it would be, or maybe hasn't happened at all yet."

Turning to Andrew, he said: "I don't suppose it would do any good, Andrew, but could you try and find out from Klaat after this meeting why his 'desire reduction programme' if I can put it that way, doesn't seem to be working properly in many parts of the world?"

Let me know if you get any sort of helpful response from him."

Turning back to address the whole meeting again, he went on:

"Either way, this extensive attack on their women back home is, of course, another reason why a lot of the immigrants are leaving. It's too early to speculate how this cultural change will resolve itself, but immediately it results in our loosing quite a slice of our workforce...

"Our first response to this must be to replace these missing workers from within our own people, particularly those who could, but prefer not to work. This will obviously take some very careful handling to ensure its success.

"Another aspect of this is that we will have to return to manufacturing a lot more of the goods ourselves that we need, rather than relying on imports, as we do now for some 80 percent of these.

"This, in turn, will need resurrecting or rediscovering earlier skills and manufacturing methods for achieving this, as well as building and equipping the necessary factories.

"To this end, we may well have to recruit workers who have these skills but who have retired or moved into other activities when their lifelong skills were no longer required and they were made redundant.

"Another incipient problem appears to be that several countries we rely on for our food imports are experiencing considerable shortfalls in production for various domestic reasons. They will thus be cutting down on exports to ensure they can feed themselves. This, in turn, means we must gear up our own farming to provide for our own food supplies.

"The reduction in the number of babies being born, though not of immediate (i.e. within the next few weeks) concern, will entail redeploying quite a number of people currently employed in this whole sector, from hospitals to industries producing baby and childrens' needs. To this end also, we can cut back on the previously seen need to build a great number of new houses, and again deploy the construction workers who would have been employed on this activity into agriculture or manufacturing."

"Well, I think that has given you a few pointers in the direction our government is going to have to move. To those who criticise us by saying we're just 'turning the clock back', I make no apology because of the vastly changed circumstances we now find ourselves in. It has many analogies to how we lived successfully in the past, so returning to many of those methods will give us a good start. It doesn't, of course, rule out using our current or new technology where appropriate and where it can be shown to work.

"Filling in the details of how this is to be achieved is down to you ministers and your departments, as well as identifying all the many other areas that I have not specifically mentioned, but will become apparent as you develop the required strategies for your particular briefs."

He paused, and looking round the table fairly slowly added: "I will stress again, that each and every one of you here has got to consider every aspect of what is likely to happen, and proposals as to how we will deal with this, as deal with it we must.

"We will need to co-opt as many of our 'think tanks' and universities, who have expertise in all of these fields, as possible. It will be also up to them to identify as many as possible of the, to quote Donald Rumsfeld the one-time American Defence Secretary, 'unknown unknowns' so that we do not have too many unpleasant surprises.

"To this end, the Home Secretary will set up meetings with these bodies to try and get at much co-operation from them as possible.

"There is another unfortunate aspect that should be borne in mind. As these new conditions start to become significant around the world, it is regrettably more than likely that some countries will resort to war to get their supplies, be it food or raw materials. So our defence capability across the armed forces must be maintained. Depending on how the world deals with all the likely problems, we will have to keep this requirement permanently under review.

"That is all I have to say on the matter at this time, and what with Professor Kowalski's demonstration, should be more than enough to get all your best ideas flowing. I intend to hold another cabinet meeting in a week's time to review progress, and I hope to confirm the layout of an overall first-pass schedule as to what we have to do and when, and for which I will need all your individual department's input. I have set up a special secretariat to collate these and to whom you can address any questions. You will find all the details of this new group in this memorandum, so please help yourselves to a copy as you leave.

"One final word. Just at this minute everything out there seems to be continuing as normal. But make no mistake. We may well witness a sudden domino effect in many areas of our industry and indeed our civilisation itself resulting in their collapse, so be prepared for the worst. Try to foresee any such looming disasters and forestall the worst effects by precipitous action on the part of each of you and your departments. My one slight comfort in all this is that I think I have got a damn good team around me here who I'm sure will do all you can to guide our country through the coming difficulties that we will face.

"Thank you all and good morning."

With which comment the PM got up to close the meeting and left the room.

After the PM had left, there was an unaccustomed near silence as they all thought about what had been said and how it affected them individually, before they too started to leave the cabinet room.

Andrew returned to Ecowotsit and told his staff about the meeting, and then remembered he had to contact Klaat about the apparent failure of his 'libido control system'. Not quite as he had expected, Klaat said that there had been a few small difficulties in getting the system to operate as intended, but that they hoped to have it implemented very shortly. Andrew permitted himself a slight smile to hear that things could still go slightly awry and were not always perfect, even in such an advanced civilisation, as happened rather more often here in our world. He decided against making any remarks about that, and just asked if Klaat could let him know when the system had been perfected.

CHAPTER 24

End Game

Over the next month the Ecowotsit department gradually settled down to its new role and started to receive reports which they disseminated to the PM's new secretariat for distribution. They also tried to find answers to questions from various government departments as to how some specific problems were being dealt with by other countries. They were also particularly concerned with trying to establish and where possible, remedy trade disruptions that could have a serious impact back home, typically imports of food.

They also started to receive some reports about some 'unintended consequences' of the Klaat regime. In some countries where 'human' rights should perhaps be called 'men's' rights, it was getting to be generally recognised that only those women with less than two children were worth pursuing to satisfy the need for the men to demonstrate their siring prowess. The other side of this coin was that those women who already had two children were considered fair game for sex without producing any permanent reminders of the incident, in the shape of babies. It would become apparent, before long that this would result in soaring rates of sexually transmitted diseases, as any precautions, such as the use of condoms, that may have previously been taken, either to avoid a pregnancy or disease, were now often ignored.

A particularly barbaric aspect came to light from one of the unofficial reports that Pat O'Hanlon managed to get out of the country he was visiting, though obviously was not contained in any official government statement. Apparently, a radical fundamentalist offshoot of the Taliban (who they didn't consider to be radical enough) and calling itself the 'Mohammed's Real Disciples' were solving the problem by kidnapping women. This involved a group of two or three of them, accompanied by a compliant Iman, hunting around for any woman who was of childbearing age. Having found one, the Iman performed an immediate 'marriage' ceremony and the unfortunate woman wasn't seen again by her family. In some cases, if there was a lack of suitable girls, the husbands of otherwise suitable women were told to divorce their wives then and there, who were then immediately remarried to one of the hunters, under the auspices of the Iman. Any husbands who objected to this were shot out of hand.

On receiving this, John showed it to Andrew, who having read it, said: "God it's almost unbelievable what some men can justify on the basis of religion," shaking his head in disbelief at what he'd read.

"Yes, isn't it – it makes me sick at times reading about some of these practices," said John.

About the same time these reports were being received, Denise Carter told the Professor that experimental rice plants they had been growing had exceeded by far the amount of rice the plants normally produced, apparently in line with what Klaat had promised. She was still trying to fathom what had occurred to these experimental plants that caused their increased yield, but so far had not been able to explain it. Did Andrew think that despite saying they were not going to tell us how to get round problems brought on by the Klaat regime, he might have had something to do with this?

Andrew said he supposed it was just a possibility, though Klaat had been noticeably unco-operative in providing any specific information to earlier questions. However, it was excellent news, and he would inform the relative minister so that large scale production could proceed, which, in turn, would help not just those countries that relied on rice as a staple food stuff, but also the UK's balance of trade figures which, in turn, would help imports of items the UK needed.

After he'd been in the job for about two months, Andrew realised that his administrative functions as head of this new Ecowotsit team was beginning to get him down. He found himself thinking of the work he could have been doing back at his university and how much more intellectually satisfying and challenging he would find it to be back in the academic world rather than keeping pace with his current day-to-day administrative duties. Even the need to keep him in his position due to his unique function for communicating with Klaat had become less and less necessary since the automatic link had been set up. And, anyway, as Klaat had said, John would become the box's keeper if Andrew could no longer fulfil that function.

He was having one of these introspective thoughts on the Monday afternoon after their usual progress meeting in the morning, when he got the telephone call.

"Professor Kowalski?"

"Yes – who's that speaking?"

The voice went on: "We have kidnapped your wife and if you want to have her back, you will go to Waterloo station at four o'clock this afternoon and await a call from the public phone box by platform 11. You will bring with you that aluminium box thing that you use for demonstrations. If you do not comply, you will not see your wife alive again," after which the caller hung up.

"Hello! Hello! Hello!" Andrew shouted back down the phone until he realised it had been cut off.

For a second or two of near blind panic, Andrew, who had never had such a serious threat to contend with, sat frozen in his chair, his mind in a turmoil. The box? He hadn't seen it in days – he hadn't needed to contact Klaat since all the messages were dealt with automatically. How could he get it and go to Waterloo?

Eventually, he shouted out to John, who fortuitously was walking past Andrew's office at the time:

"John! JOHN!"

John came running into the office wondering what could possibly have upset Andrew so much.

"Whatever's the matter?" he asked.

"They've got Myra," he replied, "and they're threatening to kill her. What am I going to do?"

"Who have? Why? What's happening? You're not making a lot of sense, Andrew. Calm down a bit and tell me what's happened."

It didn't take long for John to hear what had happened.

"So they want the box?" he asked. "Well, get onto Klaat NOW and tell him about it!"

Still in a bit of a state, Andrew said: "I don't know where the box is and I haven't spoken to Klaat for quite a while, I …"

At that moment, the box appeared beside Andrew's chair and Klaat's voice came from it, saying: "Don't worry, Andrew. It appears there is a fairly large group of would-be dictators and similar power hungry men who think that they could profit very nicely from my box. I fear they are about to be severely disillusioned about that any minute now. Take a taxi to this address where you'll find Myra. She's okay, but the sooner you get to her the better."

The printer on his desk suddenly started up and a page appeared with an address on it.

"She hasn't been physically harmed but is very worried and scared, not knowing what is going on. She is expecting you fairly shortly and will tell you what happened to her."

Klaat continued: "Enough of the people involved indirectly with this attempt to take over my box, or who even knew about it, will be made aware of what has happened to the main group behind it, so that they will never, ever, even want to *think* about it again. I won't go into details, but they will be afraid of their own shadows for a long time to come and will spread the word, and the continuing fear, of attempting anything like this again. And as for the perpetrators, well, there will be the occasional report of some fairly well known people who have just vanished and others who will probably feature in the 'Missing Persons' files for a while before their cases will be 'closed'. You can be sure none of them will ever be heard of again."

"I hope you have a happy meeting with Myra. Goodbye." After which the box vanished.

John said: "Well, you'd better be on your way. I wonder if the crooks behind this will ever know what hit them, remembering what happened to the three thugs who tried to take the box from you before?"

Andrew found Myra safe, but somewhat confused and upset. He hugged her and held her close asking: "Are you okay, darling – they haven't hurt you, have they?"

She started crying a bit with relief and said: "No, I'm fine now that you're here," and then went on to describe briefly how she had been grabbed and bundled into a car and felt really frightened. Finally, after a few threats to keep quiet, they put her in the room where Andrew had found her.

"Then a curious thing," she went on, "one of the men came into the room a little later and he looked as though he was in a trance. He told me to wait in the room for a while as you would be coming to collect me, then went out, leaving the door, which had been locked previously, wide open. I saw him leave the flat, followed shortly by two or three others, who all moved as though in a trance. I didn't know what to make of it, as they were certainly far from in a trance when they picked me up, in fact were very aggressive. Anyway, after a while, I realised it had gone very quiet so left the room to have a look around. I found the flat empty, though curiously it looked as though they'd been eating a meal in the kitchen but had left rapidly while in the middle of it. So as there didn't seem to be much point in running away as you were coming to fetch me, I thought I would stay put for a while and wait for you. If you hadn't come, I'd have made my way home, anyway.

"Well, I'm more relieved than I can tell you. Are you sure you're okay?" asked Andrew.

"Yes, really, I'm fine now that you're here," she replied, taking his hand and pulling him to her to give him a hug.

Andrew hugged her and then kissed her before saying:

"God, I'm so relieved you're okay, when I had that phone call I was terrified that they would hurt or even kill…" He left the rest unsaid and kissed her again, then said:

"Come on – let's go and have a drink in the first pub we find and then we'll go home."

Over the drink, Andrew told her what had happened as far as he knew it. He finished up by saying:

"Well, this has finally made up my mind for me. I've been thinking of leaving this job and going back to my work at the university for quite a while now as I'm fed up with just doing damn admin work all the time, so I will hand in my notice tomorrow. I think it would be nice if we used the opportunity to go away for a week as I know it's been a stressful time for you as well as me, living in a flat here in town and only getting home for the occasional weekend when my work allowed."

True to his word, the next morning he asked John how he'd like to take over running the department. John said he would be delighted, and Andrew said he would recommend that he be given the job. He then made an appointment to speak to the Prime Minister to explain why he wanted to quit and suggesting that John should take his place. He added that obviously he could be contacted at any time should it be necessary. The PM, who was himself under a terrific load of responsibility, said he could quite see why Andrew would want to leave, and that unofficially, he quite envied him in being able to do so. So the changeover was agreed, John would take over, and Andrew would leave as soon as convenient, probably by the end of the following week, leaving time for a clean handover. The PM concluded their meeting by saying:

"Well, I suppose it just remains for me to thank you for all the excellent work you've put in and to wish you well back in your academic work. It looks as though our new arrangements and policies are generally leading us in the right direction, and though we have a hell of a long way to go yet, I feel we are starting to get there, in no small part thanks to the work you and the Ecowotsit team have put in. So goodbye and good luck!"

One of the first tasks of the handover to John was to ask Klaat to arrange for John to become the sole operator of the box. Just after they had sat down in Andrew's office and were discussing how best to put their request to Klaat, the box appeared alongside John. They were both a bit surprised at its sudden appearance and John was about to remark on this when Klaat's voice came over.

"Well, good morning to you both and I see that you, Andrew, want to hand over your position with Ecowotsit to John."

They both looked at each other with raised eyebrows: how could Klaat possibly have known about their proposed changeover?

Klaat continued: "I have to say that I agree with you, both on your reasons for wanting to get back to your academic work, Andrew, and for handing over your sole control of my box to John. We are happy with that transfer and feel that John is the best person in your organisation to take over this responsibility. John, we are very pleased to have you work with us."

John, delighted at this compliment, replied: "Thank you for your confidence in me and ..."

But before he could finish, Klaat came back in and said:

"Andrew, I am instructed on behalf of my organisation to express our gratitude for the excellent way you have helped us to get our message across to the peoples of your world. The results so far have been all that we could have wished for. So with our sincere wishes for great success in your return to academic life, we will say goodbye."

With which, the box closed itself, moved back alongside John again and then vanished.

After a few seconds pause and shaking his head in slight disbelief, Andrew said: "Well, that was a bit easier than I thought it would be. So good luck with your new found position, my friend!"

"Thanks, Andrew," replied John. "I think the enormity of what I just agreed to will take a while to sink in!"

After a further fairly hectic week handing over his workload and making arrangements with the university for his return, Andrew and Myra went off for a quiet holiday in a country inn in Suffolk where they had enjoyed happy holidays in their younger days. After a couple of days relaxing, enjoying long walks in the countryside and shaking off the stresses of their recent life and events, they found to their delight that the renewal of their relationship, started in Washington had not been a 'one-off', and they thoroughly enjoyed exploring and cementing it further.

The End (...of the beginning...)